A Dream for

Harper

A Dream for Harper

Willow Wood Brides: Book 3

by

Teresa Slack

Read the story that started it all.

Thank you for buying one of my books. To get to know me and my books better, I'd like to give you a free download of A Promise for Josie: A Willow Wood Prequel. Simply follow the link and sign up for my newsletter to get the free download.

Also by Teresa Slack

Legacy of Faith

Tender Blessings Series:

Love Begins
A Little Goodbye

The Ultimate Guide to Darcy Carter
Runaway Heart
Joy Redefined

What readers saying about Willow Wood Brides

"Lots of twists and turns and suspense."

"This is the book for you. If you are looking for a good story, then this is the book for you. It has it all. Romance, adventure, laughter, and tears."

"I was up til 2:30 am reading this book!! The suspense, romance, and unexpected twists make this book intriguing and fun to read! ...Can't wait for the next book in the series!! "

"I loved everything about this book! ...Love story, a mystery, the Old West and Christian faith!! I love everything Slack writes and this was no exception! She draws you in and makes you want to live in the worlds she writes! You will fall in love with her characters."

"Excellent storytelling of a western romance. Compelling and unforgettable characters will fill your imagination with images of life in the Old West."

"Great story about a young lady grieving for the man she loved. Her father sent for a cousin to be a companion for her and help her out of her depression. The cousin and a ranch hand try to unravel the mystery of what happened to him. There is a lot of unanswered questions and quite a bit of shock as they unravel what happened."

"**I couldn't put this book down.** Another Willow Wood heroine. Leaving her home and family to selflessly care for a cousin she didn't even know she had. The story plot was fun and mysterious, filled with twists I never expected! A must read! I am looking forward to the next Willow Wood story. This author never disappoints me!!"

"**A nice change of pace** will keep you hooked."

"**This is my first encounter with this author,** and I have to say that I quickly ran off to find other books by her when I finished this one. This book definitely made me fall in love with a new author and a new series."

"**Hard to put down.** The author kept my attention through the whole book. Can't wait to read the next one."

"**Storytelling is spot on...** Wonderful characters, action, and great dialogue. A few funny moments and some scary ones too."

"**Well written! Funny!** Always a Christian theme makes them so much better. Plus, frontier days or mail order brides are my favorite."

"**Most enjoyable read from an author new to me.** This was the first book I have read by Teresa Slack. I enjoyed is immensely. Teresa has spun a story that is exciting and draws your interesting from beginning to end."

"A must read for those who enjoy historical western romance kindle books from Amazon at a special price and from a delightful author who keeps me wondering what next for the characters. A very enjoyable event-filled story to read and enjoy."

"Slack's characters are well developed and she tells a wonderful story. I am looking forward to reading the entire series! I highly recommend this book and hope you enjoy it as much as I did!"

"Storytelling is spot on... Wonderful characters, action, and great dialogue. A few funny moments and some scary ones too."

"Well written! Funny! Always a Christian theme makes them so much better. Plus, frontier days or mail order brides are my favorite."

"A must read for those who enjoy historical western romance kindle books from Amazon and from a delightful author who keeps me wondering what next for the characters. A very enjoyable event-filled story to read and enjoy."

"Slack's characters are well developed and she tells a wonderful story. I am looking forward to reading the entire series! I highly recommend this book and hope you enjoy it as much as I did!"

Dedication

In memory of my sweet friend and sister in Christ, Unia Faye Williams. You impacted so many people while you were with us. We miss you every day.

Chapter One

Kentucky, April, 1891

Harper Dixon's heart sank the instant she saw the look on Ma's face. Something was wrong. She straightened her spine as if she hadn't noticed and crossed the faded kitchen floor to the sideboard to deposit the basket of collard greens she'd gathered from the edge of the garden.

Ma tucked a dishtowel into the sash of her apron and turned her full attention to Harper. "Sit down a minute, love. I got something to talk with you about."

Just as she thought. Whatever was on Ma's mind wouldn't likely work out well for Harper. She dumped the greens into the sink. "I should wash these first and put them on—"

"They can wait a few minutes." Ma went to the scarred pine table and patted the spot next to her.

Harper glanced at the greens. Through the open window above the sink she heard her three younger sisters and little brother talking and teasing each other as they worked in the garden, scraping shallow rows in the rocky soil. It wouldn't be long before their grumbling bellies reminded them they'd been working all morning and lunch was overdue.

The inopportune time of the conversation, along with the look on Ma's face, made a lump of dread settle in Harper's stomach.

Regardless, it didn't occur to her to disobey or question Ma's request. She pulled out the chair Ma indicated. As soon as she was seated, Ma covered her hand with her own.

Someone was dead. Or nearly so. Or a train had derailed on the other side of the mountain and ran into the family's church. Or a famine somewhere in the world had orphaned a town's children and Ma wanted to take some of them in.

No inconsequential matter explained the grave expression in Ma's typically peaceful deep blue eyes that reflected Harper's own.

"There's no future for you here, Harper. You deserve better than to spend your life in this house waiting for something that'll likely never happen."

Harper's eyebrows slid together. What did that have to do with someone dying?

"Ma?"

Ma looked toward the door, either to make sure the younger children couldn't hear or to escape through it herself. She sighed and turned tired her eyes back to Harper. "The only respectable young men around here have either found a wife already or taken off in search of something better. Those that haven't spend their time brewing corn whiskey or looking for a less than honorable way to make a living. I don't want you to waste your time hoping to change one of them into a proper husband."

"I'm not looking to change anybody into a husband. Not now, anyway."

Ma went on as if she hadn't spoken. "You're twenty years old, Harper. You've always been my dreamer. Your dreams will never come true here."

Why was Ma telling her this? Yes, she was a dreamer. Her sisters often teased her for having her nose in a book or her head in the clouds. But she never thought of leaving the Kentucky hills like some of her friends had. Some stopped going to school as soon as they were old enough to marry a hill man and start their own families. Others headed north to find work and hopefully a better life. Not Harper. She also imagined a future home and family with a faceless man God had waiting for her. But she never dreamed that future would happen anywhere but right here.

Tears glistened in Ma's eyes. "I want to give you a better life than what I had. If not better, at least…different."

"What? I don't understand. This is my life, Ma. I don't need a better one, or a different one."

"But you deserve it. And whether you want it or not, I'm going to do whatever I must to give it to you."

The knot of dread in Harper's stomach doubled in size. "What are you saying?"

"I'm saying you were born for something greater. You're smart. And strong. The other children are too. All my children are a notch above the rest. Not a lazy one in the bunch. But you..." She bit her lower lip. Her expression turned urgent. "I see myself in you the most, Harper. Maybe that's why it matters so much that you have the opportunities I didn't."

Harper shook her head to clear the cobwebs. "I'm sorry, Ma, but I still don't understand. Have I done something wrong? Are you putting me out?"

Ma's gaze softened. She looked deep into Harper's eyes. She clutched Harper's hands and pulled them toward her. "We don't got no money."

Harper didn't need Ma to tell her that. It was obvious from the worn handmade rag rugs on the floor to the newspapers on the walls to muffle the drafts all the way up to the water-stained ceilings.

Ma's gaze swept the kitchen. "Times are hard. We got more mouths that want fed than we got food to put in them."

She released Harper's hands and dug at a broken fingernail. Harper's heart pounded. Even with Joan married, Patrick living on his own, and Davy and Billy working at the sawmill, the family still had a hard time making ends meet. Harper remembered plenty of nights—some not so long ago—she'd gone to bed hungry because there hadn't been enough food on the supper table. But her parents never turned away someone in need, especially a member of the family. Was that what was happening now? With no money and no sign the situation would improve, they had decided she, as the oldest one not bringing in money, would have to go.

Ma gently shook her head. "Harper, you're more special than what you'll ever amount to around here. Your dreams are bigger than these hills. You gotta fly, little bird."

Harper had always shared a kinship with her mother the other children didn't. Like Ma, she was thoughtful and creative. Out of the five Dixon sisters, she looked the most like Ma, too, with her wavy blond hair and twinkling deep blue eyes, though she hadn't seen much of a twinkle in Ma's eyes in more years than she could count.

Ma went to the oven and opened the door to slide in a pan of cornbread. She turned back to Harper but stayed by the stove. "I don't want you to marry the first boy who asks just to help your Pa and me out. I don't want you having babies and trying to dig food out of these hills to feed them." She squared her shoulders. "I'm going to save you from this life."

"Save me?"

Ma reached into her apron pocket and drew out a folded sheet of heavy paper. She unfolded it and carried it to the table. "This came last week. It's from my cousin Hugh. He lives in a town out west in Idaho."

Idaho? That was clean on the other side of the country. Harper had barely heard of it and wasn't sure she could find it on a map.

"You've never met him," Ma said. "None of you children have. I haven't seen him in years myself. Not since he left the hills…"

When Ma's gaze drifted to the window, Harper broke in. "What does he want? Why did he write after all this time?" She feared she already knew the answer.

Ma sank into the chair she had vacated. Her eyes lit up with something akin to eagerness for the first time since the conversation began. "He needs our help. He has a daughter. She's a few years older than you. The girl...she has...problems."

"Is she sick?"

"Not in a way you think. Hugh thinks it would do her good to have someone move into the house to stay with her. A companion. She doesn't have a ma. Hugh's wife passed away when the girl was young. Hugh wrote she had her cap set on marrying a young man. Then he up and left the way restless fellas sometimes do, and the poor girl never recovered."

Harper was immediately intrigued by her Idaho cousin. The hills around her home were filled with Dixon cousins of every variety. But she'd never heard of one on the other side of the country. And to think the poor girl was all alone with no ma to help her through, grieving and mourning a young man who'd left her practically at the altar.

Indignation rose inside her. When someone shamed a Dixon, he shamed the whole clan. Why, she had half a mind to head out to Idaho to assure her cousin she was better off without the shiftless snake. Life just wasn't fair, especially to women. Men had means and opportunity to do whatever they wanted while the women left behind had to pick up the pieces and face their shame all alone.

"Hugh says she suffers from melancholy," Ma continued, "and he's right worried about her. Anyway, he asked..."

Harper's breath caught in her throat. Was Ma about to suggest what she'd just been thinking of doing? She hadn't meant it, of course. She couldn't go to Idaho or anywhere else to convince a cousin she didn't know that no good-time Charlie was worth shedding one single tear. She couldn't convince a dog to howl at the moon.

"He asked if I'd send you."

Now that the words were out, Ma hurried on. "It's a wonderful opportunity, Harper. An adventure. You'll meet all sorts of new people, see new things. You might even meet a young man of your own. You'll live at Hugh's house. He said he'd pay you a small stipend. It would be nice to have your own money for once, wouldn't it?"

Harper stared at her mother's mouth moving, but she could scarcely believe the words coming out of it. Ma was talking like it had already happened. Like Harper had agreed to go. She supposed she would if Ma and Pa wanted her to. She'd not been raised to refuse them anything. But she wasn't qualified to help a woman who'd been jilted. What did she know about matters of the heart? She'd never been in love.

"I don't know anything about taking care of someone who's…sick."

"She's not sick. She's sad."

"That's even worse. How does Hugh know about me? What if he doesn't like me? Will I be stuck out there with no way home? Will they treat me like a servant? What if the daughter doesn't want me there? What's her name anyway?"

Mama scanned through the closely written lines. "Ellie," she answered, ignoring the other questions.

"Hugh says she's very intelligent. She was always the top of her class. Her mother was artistic and Ellie shows the same talent. I'm sure the two of you will have a lot in common."

"How? I'm not accomplished at anything. I'm certainly not educated."

"Don't sell yourself short, Harper. You're very bright. You're a quick study."

Harper took a deep breath as tears threatened. "If I go, Ma, I'll probably never come back."

Ma's lips pulled into a frown. Harper regretted her words, but part of her wanted Ma to hurt too.

"It breaks my heart that I have to consider sending you so far away. Your pa and I won't force you to go, but it'll break my heart more to have you stay. I don't want you to give your life to these hills. I want you to be somebody. I want you to have what your brothers and sisters will probably never have."

"What about Pa? What about Doris May and Sophie and Lottie? Who'll help you take care of Little Walt?"

Ma lifted her chin. "It's high time I taught your sisters to do more around the house instead of relying on you so much. You make everything easy on me, Harper. But it's time for you to go out and chase your own dreams instead of taking care of all of us."

A shuddering sob tore through Harper's chest. Instead of taking care of the people she knew and loved, Ma wanted her to go to Idaho to take care of a cousin who may not want her.

"If this is what you want..." she said softly, praying her mother would hear the despondency in her voice and forget the whole thing.

"It's the only chance you have, Harper. I don't want it for me, I want it for you."

"Where is it in Idaho?"

"In a little town called Willow Wood. Doesn't that sound lovely?"

It didn't sound lovely to Harper. It sounded far. She wanted to tell Ma she wouldn't go. She planned to stay where the view outside her bedroom window never changed. She wanted to smell the trees in bloom in the spring and feel the crisp earthy leaves under her feet in the fall. She wanted to watch her sisters grow up and fall in love. She wanted to watch Little Walt become a man. If she went to Idaho, she'd miss everything that mattered. But Ma was right. If she stayed, she wouldn't have much of a life herself.

She forced her focus onto her cousin Ellie. The young woman needed a friend. A listening ear. Was this what God wanted her to do with her life? Put her own needs and dreams aside for those of another? By doing so, was there a life waiting better than anything she ever imagined?

"Hugh assures me Willow Wood is quite civilized for a frontier town," Ma added hopefully. "From what I gather, he's a successful businessman. He probably knows all sorts of eligible young men."

If he knew so many eligible young men, why had his daughter fallen in love with a rogue?

When she didn't speak, Ma went on. "Your pa and I will support whatever decision you make. Just know you'll never have a chance at a better life if you stay. What you see right here is all you'll ever have."

Harper braced her hands on the table. "Are we finished? May I go?"

Tears pooled in Ma's eyes. She nodded.

Harper leapt up from the table and ran out the door, past the garden where her sisters and little brother stopped their work to stare after her.

She didn't stop to answer the questions they called after her. She needed to think, to pray.

Ma believed a grand life awaited her in the west. Dreams. A friend. A future. Love. Was it true? The image of a faceless cowboy with long legs and a broad chest, strong hands and a heart that would cherish hers, flitted across her mind. Did such a man exist? Did she care enough to find out?

She knew what she'd miss if she left home, while she had no idea what she'd lose out on if she stayed.

Chapter Two

Two months later

"Excuse me. Are you Miss Dixon?" Harper turned to look at the only other person on the platform. She had noticed the clean-cut cowboy from the train when it pulled into the station. Though anxious to meet her Lundy cousins, she had taken a few moments to size him up from the privacy of her seat. A hat shaded his face so she couldn't make out many details from inside the train. Now she could see chiseled features with the most startling aquamarine blue eyes she'd ever seen on a grown man. Russet brown hair curled upward from beneath his faded hat and framed his angular jaw, which sported a clean shave. He smelled pleasantly of pine from the shave, a refreshing change from the stale air on the train.

While not overly tall, he was rugged and manly with broad shoulders, a trim waist, large hands, and worn boots that suggested he worked hard for a living. He reminded her of everything the dime novels suggested she'd find in a western man, except for maybe those eyes.

He also looked like he was waiting for someone. Since there were only two other passengers remaining on the train from the last stop, Harper had wondered if he was here for her. She immediately dismissed the notion. Her cousins, or at least one of them, would surely meet her after the long, arduous trip she'd endured for their benefit.

A shabbily dressed older man had disappeared into the depot. He didn't look like he could afford to pay for a cousin to come all the way from Kentucky. Surely he wasn't Cousin Hugh.

There were no young women in sight. Had Ellie not come to meet her either? Disappointment fluttered in Harper's stomach. Speculation had kept her head whirling during the last four days on the train. She spent the time wondering about her relatives and imagining her new life with them in Willow Wood.

She pictured them as warm and friendly like the family she left back home. She figured they were devout and followed the edicts of Holy Scripture. Ma didn't know if they lived on a ranch or in town. Harper had never lived in town; that might be interesting, though she would be more comfortable on a ranch or even a small farm. Wherever he lived, Cousin Hugh was obviously successful and possessed at least a modest extra income. Whatever she was about to walk into would be different than anything else she'd ever experienced.

She had thought much about Ellie and tried to picture the other woman. Since she needed a companion, Harper imagined small and frail. Maybe she spent her time reading or creating cross stitches. Harper hoped they would spend time outside. If the family lived on a ranch, Ellie was probably an accomplished rider. Harper loved to ride and could easily spend an entire day on horseback. She hoped the family owned an extra horse so the women could travel the surrounding countryside whenever it suited them. She tried not to get her hopes up. Keeping horses for anything other than necessity was more than many households could afford, even businessmen like Cousin Hugh.

Ma said his family moved west when he was in his teens. That was the extent of her knowledge. She didn't know what he did for a living or if he had a wife at home and other children. Harper figured it wasn't likely since he sought a companion for Ellie, unless the rest the other children had already grown and moved off of the house.

Would she meet more cousins? Aunts and uncles? The Idaho mountains could be filled with more Lundys for Harper to get to know.

The cowboy in front of her could even be one of them.

Before identifying herself to him, she scanned the empty platform one more time. It looked like her questions would have to wait. The cowboy moved a toothpick to the other side of his mouth. Doubt and curiosity clouded his face. His gaze traveled from the scuffed shoes her sister Joan had given her, past her faded gray dress, to the navy blue hat, from which escaped dark blond wisps of hair she had tried to wrangle back into the bun at the back of her neck before exiting the train. After the last four days of travel, the cowboy could consider himself fortunate she didn't collapse at his feet in a grimy, sweaty heap.

"Yes, I'm Harper Dixon." She resisted the urge to straighten her hat. She was beyond the help of a straightened hat.

He touched a finger to the brim of his Stetson and dipped his head. "Logan Kinski," he said formally without warmth or greeting. "I work for your uncle Hugh. He sent me to fetch you."

So, he wasn't a cousin. For some reason, the fact brought her a measure of happiness.

"He's not my uncle. He's my cousin."

"Pardon, ma'am?"

"Mr. Lundy. He's a cousin of my mother's. That makes him my cousin, too, not my uncle."

"Oh." A hint of a smile softened his expression. Harper's stomach tightened further. Smiling like that, he was downright handsome. She wondered briefly what she could do or say to bring that smile back to his lips.

"Begging your pardon, ma'am, but we don't stand much on proper titles out here. Mr. Lundy's considerably older than you so folks are gonna assume he's your uncle. Besides, when he told me this morning to fetch you, he called you his niece, so it looks like that's what you are from now on."

Harper wasn't sure if she should take offense at the cowboy for correcting her or at her cousin for deciding she'd call him *Uncle* because he preferred it. It was hard to stay offended at either of them, though, with those blue eyes fixed on her, warming her all the way down to her aching feet.

"I reckon *Uncle* is as easy as *Cousin*."

"I reckon it is." He offered another smile so quick Harper almost wondered if it was wishful thinking on her part.

This man was all business, she decided. She wouldn't judge him too harshly for his lack of enthusiasm in meeting her. He probably had other work to do after delivering her to the Lundys. She still couldn't believe they had sent a hired man to pick her up instead of doing it themselves. If a relative traveled halfway across the country to visit the Dixons, the whole family would turn out to meet them.

His plaid shirt strained against muscular arms as he reached for the battered valise a woman from church had donated for Harper's trip. She gladly relinquished it. She'd been carrying the valise so long she wasn't sure her hand would unfurl from around the handle.

He was only a few inches taller than her. So much for the long-legged cowboys she envisioned while preparing for her journey. She had quickly learned long legs and good looks didn't necessarily account for character, though. She encountered plenty of long-legged cowboys, ranchers, and rail workers along the way from Kentucky. She kept to herself as much as possible while traveling but had still been jostled in crowds, leered at, and even witnessed a bloody fistfight in an alley as the train pulled into a remote station in Missouri. Her opinion of the male of the species had taken a beating since leaving home.

"The rig's over here, ma'am."

He pivoted and started across the boardwalk. Harper clutched her skirt with one hand and set her hand on her head to keep her hat in place as she hurried to keep up with him.

They reached a fancy carriage attached to a pretty sorrel horse with a flaxen mane and tail. The buggy looked as if it had never seen road travel. The sides were a vivid royal blue, and the polished, creamy leather seats gleamed in the sunlight. Harper had never sat in such a fine carriage. She hoped her dusty clothes wouldn't leave marks in the leather.

Who exactly was Hugh Lundy? She knew he was a man of means when she saw how much money he sent to cover her traveling expenses. The amount could've gotten her and a few brothers and sisters to Willow Wood. Still, she hadn't expected a show of wealth like this.

What would he think when he laid eyes on her second-hand wardrobe and valise? What if her simple ways and the twang in her voice embarrassed him in front of his neighbors and business associates and made him question his decision to bring her here?

What of Ellie? If she was used to fancy carriages and a hired man who ran her errands, she would be mortified at the sight of Harper. She might've gone to a fancy university for young ladies. What would she think of Harper's eighth grade education from a three-room schoolhouse in the Kentucky hills?

"You don't need to call me ma'am," she told Mr. Kinski as he swung her valise into the space behind the seat. "Please, call me Harper."

"Excuse me, but I never heard of a woman named Harper before."

"Neither have I," she said with a smile. "When I was a girl, I wished I had a common name like Sally or Mary. Now I'm glad Ma chose something out of the ordinary."

He tilted his head to study her from under the brim of his hat.

Harper pursed her lips. She couldn't tell if the man found her strange for giving him an intimate glimpse into her life, or he just didn't like her. He probably thought nothing of her at all. She was just another chore on his list of jobs to do today.

He stared a moment longer before giving a short nod. "Well, if it suits you, it suits me too. I'll call you Harper and you call me Logan."

His rough expression softened. He took hold of her elbow to guide her into the carriage. She hoped it meant he didn't dislike her or find her strange. She could use an ally as she entered her cousins' foreign world. "I'd be pleased to, Logan."

She tried to ignore his calloused hand on her elbow. He wasn't the first man with whom she spent time alone. She'd had beaux back home. It never took more than one or two encounters, however, for her to lose interest. Maybe it was Ma's suggestion the man of her dreams waited for her in Idaho that made her heart race at Logan's innocuous touch.

Perhaps she was just tired from the trip and her weary bones required assistance to climb into the carriage.

With effort, she focused on the heady scent of new leather instead of the man beside her. The carriage seat creaked under her weight as if hers was the first backside to settle into it. Logan circled the back of the rig and hoisted into the seat beside her.

Harper folded her hands in her lap as he set the buggy in motion. She told herself it wasn't Logan who made her anxious but the thought of meeting her Lundy relatives.

"Is Cousin...Uncle Hugh working today?" A demanding schedule was a better excuse for not picking her up himself than plain disinterest.

She had two months of preparation and four days of exhausting, sometimes nauseating, train travel to think about how this move would change her life and Ellie's. She shouldn't be irritated. She had no right to condemn them for not picking her up when she didn't know what challenges Ellie's mental state caused the family. Uncle Hugh wouldn't have reached out to Ma unless he believed the situation was dire. Harper had prayed God would give her wisdom, patience, and discernment upon meeting her cousins. Now that she was here, she needed to stop feeling sorry for herself and learn how she could help Ellie.

"It's Wednesday," Logan said without looking at her. "That means he's working. Your uncle is always working."

Harper didn't miss the disapproval in his voice. Was Hugh the kind of man who put work above all else? Had it affected Ellie's inability to recover from losing her beau?

"Have you worked with my uncle for a long time?"

Logan gave her a brief glance. "Three years, since I came here from Indiana."

Indiana. So, he wasn't a true western man. Too bad.

"You're not originally from Willow Wood?"

His chest rose and fell as though conversation with a chatty cousin was not how he wanted to spend his day.

"Most folks aren't," he said. "They come for the work. There's plenty of it if a body isn't afraid of a few blisters."

"What exactly does my uncle do?"

Logan whipped his head around to stare at her. "You don't know?"

She drew back at the intensity in his gaze. How could she know? She just got here. "Ma hasn't seen him since they were children. All she knew was he owns his own business. I'd never even heard of Hugh Lundy until he sent for me."

"And you came without question?"

Oh, she'd had questions all right. A hundred at least. But she couldn't tell a perfect stranger Uncle Hugh's offer was a godsend to her family. She couldn't tell him what a blessing it was for them to have one less mouth to feed and one less pair of feet to keep in shoes. How could she not accept Uncle Hugh's generosity when the most basic comforts for such a large family were often outside Ma and Pa's means?

Though there was no shame in poverty, Harper would keep the extent of her need to herself. The last thing she wanted was for Logan Kinski or anyone else in Willow Wood to feel sorry for her or to judge her parents.

"Did Ellie know you were coming after me today?" she said instead. "I expected her or Uncle Hugh to pick me up."

"Ellie doesn't leave the house."

Was he serious? If so, this job could be too big for her? She'd never met a recluse. She wouldn't know how to deal with one. "Do you mean ever?"

"Yes, ever. She doesn't go anywhere."

The scope of Ellie's melancholy was worse than Harper thought. "Not even to church?"

He grunted. "Especially not there. I thought you knew."

Harper swallowed her frustration. Logan either didn't want to talk, or he worried about divulging secrets about his employer's personal circumstances with someone he didn't know he could trust. Whatever his reasons, she needed to know as much about Ellie's condition as she could before they reached the house.

"All I was told was Hugh—Uncle Hugh—wanted a companion for Ellie."

Logan straightened in the seat and turned to look at her. His bright blue eyes—the color of a morning sky the moment after a lightning strike—penetrated hers.

"She needs a friend. A true one."

Harper blinked in surprise. "I wouldn't dream of anything less."

His expression didn't falter as he studied her. Harper stared right back with the same determination. What was this man's problem? She was here to help, or at least she hoped to.

"Is there any other family in the house? Brothers? Sisters?"

The furrows on his forehead deepened. He shook his head.

"Does she have friends she can confide in?"

"Not anymore."

Harper clenched her jaw at another half answer. Why was it so hard to get information? She prayed Ellie wasn't as difficult to deal with as this man. "What happened to them? Did they desert her in her time of need?"

He looked back to the road and exhaled slowly. For a moment she thought he wouldn't answer. She considered grabbing the buggy whip from the floorboard and smacking the back of his hands with it.

Finally, he turned back at her. His eyes had gone from suspicious to sad. "Ellie used to be a very social person. She held everyone in town in the palm of her hand. Now she has no interest in seeing anyone. Her friends eventually got the hint."

"Because of her young man?"

"You could say that."

She waited. After a moment it became apparent he wasn't going to say more.

"Did you know him?"

"He and I came to Willow Wood together."

It was Harper's turn to have no answer. So much became clear. She had already decided the beau who abandoned Ellie wasn't worth missing. Now she discovered this irascible man had known him well.

"Matthew was my best friend," he affirmed. "A few years ago, he decided to come west and asked if I would join him. I had nothing holding me in Indiana so here I am."

"Did Matthew work for Uncle Hugh as well?"

He nodded.

"Is that how he met Ellie?"

"Ellie and Matthew planned to marry," he said at length. "Your uncle wasn't pleased."

Uncle Hugh hadn't mentioned that in his letter. "Why not?"

Logan motioned to his clothes with a wag of his chin. "Matthew and I weren't in the Lundys' class."

Nor am I, Harper thought. Aloud, she said, "Did Uncle Hugh have a more suitable mate in mind for her?"

"A whole cadre of them, I imagine." Logan fixed his suspicious gaze on her again. "You sure ask a lot of questions."

"That's because I have a lot of them. I came all this way to help Ellie, and that's what I intend to do.

Chapter Three

Logan Kinski looked from the young woman's dry, chapped hands clasped in her lap, to the hard set of her jaw. She was agitated, that much was sure. He wouldn't apologize if he had offended her. The first he'd heard her name was yesterday when Mr. Lundy directed a terse; "My niece is arriving on tomorrow's 10:40 train. I need you to pick her up." at him.

Logan's first reaction was to wonder why Mr. Lundy wasn't picking his niece up himself. He couldn't imagine sending a stranger to pick up one of his kin like a piece of furniture from a fancy store back East. But that was Mr. Lundy for you. He hadn't even sounded interested in the woman's arrival. He probably would've shown more enthusiasm over a piece of furniture.

Logan had learned long ago not to waste energy pondering Hugh Lundy's motives or methods about anything. The only thing that seemed to matter to the man was money, and he'd accumulated plenty of it over the last thirty years. What business did someone like Logan, who barely had two nickels to rub together, have questioning a man who had achieved Mr. Lundy's level of success? The Hugh Lundys of the world hired the Logan Kinskis to stand on station platforms and wait for relatives instead of wasting a work day doing it themselves.

From the look of the little blonde's plain cotton dress and outdated hat, he deduced she was a country girl. She had a cute southern drawl that tickled him all the way down to his toes, though he had no intention of letting her know it.

He sure couldn't imagine what type of help she thought she could offer Ellie. How much did she even know about the situation? How much had Mr. Lundy told her about Matthew Dunleavy, the beau to whom she referred?

Logan's lip curled in distaste as he shifted the toothpick in his mouth. A suitable mate, indeed. Mr. Lundy probably danced in the streets after Matthew left town. He sure didn't act like he cared that Ellie was left heartbroken and miserable. Just annoyed. This wisp of a thing in the buggy beside him was Mr. Lundy's solution to an inconvenience. Logan knew Ellie never would've sent for her. He doubted Ellie knew she was coming.

He grimaced again. Ellie had enough people in town whispering behind her back about how she still grieved for a man who nobody'd seen hide nor hair of in two long years. Two-faced people who smiled at Mr. Lundy and fawned over his wealth, only to gossip and speculate about his daughter the minute he walked out of earshot.

Ellie sure didn't need a far-flung cousin moving into the mansion with plans of doing the same thing.

Before Matthew disappeared, making Logan wonder what had chased him out of town this time, he had asked Logan to watch over Ellie, should the need arise.

At the time, Logan figured Matthew was paranoid again. A man got that way when he spent his evenings with the type of characters Matthew did. Men who wouldn't hesitate to draw on someone who won too big or talked too much.

After he disappeared, Logan figured the same thing happened that drove them out of Indiana three years ago. Leaving Indiana had been one thing, but leaving without a word of explanation for Ellie was more than Logan could fathom. He could never walk away from a woman who loved him like that. But Matthew didn't think the same way. He was who he was. He acted with no thought or concern about the consequences or who got hurt. Wherever Matthew was now or what he was doing didn't matter to Logan. All that mattered was protecting Ellie, and he'd continue to do it.

He stole another glance at Harper. She didn't look like a threat. At a couple inches over five feet tall and narrow as a willow branch, he figured the first stiff wind would blow her back to wherever she came from. Dark blond hair hung in limp strands around her heart-shaped face. The pale freckles sprinkled across her straight nose and cheeks gave her an innocent air. He wasn't fooled, though. Behind the telltale, dark smudges of weariness, her deep blue eyes were sharp and intelligent. She might look like a shy country girl out of her element, but he believed she was here for more than she claimed.

No matter how innocent she looked, he wasn't about to stand by while a doe-eyed interloper with false promises and feigned compassion plunked down in the middle of a comfortable situation to take advantage of someone who had already suffered enough.

Harper's inquisitive eyes darted in every direction as the carriage moved away from the station. Her wide-eyed eagerness convinced him his worries were well founded.

The gentle breeze carried a scent of roses in their direction. Laundry swayed easily on lines stretched across porches and backyards. Flowerboxes burst forth with color as vibrant as the rainbow. A smartly dressed man sat on a chair on a front porch smoking a pipe. Children too small for school ran across yards hollering at each other.

Logan stared after them. It seemed like it hadn't been that long ago since he and his brother were the ones chasing each other around the yard, fighting over a ball one minute and wrestling playfully in the grass the next. Then in 1882 Larry joined the Army and never came home. Ma fretted that he had been killed. Logan suspected Larry joined up in order to make a clean getaway. Ma grieved her favored son until her last breath. Logan doubted she would've suffered as much had he been the one to leave home instead of

Larry. Though he scarcely admitted it, even to himself, he always wished Ma would realize he was a good son, too, and worthy of her love.

He had stood next to her death bed that last day and waited for her to tell him she loved him. She didn't say the words, even after Logan did. Once the pain subsided, he realized it was just as well. Lying to him would've been worse than her not loving him.

A week after he and Pa put her in the ground, Matthew Dunleavy rode into the yard late one night and said he was leaving town. Logan didn't hesitate when Matthew asked if he wanted to go. And he hadn't looked back.

Larry was gone or dead; Logan wasn't sure which. Ma had died and taken his last hope of love and acceptance with her. Pa was wrapped so tightly in his own despair over a life that turned out as wrong as it could get, Logan knew he wouldn't be missed. Matthew had been closer than a brother anyway. The only one Logan could count on. Matthew needed him. The choice had been easy.

He turned the rig down a side street bypassing the main thoroughfare. At the end of another street he turned away from a quiet residential street. Out of the corner of his eye, he watched Harper's head turn to gaze, almost with longing, at the row of pretty clapboard houses they were leaving behind.

An industrial district came into view. Harper's gaze snapped forward. She pointed at the massive structure bustling with activity. "What's that?"

He knew the imposing factory would get a reaction. He came this way intentionally to see for himself how important money and prosperity were to her.

"Trego Leatherworks," he answered. "They make reins, halters, buggy seats, and the like."

"It takes up the entire block."

"The factory's been in business nearly as long as Willow Wood has been here. Just about everyone who doesn't work at the mines or for the railroad works here. It's run by the Trego sisters."

Harper gasped. "Sisters? Do you mean women oversee an operation this size?"

"Yup. Two of them. Actually, the oldest sister, Belinda Trego, does most of it. The younger sister isn't involved much. Word around town is she's an owner in name only."

Harper looked impressed, regardless of how unbalanced the work was.

"I've never known of a factory owned and operated by women."

Logan hadn't either, but he didn't say as much. The horse plodded along the busy street offering them time to watch the outside operation. Large wagons backed up to loading docks, where men either loaded or unloaded them of various products. The heavy tang of leather and smoke hung in the air. Windows along the roofline of the large building were open to take advantage of the breeze. The shrill cry of machinery and loud masculine voices vibrated around them.

"Do women work there too? I mean, besides the sisters?" Harper asked.

He nodded. "On the inside, maybe. Packing boxes and working the sewing machines and the like. Most of it is heavy work, so I don't imagine many women can handle it. Why? Are you looking for a job?"

"Certainly not," she exclaimed. "I told you I was here for Ellie."

He nearly broke into a smile at the indignation on her face. She sure was a pretty thing, especially with those spots of color on her cheeks. He lifted a shoulder in indifference. "I was just checking."

They rode on in silence for a moment. Logan almost regretted teasing her. Then he reminded himself what she was doing here, and irritation washed over him all over again.

"I didn't know what to expect when I got here," she finally said. "I didn't know if Willow Wood was a rustic frontier town or a booming industrial center."

"Guess it's a little of both."

At the end of the street, the noise level increased further as the rumbling of train cars and train whistles split the air.

On the far side of the railyard was a large building fronted with massive glass windows. Logan pulled the rig to a stop and focused on Harper to get her reaction when he announced where they were. If she had been truthful about her mother not telling her what her uncle did for a living, she was in for a shock.

"This here is the headquarters of your uncle's company. Lundy List Railroad and Mining."

Harper gasped aloud. Her gaze traveled up the front of the building to the words *Lundy List* etched in stone across the façade.

"This is...my uncle's?"

He had to admit she looked taken aback. He wasn't convinced, though, she wasn't putting on an act. Maybe she knew he was wealthy but didn't know the extent of it. Well, now she did.

"Partly. This is the headquarters of the company's holdings. Your uncle and Hershel List own and operate the railyard as well as most of the mines in the area."

It took a few moments for her to find her voice. "I had no idea. Ma said he was successful. She said he was a self-made man. I don't know how I'll tell her about all this."

Doubt crept into Logan's head. She sure did look bumfuzzled. Either she was a skilled actress, or she truly had no idea her uncle was one of the richest men west of the Mississippi.

"Mr. Lundy doesn't work here in the office much of the time. He usually works in the field overseeing the mining operations. He and Hershel List are single-handedly responsible for bringing a railroad spur to Willow Wood. Without them, it wouldn't be much of a town here."

They watched the hustle and bustle outside the railcars and warehouses for a few minutes as men and machinery moved around the massive yard. When Logan clicked his tongue to spur the horse forward, he kept a wide berth of the activity. At the end of a long string of warehouses, he turned the rig back toward town. The noise level faded into the background.

"I had no idea it would be like this," Harper said almost to herself.

Logan cocked his head in wonder at the tears in her voice.

"What would be like this?" he asked.

"Willow Wood. I thought…" She shook her head at the futility of her assumptions.

He felt a little guilty for his earlier suspicions. Maybe she had no nefarious intentions. But he wasn't convinced she wouldn't try to worm her way into her uncle's good graces—and some of his wealth—now that she realized how much there was.

"It isn't much different from any other frontier town, I expect. Noisy and busy. Full of honest, hard-working folk trying to make a place for themselves."

"Like home, I reckon."

They rode in silence for a few moments. "What does Ellie do to occupy herself?" Harper asked as Logan urged the horse around another corner. "Uncle Hugh didn't tell us much about her. Other than writing she was intelligent and artistic, he didn't provide many details."

Logan sucked air between his teeth. What was there to say? Matthew was gone. Ellie was here and might never get over losing him. "I told you she doesn't leave the house."

"Surely she must do something. What are her hobbies? Does she receive visitors?"

He shook his head. "You'll be the first visitor she's had in a long time. As far as hobbies, the only one I ever knew of was going to parties. She sure doesn't do that anymore. She used to paint and draw. She sketched trees and owls and the mountains and such. I haven't seen her lift a pencil or a brush in a long time." He shrugged. "She has an artistic bent like her ma."

"What happened to her mother?"

"She passed away when Ellie was little. I never knew her, of course. You'll have to ask Mrs. Philips about her."

"Who's Mrs. Philips?"

"The housekeeper."

Harper's face whitened under her freckles. "How many staff does my uncle employ?"

"Not many. Mrs. Philips and me. There's Patty and Gwen, the maids. Burt tends the gardens this time of year. There are always a couple local boys who work the stables. Mrs. Philips told me she used to bring in additional cooks and bakers when the family entertained. That doesn't happen anymore."

Harper looked overwhelmed. Logan wondered if she'd burst into tears. He sure hoped not. He wanted to tell her she needn't fret about living in a big house with servants and stable hands. It had been intimidating to him at first, too, but he got used to it quick enough.

The horse lowered its head as it began the gradual assent up the hill toward the Lundy mansion. A stone wall that surrounded the house began at the corner and rose in height along with the hill. On the other side of the wall a tall hedge of trees was in full leaf, completely obstructing the view of the estate from curious neighbors. With no guidance from Logan the sorrel turned through a wide gate onto the manicured grounds.

"Oh, my. Is this..." Harper's eyes were as wide as silver dollars. She couldn't finish the question.

"Yes, your uncle lives here."

Her face lost what remained of its color except for the two pink dots on her cheeks. "Oh, my." She couldn't seem to say anything else. Apparently awestruck, she gazed up at the three-story stone house, her eyes hungrily taking in the sight.

Logan's hands tightened around the reins. Just as he thought. It didn't look like she'd have any trouble getting used to the ostentatious wealth in front of her.

Chapter Four

Harper had never seen anything like the house and grounds. She had never even read a fairy tale that compared in beauty and splendor. She couldn't really call the structure a house. When the paved drive angled gently upward and the house came into full view, she nearly fell out of the carriage. She hoped her shock wasn't evident to Logan. It looked like every person in her small town could fit inside the mansion. It was inconceivable it all belonged to one family. *Her family.* Any girl growing up here would surely see herself a princess. A fairy princess in a glittering ballgown, hiding her face behind a lace fan and waiting for her prince to kneel in front of her and kiss her hand.

A handsome prince, who in Ellie's case, had turned into a frog.

The house's façade was made from tan river rock and painted wood that complemented the natural stone. Deep brown slate shingles on the roof and eaves encompassed the doors and windows. Ivy crept up the shady side of the house near a carriage house painted in the same colors. The ivy and carefully planted trees made the side entrance cool and inviting. Not like the front of the house, which reminded her of a severe, stony face scowling down at her.

She wondered for a moment if Uncle Hugh was like the house his wealth represented. Cold and impersonal.

Her stomach clenched tighter with each rotation of the wagon's wheels. She was bone weary from the train trip, and she missed her family. She had never spent as much as one night away from home. Two years ago as Joan prepared to marry, she and Harper spent weeks running back and forth from the farm to what would become Joan's new home. Yet each night the girls were home and in their own beds, surrounded by little sisters.

She regarded her red, work-roughened hands in her lap and fretted again about what Uncle Hugh would think of her. If he considered Logan and Matthew below his station, what would he think when he saw her? His household staff was probably better dressed than she was.

Logan must've read the trepidation on her face. "You needn't worry about the size of the house. Most of the time, you'll forget anyone's in there with you."

If his last statement was meant to comfort her, it had the opposite effect.

He stopped the carriage in the shade at the side of the house. Before he climbed down, he pinned her with a grave look. "Do me a favor, Harper? Bring Ellie back from the dark place where's she's gone. She needs to know people still care about her."

Before she could formulate a response, he jumped down from the carriage and hurried around the back end to help her off on her side.

When her feet were on the ground, he took her bag and went to the back door and pushed it open.

"We're here," he called out. He stepped back to let Harper enter first.

"No need to shout," a woman called from the next room. "I'm right here." A short, rounded woman wearing a white cap and matching apron over a faded green dress stepped through a doorway, her arms wrapped around a large crock.

Logan set down the valise and jumped away from the door to help. "I'll take that." He whisked the crock out of her arms and carried it through the doorway into the kitchen. The woman followed, leaving Harper alone in the entryway. She picked up her valise and went after them.

"Be careful." The woman's face bore a warm smile as she admonished Logan. "You spill the flour and there won't be any pie crust to go with the cherries Burt picked yesterday."

Logan set the crock on the counter. "You should've told me it was for pie crust. I would've handled it like a newborn babe."

"Oh, you." The woman's gaze traveled to where Harper stood in the doorway. "You must be Harper." She crossed the sparkling kitchen floor.

Logan left the counter to make introductions. "Mrs. Philips, this is Harper Dixon. Miss Dixon, this is Mrs. Philips, the housekeeper. If you need anything, she's the one to get it for you."

Mrs. Philips gave him a long-suffering sidelong glance but didn't correct him. She turned a warm, welcoming smile on Harper as she reached out to grasp her hands. "You are a sight for sore eyes, girl. I pray you can make a difference around here."

Harper lifted her chin. She wouldn't be here if she didn't think she could help her cousin, even if Logan didn't share her confidence. She needed to be realistic though. He and Mrs. Philips knew the severity of Ellie's melancholy. They knew her temperament. The only thing Harper knew was Ellie hadn't cared enough about her arrival to meet her at the station.

"It's a pleasure to meet you, Mrs. Philips."

Mrs. Philips stepped back and let her gaze travel down Harper's worn dress. There hadn't been money or enough time for Ma to make her a proper traveling suit. This was the nicest dress she had. Like her sisters, she had never owned more than three dresses at a time in her life.

"One to wear, one to wash, and one to mend," Ma always said.

"It's lovely to have another young woman in the house," Mrs. Philips said with no judgment in her eyes. "You must be hungry. I know Logan is."

"Easy guess," Logan said.

Mrs. Philips laughed.

"Will Ellie join us for lunch?" Harper asked to drown out the sudden growling in her stomach. She was anxious to meet her cousin and thought it might go easier if Mrs. Philips and Logan were here to help break the ice.

Logan exchanged a glance with Mrs. Philips. "I'm going out to unhitch the rig. When I'm finished, I'll take your bag upstairs. Then I'll join you for lunch."

"That isn't necessary. I can take it upstairs."

"It's my job," he said as he turned and headed outside.

"I reminded Ellie you were arriving today," Mrs. Philips said, seemingly oblivious to Logan's departure.

Ellie knew she was coming; she just didn't care.

"I'll show you where you can wash up while I set out your lunch," the housekeeper continued. "You and Logan can eat here in the kitchen if you don't mind. You'll have dinner in the dining room with Mr. Lundy and Ellie tonight. He told me this morning he'd be home promptly at six for dinner."

Dinner at six. Harper wondered what was she supposed to do between now and then if she couldn't meet Ellie? Had Uncle Hugh drawn up a list of responsibilities? It seemed a sin to sit around all day while one person toted her bag and another prepared her food. She would never get used to this big, cold, empty house.

•••

Mrs. Philips refused Harper's offer to help clean the kitchen after lunch. As soon as she took her last bite, the housekeeper showed her upstairs to a large airy room that faced the street, or what she could see of it over the treetops. The room was more simply appointed than the rest of the house but still so fancy Harper was nearly afraid to sit on the furniture. The walls were covered in a delicate gold damask pattern. A deep purple valance with the same damask design topped a gauzy curtain over the window. An ivory counterpane patterned with a muted lavender filigree covered a bed bigger than Ma and Pa's back home.

After Mrs. Philips closed the door behind her, Harper stood in the center of the room and tried to get her bearings. The entire last four days threatened to crush down on her.

She gazed up at the ceiling, so high above her head she doubted she could reach it if she stood on the bed and jumped as high as the mattress would allow. The only sounds she heard were the tapping of tree branches on the side of the house, creaking and settling of floors and walls, and a lone bird on her windowsill. Everything about the house was so big, so solemn, so cold, despite the sun's warmth pouring through the window, it felt more like a museum than a house.

The only artwork was a painting of snow-capped mountains against an azure sky in a heavy scrolled frame. Logan had said Ellie used to paint nature scenes. She went to the painting to study it closer. It looked professionally done, though she was no judge of artwork. A few illegible scratches along the bottom could've been the artist's signature. Or they might've been the bark on a tree. She wasn't sure.

While escorting her upstairs, Mrs. Philips had told her Ellie was in the next room. Harper held her breath and put her ear against the wall. A braver companion would walk over and introduce herself.

Even if Harper were brave enough to march next door and announce herself to someone who obviously wasn't interested in meeting her, she had noticed the way Logan and Mrs. Philips avoided talking about Ellie at lunch. Every time she attempted to steer the conversation in that direction, they exchanged glances, and Mrs. Philips would ask about her brothers and sisters or her journey to Willow Wood. It didn't take long to realize the subject of Ellie was off-limits.

Hearing nothing through the walls, she removed her shoes and stretched out on the bed, careful not to wrinkle the counterpane. A full stomach and warmth from the sun through the curtains made the fatigue of the last few days impossible to ignore. A headache pressed at the back of her eyelids.

Tonight, she would meet Uncle Hugh. And Ellie, she hoped. She should take advantage of the chance to rest.

She tried to relax into the soft mattress. At home, Ma and Pa slept on a feather mattress while the children slept in shuck beds. Over the years, Harper had gathered her share of green corn shucks to stuff into mattress ticking. It made for relatively comfortable sleeping once she molded her body into the shucks, especially with a sister or two nestled beside her for warmth.

This bed didn't make noise, unlike a shuck mattress which awoke everyone in the room when someone rolled over. How would she ever fall asleep without Doris May's knee in her back or Sophie's snores lulling her to sleep?

She blinked away tears and tried to ignore the homesickness. She was twenty years old; too old for crying for her mother. So far, her journey hadn't worked out the way she expected. No one here was happy to see her, except for maybe Mrs. Philips. Logan said Ellie didn't have visitors and she didn't go to church. How would Harper meet anyone, hidden behind stone walls?

Tears filled her eyes, despite her determination not to give in to them. Ma had said her dreams would come true here. Harper snorted at the ceiling twelve feet above the bed. She was alone. For the first time in her life, one of her brothers or sisters wouldn't crash into the room making demands. Ma or Pa wouldn't yell for her to come lend a hand with something.

She pushed away the self-pity. She wasn't alone. No matter how it looked on the outside, God was with her. She blinked away her tears and prayed for forgiveness for forgetting that. For whatever reason, she was here. God had placed her in this strange place. He had put her on Uncle Hugh's mind because Ellie needed help.

The dreams that would come true inside this house might not belong to her at all. Her purpose in Willow Wood could be to awaken the dreams inside Ellie. Was that what the Lord planned for her?

Harper rolled onto her side and stared at the painting across the room. God knew why she was here, even when she didn't. If she were a single brushstroke on a canvas, she couldn't see the whole masterpiece. But the Master saw. The details had been worked out long before she boarded the train. Before Ma received Uncle Hugh's letter.

A sense of peace washed away Harper's homesickness as she pulled a corner of the counterpane over her shoulder. She was here to help the Lundys, not wallow in loneliness. She wouldn't fret over Logan's suspicions or Uncle Hugh putting work ahead of meeting her at the station. She would focus on the Lord and what he asked of her.

She murmured a prayer of thanksgiving for her safe journey and let sleep overtake her. Her dreams would have to take care of themselves for now.

Chapter Five

"Harper."

The tall man stood and circled the large dining table with a few long strides.

Harper's breath caught at the sight of him. Hugh Lundy looked just like Grandpa Ferguson, Ma's pa, who had passed away when Harper was twelve. Hugh had the same wide nose, square jaw, and piercing ebony eyes of the Cherokee nation whose lineage had influenced Ma's family for generations.

She had peeked into the dining room earlier during Mrs. Philips brief tour before she was shown to her room. Now, with the table laid out with fine china, crystal glasses, and candlelight, she wished she could eat in the kitchen with Mrs. Philips. What if she broke something? Or brushed her sleeve through the butter?

Or spilled gravy on the linen tablecloth? Or chose the wrong fork? From where she stood, she counted six pieces of silver positioned around her plate. At home each person had one. Two if the meat was tough.

To the right of Uncle Hugh's chair sat a slim woman who reminded Harper of a fragile porcelain doll. Her coppery brown hair was pulled into a loose chignon at the nape of her neck highlighting delicately chiseled features. She wore an ivory-colored dress with ecru pinstripes and maroon piping. Harper couldn't make out further details since the woman's head was lowered, and she stared at her empty plate.

Ellie.

Harper studied her profile as best she could and looked for a resemblance like the one shared between Uncle Hugh and Grandpa Ferguson. Did they have things in common? A few months ago, she didn't know she had a cousin in Idaho. Now that she was here, she was bursting with curiosity. From the way Ellie kept her gaze fixed on her plate, the curiosity was one-sided.

Uncle Hugh took Harper's hands and gave them a brief squeeze before motioning her to the empty chair opposite Ellie.

He waited until she was seated before resuming his seat at the head of the table. "It's a pleasure to have you in our home. Isn't that right, Ellie?"

He barely glanced at his daughter, as if he didn't expect a reply. He wasn't disappointed.

In Harper's house, a child never ignored a question posed by an adult, even a grown child answering a trivial question. Ellie did not lift her head or acknowledge her father had spoken.

After an anxious moment for Harper, she looked back at her uncle. "Thank you, sir. It's a pleasure to be here."

She wouldn't exactly call the experience a pleasure, but it wasn't terrible either. Yet.

Uncle Hugh smiled in response. He snapped open his napkin and spread it on his lap, signaling the start of the meal. He reached for a platter of roasted beef in front of him without offering a prayer. Harper hesitated a moment and then began filling her plate. Maybe they prayed after everyone's plates were ready.

They didn't.

Ellie dutifully put a small portion of several dishes on her plate and preceded to push the food around on her plate with barely a nibble of anything reaching her lips.

Harper silently breathed her own prayer and began to eat.

"I trust you found everything in your room to your satisfaction," Uncle Hugh said as he cut through his roast.

The meat was so tender it only required a fork for Harper to cut, but a knife and fork looked more civilized. Next time she would exercise a little more decorum. At lunch she had sampled Mrs. Philip's cooking, but the roast, with baby red potatoes and carrots, practically melted in her mouth. She wondered if food always tasted better when someone else did the work of preparing it.

"Yes, sir. Very satisfactory."

She glanced at Ellie. Ellie hadn't spoken or looked directly at anyone. Ma said Ellie was a few years older than Harper. Harper figured she was about twenty-five. Dark smudges under her large cocoa brown eyes indicated a person who didn't get enough sunlight or food. The natural copper highlights in her thick full hair were faded and had no luster. It was easy to see she was a beautiful woman, if only she'd put on a few pounds and step outside. A smile would go a long way in improving her appearance as well.

She glanced at Uncle Hugh who chewed methodically at each bite he put in his mouth. Was he as doubtful of her ability to help Ellie as everyone else? What if Ellie never warmed up to her? Would Uncle Hugh send her home? Ma would be disappointed if she couldn't make the position work. Whether Ellie wanted her here, she needed her, and Harper was determined to make a difference in all their lives.

She steeled herself and looked across the table. Before she could talk herself out of it, she burst out, "Perhaps we could go for a walk tomorrow. Logan showed me your father's company headquarters. I'd love a tour of the neighborhood sometime."

Though she didn't lift her head, Ellie's shoulders stiffened, and her eyes widened. She shot a quick glance at her father before turning her gaze back to the food she hadn't been eating.

Uncle Hugh swallowed his food and pulled his mouth into a frown. Harper knew immediately her suggestion was not appreciated. "If you need anything from the stores, ask Logan or Burt to pick it up for you."

"No, I...it isn't that. I just thought, if the weather is nice, we could..."

"Logan can walk with you around the neighborhood if you require an escort," Uncle Hugh said. "Or hitch the carriage and take you wherever you need to go."

She didn't need an escort. She needed Ellie to stop feeling sorry for herself and get out of this house. She needed Uncle Hugh to stop babying his daughter.

"If all you want to do is enjoy the weather, there's no need to leave the grounds," he continued. "The property encompasses the entire block. The gardens are exquisite this time of year, and there are several walking and riding trails. If you want a mount, just tell Logan."

Harper shook her head as she tried to envision the expanse of the property. She gave up and looked across the table at Ellie. Her downcast eyes were wide with terror. The hand clutching her fork was white knuckled.

Guilt colored Harper's cheeks. She hadn't meant to scare her. She only wanted to extend her friendship. But if Ellie never interacted with anyone, how did Uncle Hugh expect her to recover?

"I don't need to go anywhere. Maybe another time."

Over Ellie's shoulder, she watched Mrs. Philips transfer cherry tarts to serving dishes. The woman shook her head in defeat. Harper was heartened to know she wasn't the only one in the house who wondered if the situation would ever improve.

Chapter Six

Uncle Hugh was gone by the time Harper got downstairs for breakfast the next morning. Mrs. Philips was preparing a tray to take up to Ellie.

"Isn't Ellie coming down for breakfast?" Harper asked.

"Ellie never was much for eating in the morning. Even more so now. Just toast and tea usually."

Harper barked out a laugh. She caught herself at Mrs. Philips' reaction and put her fingers to her lips. "I'm sorry. I didn't mean to laugh. Everybody in my house wakes up famished. There are so many chores to do before breakfast, and lunch is such a long way off, we eat like soldiers preparing for battle."

She knew it was poor manners for a young lady to admit she was hungry, no matter how much so she was, but Harper was tired of pretending she was someone she wasn't. She'd been walking on eggshells since stepping off the train yesterday. The sooner everyone in this stone palace got to know the real Harper Dixon, the better off they'd all be.

Mrs. Philips apparently thought so too. She laughed in appreciation as she poured honey into a tiny crock and set it on the tray next to two evenly browned slices of bread. "You remind me of when I was a girl, Harper. I grew up on a farm near a little town called Scottstown not far from here. I had six brothers, so I didn't have many chores outside to do. But my, my, the food those boys could put away. Mama and I would cook pounds of potatoes and slabs of bacon and dozens of eggs every morning. There wasn't a crumb left when they headed out the door to work."

"Sounds like home, though we girls had as much work to do outside as the boys."

Mrs. Philips laid the towel over the tray and set a hand on Harper's cheek. "Makes you miss home, thinking about these things, doesn't it?"

Tears pooled in Harper's eyes. She quickly blinked them away

"I'm sure you're worried about how they'll get along without you."

She nodded again. "So much."

"I know they miss you, but you're needed here too."

Harper straightened her shoulders and hugged the older woman. "Thank you, Mrs. Philips. I would love to hear more about that farm in Scottstown whenever you have time to share."

"Girl, I have more stories than you have hours to listen. With six brothers, they were always coming up with something. Whatever mischief one didn't think up, another one would."

"I look forward to getting to know them through your stories." Harper took hold of the breakfast tray. "In the meantime, I'll take this upstairs to Ellie?"

Doubt creased Mrs. Philips' brow. "What about your own breakfast? You said you wake up hungry."

"I have to work up my appetite first. Uncle Hugh didn't send for me so I could sit in this kitchen and watch you work. If Ellie and I are to become friends, she has to get used to seeing me around the house."

Mrs. Philips looked from the tray to the early stages of lunch preparation spread out on the counter. "I suppose it would be all right."

"Perfect." Harper nearly snatched the tray away from her. Not only did she want something to fill her long morning, it would give her a chance to talk to Ellie without Uncle Hugh making everyone uncomfortable.

"Knock before you go in," Mrs. Philips admonished as if Harper had never entered a person's room before. "Set the tray on the table by the window and go. Don't expect her to talk with you."

Harper would probably fall over from shock if she did. With trembling hands, she carried the tray as quickly and carefully as she could across the wide foyer to the staircase. Outside Ellie's room, she balanced the tray against her hip and knocked.

Silence. She knocked again and cocked her head to listen. Impatience swelled inside her breast. This was ridiculous. She couldn't stand here all day. Unlike

Ellie, she had things to do. Well, she might not have anything to do at the moment, but she'd think of something.

She gave the door another quick rap and turned the knob. Though the sun was well on its way across the eastern sky, the room was cloaked in darkness. Harper was tempted to march across the room and fling open the curtains the way Ma would if she or one of her sisters lounged in bed while the world spun on its axis, filled to overflowing with people with real problems.

She reminded herself she wasn't her mother, and this wasn't her house. She didn't know what Ellie was going through. She had never been in love. She'd never had a man walk out of her life as if she were no more important than a pair of shoes he'd outgrown.

She listened for signs of life coming from the four-poster bed, twice as big as the one she shared with Doris May—and Sophie and Lottie when the nights were so cold they needed to double up on the blankets. Hearing nothing, she crossed the room as stealthily as she could. Her eyes grew accustomed to the darkness by the time she reached the table near the bed, and she managed to avoid stubbing her toe.

"Breakfast," she announced in little more than a whisper, her voice stark in the stillness. Feeling emboldened, she spoke again. "Mrs. Philips sent it up."

She stood motionless over the bed, half tempted to tell Ellie to get up and get dressed and stop wasting the day. But if Uncle Hugh wanted someone to yell at her, he could've done it himself and spared the expense of sending for Harper.

"You should eat it before it gets cold," she prodded.

"Thank you, I will," came the quiet reply from the bed.

Harper nearly shrieked aloud. These were the first words she'd heard Ellie utter. Should she stay? Offer to keep her company? Open a window to show Ellie what a beautiful morning it was?

Instead, she would take her victories where she found them. "Mrs. Philips will be glad to hear it," she said to the shape in the bed.

At the door she turned back. "I'll be downstairs or in the garden if you need anything. Or if you would like to join me."

Ellie's reply was a murmur Harper didn't understand.

She thought about asking again, but Ellie was a grown woman. If they were to become true friends, it wouldn't be by pestering or coercion. She closed the door behind her with a soft click. She doubted Ellie would join her in the garden, but she had said thank you. That was something.

Chapter Seven

Harper had never seen a more enchanting garden that belonged to just one person. As she walked the perimeter of the rock wall surrounding the Lundy property, she marveled at the manicured lawns and flowerbeds. Uncle Hugh was right. Several walking trails meandered through the garden, among rose bushes in full bloom. She bent close and inhaled their heady aroma. She thought about picking a few to take to her room, but it wasn't her place. Uncle Hugh or Ellie might prefer to come outside to enjoy their beauty.

She brushed her hand across a velvety blossom and resumed walking. More than likely, the roses would wither where they stood, having no one to enjoy their beauty and fragrance unless the groundskeeper cut a few to position around the house.

As she walked, she studied the ground for a weed to pull or a clod in the soil to break apart. She found none. She sighed in frustration. What was she supposed to do all day? She'd never known the luxury of idleness. At home, Sundays were the closest she came to leisure. Even then, cows needed milked, vegetables on the vine needed picked, livestock needed fed, not to mention the family. She supposed she should relish the inactivity. Instead, it made her want to scream.

The ring of a hammer on metal reached her ears. She left the stone wall and headed toward the stables where the sound originated. She peered around the corner into the gloomy interior. The familiar smells of horseflesh, hay, and leather reminded her of home and drew her inside.

Three walls enclosed a small blacksmith shop in the corner of the large barn. Logan stood over an anvil in the center of the room, sharpening a shovelhead. Harper's pulse quickened at the sight of him. She wasn't sure why. He'd been dismissive of her yesterday, nearly rude. He only really smiled while talking to Mrs. Philips.

Nonetheless, he was the only person she knew in Willow Wood, and the day was too long to stand outside alone in the sun.

"Good morning," she called so she wouldn't startle him.

He straightened and pushed his hat back on his head. Suspicion darkened his features at the sight of her.

Harper's teeth clenched. What was his problem? She hadn't done anything to him, unless he was still aggravated Uncle Hugh made him pick her up at the train station. That hadn't been her doing. He needn't worry that she would ask him for anything, even when she wanted to ride one of the horses. She could saddle her own horse. She wouldn't ask this man for a cup of water if she caught fire.

He removed the hat and combed his fingers through his hair, damp with sweat. "Good morning to you."

Despite her determination to steer clear of Logan, he was probably the only person at the estate who could tell her something useful about Ellie and Matthew's relationship.

A small forge under the open window blasted the room with heat. Sweat broke out on her forehead. Working in this room might be a bearable chore on a cold morning, but not today.

"It's too pretty outside to work in here," she said over the roar of the forge.

"I agree, but on a property this size, some things won't wait. Sometimes I think there should be more than one of me."

She chuckled. He seemed to be in a more accommodating mood today. "I believe you're right."

Logan set the hammer on the anvil. He replaced his hat and wiped his hands with a cloth from his back pocket. "Is this your first time in the stables? They're quite impressive, aren't they? Your uncle has several mounts on hand, should he or someone in the family need one. If you ever want to go for a ride or have me or one of the hands hitch a buggy, just yell."

Harper followed him out of the smithy. Wide doors stood open on either end of the large barn, allowing a refreshing breeze to dry the perspiration trickling down her back. She took a cleansing breath in the cool interior of the barn.

"Uncle Hugh told me as much last night. I don't need someone to hitch a team for me, though. When the need arises, tell me which horses I'm permitted to use and I'll take care of them myself."

"I don't doubt your ability, but your uncle won't appreciate it. He's particular about who handles his mounts and property. Around here, he's the boss, no matter who you are. Everyone does things his way."

She heard the words he didn't say. Even Ellie.

"Whatever you think is best."

Logan stuffed the rag back into his pocket. "Come on, I'll show you the horses. I suppose you can ride."

She tilted her head. "Of course, I can ride. Pa set me on a horse when I was three. Since then I've ridden mules, plow horses, calves, and even an actual saddle horse or two. I can handle myself."

His bright blue eyes twinkled. He looked as though he was trying hard not to smile. "We have a few docile horses here, good for riding through town or pulling the carriage. Then there are those who love to stretch their legs on the roads outside of town."

"Those are the ones I want to see."

She eagerly fell into step beside him as he moved to the stalls.

"Have you met Ellie?" he asked after introducing her to two mares and a long-legged roan that looked built for racing.

"Twice. Sort of."

He cocked an eyebrow.

"Uncle Hugh introduced her to me at dinner last night. She barely looked up. This morning, I carried her breakfast tray upstairs. The room was dark, so I didn't exactly see her, but she spoke to me."

"At least she let you in the room and accepted breakfast from you."

"I didn't really give her a choice. I went in without an invitation."

"Whatever it takes."

"Last night I asked if she would give me a tour of the neighborhood. Uncle Hugh jumped right in and said you could take me wherever I needed to go or buy whatever I required."

"Of course."

Harper huffed impatiently. "I don't *need* anything. The only thing I want is for Ellie to get out of the house. Uncle Hugh didn't even give me a chance to talk her into it. Her condition might improve more quickly if he didn't indulge her so much."

It was Logan's turn to blow out a puff of air. "That's not likely to happen. Mr. Lundy has indulged Ellie's every whim for as long as I've known them. I doubt he's open to advice on the matter."

"Especially from me," she finished for him.

She moved to a row of hay bales against the far wall and sat. "I feel so helpless. I don't know how to help if Uncle Hugh won't make her leave her room or put her into a situation she might find uncomfortable at first."

Logan sat beside her. "I believe Ellie is the only person in the world to get the better of Hugh Lundy. I doubt that'll change no matter how sick she is."

"Sick? You think she's sick?"

"Heartsick. Isn't that the same thing?"

Harper mulled the concept over in her mind. She'd never considered a broken heart an illness. She remembered a woman back home who had lost her husband and father in the War Between the States. Within a year of their deaths, both her children died from illness. The woman became a recluse. She paid the store to deliver what little food she couldn't grow herself or the few supplies she needed. No one in town caught more than a passing glimpse of her as she hurried to and from the cemetery where her children were buried. Eventually she wasted away to nothing until she finally, mercifully, passed away. No one in town said she was sick; they called her crazy. Maybe only rich people could afford the dignity of sickness, while poor women lost their minds.

She turned to face Logan. His shoulder was nearly against hers. Heat prickled in her cheeks, and not from the heat of the day. She resisted the urge to scoot over to put additional space between them. He wasn't the first handsome man she'd sat next to. He wasn't even the first one she'd kissed. But she wasn't thinking of kissing him. Was she?

"When did you first meet Ellie?"

"Matthew and I had just gotten to town. We had put the word out we were looking for work. Someone said Mr. Lundy needed the barn roof patched. Turned out a patch wasn't enough, so we reroofed the whole thing. It took nearly a month. That's when they first met."

"I wonder if Uncle Hugh blames himself for Ellie's melancholia."

"What do you mean?"

"If he hadn't hired you to replace the roof, Matthew might never have met Ellie."

"You could be right, though Willow Wood is a small place. We saw her around some while we worked on the roof. She didn't pay us much mind at the time. She was always coming and going with her friends. But, boy, Matthew noticed her. He always had an eye for a pretty girl. I guess it wasn't until the dance that Ellie noticed him."

"What dance?"

Logan rested his shoulders against the board planks of the barn wall. "Some of the local businesses hosted a barn dance. Pretty much the whole town went."

She nodded, thinking of her own experiences with community gatherings. Barn dances probably garnered the same level of excitement in every small town.

"Matthew and Ellie spent the whole evening together," Logan said. "It was a dream come true for Matthew. He's always been outgoing. He gets along with everyone. Has a lot of friends. Ellie was the same way. They were a perfect match."

He sat forward and propped his elbows on his knees. "After that night, Matthew was head over heels for her. All he could talk about was Ellie. He forgot every other girl in town. Whenever we were up on the roof working, he spent more time looking at the house and wishing she'd come out than hammering shingles."

He looked at Harper to make sure she was paying attention. "His attraction wasn't one-sided. Ellie kept finding excuses to come outside to see Matthew too. Those two couldn't get enough of each other."

Then why did he leave her? Harper wanted to ask. Instead she said, "What about the other girls? You said Matthew always noticed pretty girls, but he forgot them once he fell for Ellie. Is it possible he liked someone else at the same time?"

"He didn't play the field, if that's what you're asking. Matthew played hard and he worked hard. Girls liked him. They liked how he made them laugh and didn't make them uncomfortable like some fellows can. He was brought up Christian, though he didn't always act like it. But he didn't lead the girls on. He just liked a pretty face and liked the attention the girls gave back."

"Could there have been someone else though?" she persisted. "Is it possible he fell in love with another girl and left town with her?"

Logan's face hardened. "No. Matthew wasn't that kind. Not ever. He was crazy about Ellie, and only Ellie. After he met her, I don't think he was aware there was another girl in the world. If he left, it was for a job or something like that."

"If? What do you mean, if?"

Logan didn't speak for a moment. "I don't mean anything."

She studied him closely. "Where do you think he went? Would he have gone back home?"

He barked out a humorless laugh. "That's the last place he'd go." He plucked a piece of straw from the bale on which he sat and jammed it between his teeth. "Even though I knew he wouldn't have gone back to Indiana, I eventually wrote to his sister to ask if she'd seen him. You know, just to be sure. Took close to a year before she bothered to write me back. She said she hadn't seen him since the two of us lit outta there."

He leveled a look at Harper. "Matthew and his sister didn't see eye to eye on pretty near anything. There wasn't much love lost between them when we came west."

He stood and worked the kinks out of his back. He walked a few feet away toward one of the stalls and turned back to her. "I don't know what to tell you about where Matthew went or when he'll be back. It never made sense that he left the way he did without telling me. It was one thing, him leaving Ellie. But he and I—we were more like brothers than friends. I've known him my whole life. We knew everything about each other. He's the reason I came west. If he needed to leave in a hurry, I don't understand why he didn't tell me. Just like last time."

"What happened the last time? Was he in trouble?"

Logan turned to look into the closest stall. It was empty and clean, so she knew he was looking at nothing.

"I told you there was no love lost between Matthew and his family. My situation was much the same. We came here because we had no reason not to."

Harper jumped to her feet and strode over to where he stood. "But why in a hurry? Could Matthew have left here for the same reason he left Indiana?"

A muscle in Logan's jaw twitched. Harper stepped closer until she was close enough to smell the tangy perspiration that plastered his shirt to his back. "You must have suspicions about why he left without telling you or Ellie. Whatever they are could help Ellie get past losing him."

He stared at her, his jaw clenched around the straw between his teeth. "I don't know why Matthew left or where he went. Even if I did, I don't believe it would make a difference to Ellie. She needs a friend, not to keep waiting for something that won't happen."

"How do you know it won't happen? Are you saying Matthew isn't coming back? If you're sure of it, you need to tell Ellie."

"I don't know anything for sure. All I'm saying is it's been two years. If he was coming back, he would've done it by now. Matthew is impulsive. He doesn't wait two years for anything."

"Yet he expects Ellie to wait two years for him?"

He looked like he was going to say something, and then shook his head in defeat. "Matthew never expected her to wait. He'd be annoyed if he knew she was."

"He sounds like a real prince."

He took the straw out of his mouth and threw it onto the stable floor. "Yeah, well, the only one who should matter to you is Ellie. She needs someone who's patient enough to try to understand what she's going through."

Harper gritted her teeth at his slight. "What she needs is to know where Matthew went and if he's coming back. If he planned to walk away to chase some selfish dream, or to run away from trouble his reckless behavior had caused, he should've been man enough to tell her."

He exhaled long and hard. "We can't change the past. All we can do is help Ellie overcome it."

That's all Harper wanted to do, but she couldn't if Logan continued to keep things from her.

"I'm trying to help," she said.

He looked about to say something when a short man about twice Logan's age pushed a wheelbarrow through the stable doors. "Yeah, well, it was nice talking with you, Harper. I need to get back to work."

She brushed dust and straw off her skirt. "I'm sorry I kept you from it." She didn't try to keep the anger from her voice.

He headed toward the other man without another glance. Out in the sunshine Harper stomped across the courtyard toward the house. What an infuriating man. He claimed to want to help Ellie, but he obviously knew more than he claimed. Then he insulted Harper by suggesting she lacked the patience to understand her cousin.

Why was he even here? He took this job because of Matthew. Without Matthew gone, Logan could certainly earn better wages at the mines or the railyard.

Harper had found a Bible in her room on the dressing table. She would read a few chapters while she waited for the noon meal and her next opportunity to carry a tray upstairs for Ellie to ignore.

She was nearly to the back door when the truth hit her full in the face. Only one reason explained why Logan was still here mucking out stalls and banging dents out of farm implements for Uncle Hugh when better opportunities waited around every corner.

Love.

He was in love with Ellie. Without Matthew around, he could have her for himself. All he had to do was encourage Harper to help Ellie realize she was better off without Matthew Dunleavy, and he was the one worth having.

•••

Logan positioned himself so he could talk with Burt but keep his eyes on Harper over his shoulder. He didn't want her to know he was watching in case she looked back.

He had stopped wondering and worrying about Matthew a few months after he disappeared. He didn't know why he told Harper, *if* Matthew went away. Of course, he left of his own volition. When trouble didn't find Matthew, he went looking for it. Logan was sure that was what had happened this time.

Truth be told, Logan was sick of coming to his friend's rescue. Sick of playing the mother hen. Sick of handing over a week's pay to settle a debt after Matthew bet too optimistically on a horse race. Sick of waiting for his friend to grow up. Sometimes, the only way a fella learned life's lessons was the hard way.

Logan remembered the argument they'd had a few weeks before Matthew took off. He was gambling again. Not actually *again* since he had never stopped. But it was getting worse. When a miner cornered Logan in the alley outside Endicott's General Store and demanded he tell him where he could find Matthew, Logan knew the situation wouldn't reach a peaceful end.

"Someone's gonna get hurt," Logan had yelled at Matthew later that night. "If not you, it'll be Ellie. Does she even know what you're doing? You can't hide it from her forever."

Matthew had tried to laugh off his concerns. When Logan wouldn't let the matter drop, Matthew told him to mind his own business. He knew what he was doing, and he knew how to handle a hot-headed miner who didn't know when to fold.

Two weeks later the miner was dead, and Matthew was gone.

Logan hadn't told anyone. He didn't want to think about it. Matthew was a lot of things. He acted recklessly and sometimes he gambled money that wasn't his. But he wasn't a killer. He didn't possess the greed or compulsion to kill another person. If the miner pushed him into a fight, Matthew would've laughed it off and walked away, even if he took a beating in the process.

The death of the miner worried Logan, but not because he believed Matthew killed him. Matthew had run from trouble, as was his pattern, but how much trouble? And was someone on his trail? Someone who might come after Ellie if they thought she could pay what Matthew wouldn't.

From the moment Logan saw Harper climb off the train, he knew the little blonde would unsettle the tenuous equilibrium of the house. He had worried that her gentle southern smile would be his undoing. He didn't have time for a woman. He had enough to do building up the ranch he was buying off Hiram Campbell. Every day he grew more anxious to make his own getaway once Ellie got Matthew Dunleavy out of her head once and for all.

Ellie never saw Matthew for who he really was. She had loved him, flaws and all, and refused to see the truth when it was standing right in front of her.

But Harper would see. She wouldn't accept Logan's theories until she had proof. And she wouldn't stop asking questions that could endanger Ellie and herself.

Chapter Eight

That evening Harper ate dinner alone in the kitchen while Mrs. Philips finished her chores for the day. She hadn't seen Ellie since lunch when she went upstairs with a lunch tray and collected the nearly full breakfast dishes. She had attempted conversation again and reminded Ellie she would be in the room next door or downstairs should Ellie need her.

Ellie did not acknowledge the offer.

Uncle Hugh did not come home for dinner either. Mrs. Philips wasn't surprised. "Sometimes he doesn't come home at all. When he's working at the mines, he spends the night in one of the bunkhouses or a tent. That man isn't afraid to get his hands dirty."

At the kitchen table the next morning Mrs. Philips plucked another slice of bacon from the platter and held it over Harper's plate. "Care for another?"

Harper shook her head as she swallowed the last of her egg. "I couldn't eat another bite. If you keep feeding me like this, I'll have to let the seams out of my dress."

The housekeeper's smile broadened. "Good. You need some meat on your bones. I do enjoy having someone to cook for again. Besides Logan, that is. That young man always has a healthy appetite."

She took Harper's empty plate to the sink and immersed it in the soapy water. Her expression turned wistful.

"It's a shame, really. Mr. and Mrs. Lundy worked so hard to build this beautiful house. Your uncle commissioned a wood artisan from Denver to create their dining room set. I wager it hasn't been used more'n ten times since Mrs. Lundy passed away going on fourteen years ago."

Harper thought of her empty spot on the bench seat at her family's table this morning. She was sure they had lifted her up in prayer when they blessed the food. More than likely, a few tears had been shed for her the same as she shed for them.

"Our table at home gets so crowded, sometimes we have to eat in shifts."

Mrs. Philips dried her hands on a towel and joined Harper at the table. "There's no shame in missing the ones you love, child. I'll never forget how lonesome I was when I left home. I was much younger than you, that's for sure. Only fifteen."

"Fifteen?"

She nodded. "Papa had died two years earlier, and Mama just couldn't keep us all. I got a job as a laundry woman for a lady just a few houses down from here. My, but that woman was mean." She laughed at the telling. "She didn't like me, but she sure kept me around. I thought I'd work my fingers to the bone for that old battleax."

"How did you get away from her?"

"She died." Mrs. Philips laughed. "Oh, it wasn't so bad, really. I got good at laundry. And cooking and housework and gardening. I think that's why Mr. Philips fell in love with me."

"What happened to him?"

Ordinarily, Harper would never ask such a personal question to someone she'd just met, but Mrs. Philips was easy to talk to, and the conversation helped her forget her homesickness.

The older woman didn't look offended by the question. She seemed to appreciate the chance to talk as much as Harper did. "He passed away nigh to ten years ago now. Got down with the croup and couldn't fight it off." She shook her head, looking lost in thought.

Harper gave her a moment to her memories. "Did you have children?" she asked gently.

"A little girl and a boy. Our daughter died when she was two years old. Like to broke both our hearts. Our son took off to Arizona Territory as soon as he was old enough. Mr. Philips had already passed on, so I had to get over that loss on my own. It broke my heart all over again. He came back to visit once. Mentioned a little girl he was thinking of marrying.

Said he was looking to buy a spread of his own and fill it with children."

Harper propped her chin on her hand. "That's nice."

Mrs. Philips shrugged. "I don't know. I haven't heard from him in a couple years. I think he was just telling me what he thought I wanted to hear." She glanced toward the window facing the back yard.

"Anyhow, that's how I ended up at this house. When my old employer died, Mr. Lundy came and told me he had seen how clean and organized her house had been all those years. Said he was looking for a new housekeeper. His wife was in poor health and couldn't run the house the way she wanted, especially with a child to raise."

"Ellie."

Mrs. Philips' eyes instantly brimmed with tears. "My, my, she was a delightful child. Mr. Lundy gave my husband a position, too, but it wasn't long before his health started failing. Such a good man, your uncle."

"Do you have any other family left in the area?"

"Two of my brothers are still nearby. I also have a widowed sister-in-law here in town. I spend many of my days off with her."

She went to the stove for the coffeepot. She held it over Harper's cup. Harper shook her head. Mrs. Philips filled her own cup before returning the pot to the stove.

She sat again at the table. "I'm just thankful I'm able to be here for Ellie. After everything she's been through, losing her ma so early and all, it breaks my heart to think of the way Matthew Dunleavy abandoned her. She loved him so much. I thought he loved her too. I guess that goes to show you should know what to expect when you pick up a snake." She looked quickly toward the kitchen door to make sure she hadn't been overheard.

Harper glanced at the door, too, and lowered her voice. "Why would you call him a snake? Maybe he wasn't ready to settle down and did Ellie a favor by leaving."

Mrs. Philips pulled back as if Harper had slapped her. "Are you defending that man?"

"No, I just meant—"

"I agree Ellie is better off without him," she conceded. "But you've seen her. She is devastated by his leaving. If he wasn't ready to settle down, which obviously he wasn't, he could've told her face to face like a man. I never could abide a coward, and that's exactly what he is."

"Were you surprised when he took off?"

Mrs. Philips took a thoughtful sip from her coffee. "Well, yes and no. He was always a good-time Charlie. He considered himself some sort of cardsharp. He was a gambler." She curled her lip in distaste. "According to the maids, he bet heavily at the tables. And on the horses. Why, I think that boy would've bet on how many clouds were in the sky if he could find somebody to take the bet."

Despair settled in Harper's stomach. Poor Ellie. How could she have fallen for a gambler? Yesterday Logan had said Matthew left Indiana because he was in trouble. Was gambling the sort of trouble he meant? Could it have been what forced him to leave Willow Wood?

Mrs. Philips glanced again toward the door to make sure no one was listening. "Don't you dare breathe a word of this to Ellie, but I was relieved when he left. I wish it would've happened differently so it wouldn't hurt her so much. But after the time I heard him arguing with Mr. Lundy, I knew his days were numbered in Willow Wood."

Harper pushed her cup aside and leaned closer over the table. "What were they arguing about?"

Mrs. Philips drew her lips into a thin line. "I wasn't supposed to overhear, so as soon as I realized what they were talking about, I hurried past the room. But I heard enough. It was over just what you'd expect. Money. Mr. Lundy accused Matthew of only caring about Ellie to get his claws on her money. Your uncle went as far as to hire an investigator to look into Matthew and Logan."

Logan? Harper didn't want to hear that he was as much of a snake as Matthew. But if he was, she needed to know in order to protect Ellie. If he was in love with her, she wasn't strong enough to be hurt again.

Mrs. Philips puffed out her chest. Harper could tell she enjoyed filling her in on the household gossip. Regardless, Harper needed to hear it.

"The investigator told Mr. Lundy Matthew was in debt to some bad characters in Indiana. Oh, Matthew tried to deny it all right, but you can't put anything over on Hugh Lundy."

Harper gritted her teeth in frustration. So that's what Logan meant when he said Matthew had to leave Indiana in a hurry. What else was he keeping from her?

"What about Logan?" she asked Mrs. Philips.

The housekeeper stared at her over the top of her coffee cup. "What about him?"

"You said Uncle Hugh had the investigator investigate both of them."

"Oh, yes. He didn't find anything about Logan as far as I know. If he had, he wouldn't still be here, you can count on that."

Harper wasn't sure what to think. Had Uncle Hugh run Matthew off after he heard from the investigator? If he did, why not tell Ellie instead of letting her suffer and grieve for two years? Surely, she would've understood if the man was a criminal or had dangerous men trying to extract money from him.

"How terrible for Ellie," she said. "She's suffered so much the last few years. Uncle Hugh could've ended it all by telling her what Matthew was doing."

Mrs. Philips lifted a hand and wagged her finger at Harper. "We don't know that he didn't. As I was walking away, I heard Matthew yelling at him. Maybe your uncle told Ellie, but she chose to believe Matthew's version of events."

"She should've understood Uncle Hugh was trying to protect her."

"Have you ever been in love, Harper?"

An image of Logan flashed through her mind. She shook her head. "No, I haven't."

"The heart can make a young woman believe strange things."

Harper couldn't deny the sentiment. "So, Matthew could've left because Uncle Hugh threatened him or because he needed to get away from debtors in Indiana."

"Who can say? When a person lives that type of life, he makes a lot of enemies."

"There must be a reason Ellie's believes he'll come back."

Mrs. Philips shook her head. "Everyone in this town knows he isn't coming back. I think, deep down, Ellie knows it too."

Chapter Nine

Harper didn't sleep well Saturday night in her big bed. The first few nights she had been so worn out from her journey on the train, she could've slept like a newborn in the stable with the horses. Now that she had caught up on sleep, she couldn't make herself drowsy, no matter how many sheep she counted. With all the work required to keep the farm running back home, she collapsed into bed every night and fell asleep within moments as long as her sisters weren't talking and giggling. They were usually as tired and ready for sleep as she was.

All she had done at her uncle's house was carry trays of food up and down the stairs three times a day, wander from window to window, and wait for Ellie to seek her out for conversation or companionship.

She might have a long wait before that happened.

She awoke Sunday morning with red-rimmed, scratchy eyes and a headache from her fitful night of tossing and turning in the big, empty bed. Ignoring her headache, she swung her legs over the side of the bed to begin her toilette. Today was the day she looked forward to more than any other. Back home, going to church on Sunday morning was the highlight of her week. Now that she was in a new town, she anticipated it even more.

She had seen a church spire through her bedroom window and asked Mrs. Philips if Uncle Hugh or Ellie would go with her to church.

The older woman had clicked her tongue and shook her head. "I'm afraid not, child. Your uncle usually stays at the mines on Saturday night. Sunday is another workday for that man. Ellie hasn't been to church in a long time. You're welcome to go yourself or you can join me at my church. I'll have Burt hitch the carriage for you and take you wherever you want to go."

Harper thought it a terrible waste of time and resources to hitch a buggy to transport her two hundred yards when she was perfectly capable of walking, especially in such glorious weather.

"Please don't trouble Burt," she told Mrs. Philips. "If it looks like rain, I'll ask him before I leave."

She wondered briefly if and where Logan went to church. They hadn't discussed their spiritual conditions, and after their conversation in the stable the day after she arrived, she doubted they would discuss much of anything.

Another woman was in the kitchen when she got downstairs, dressed and ready for church. Harper introduced herself and fixed a bowl of oatmeal and strawberries. The woman didn't talk as she moved around the kitchen, fussing with bread dough and lunch preparations. Harper wasn't sure how to talk to her or if she should. She wondered if there was a book that explained how to interact with servants. She didn't think she'd ever get used to people doing things for her that she could do herself.

For the first time since arriving at Uncle Hugh's house, she walked out the front door. The only other time she'd seen anyone open the gigantic door was when one of the maids wiped the cobwebs away from the lintel. She felt like a princess as her worn shoes clicked across the marble veranda. It would've been a lot more fun to enjoy the opulence of the house's entrance if her sisters were here. She imagined Sophie and Lottie laughing and squealing as they ran circles on the marble tiles and up and down the four steps to the cobblestone walkway.

The huge double gate loomed ahead of her, closed as always. Too late, it occurred to her she may not be strong enough to push one side open, and she'd have to walk all the way around the house to the smaller gate that opened onto an adjacent street.

She tucked her Bible under her arm, looked around to make sure none of the stable boys or maids were watching in case she couldn't move the massive gate, and leaned her weight into it. Though nearly double her height, the gate swung open effortlessly, much to her surprise. Once through, Harper exhaled in relief, patted her hat and bodice into place, and started down the hill.

She had never walked into a church by herself in her life unless she was there to clean it. Nor had she slipped into a pew in the back and hoped no one in the cavernous building would notice her. During the service, parishioners cast quick glances over their shoulders at her. Harper smiled at each one, though the smiles she received in return were mostly stiff and uncertain. She understood the congregation's curiosity. Even though Ellie and Uncle Hugh didn't attend here, everyone in town must know by now she was staying with them. They were assuredly dying to know what went on inside the big house, but decorum and good manners forbid them from asking. At least, she hoped they wouldn't ask.

As the last notes of the closing hymn faded away, Harper stood with the rest of the congregants. A woman in a pale green dress with poof sleeves and a large stylish hat headed her way. Harper tensed. Here it came. Questions disguised as greeting.

The woman's gaze slid up and down Harper's homemade dress. It was the nicest one she owned. Last winter when Pa sold a few calves, there was enough money left for the girls to buy fabric for new dresses. Harper had chosen a tan material with a delicate paisley print in red, white, various shades of cream, and a little blue thrown in that she thought accentuated her eyes. She had loved everything about the dress, but today she felt faded and shapeless compared to the willowy brunette coming her way.

She straightened her shoulders. Church wasn't the place for vanity. She'd always seen herself as the plainest bird in every flock. She wouldn't apologize for it now. She stepped out of the pew and waited for the woman to reach her.

"Good morning," the woman said, her voice as smooth as the silk accents on the hat sitting fashionably off center on her head. "You're the Lundys' cousin, aren't you?"

Harper smiled as she took hold of the woman's outstretched, gloved hand. "Yes, I am. Harper Dixon."

"It's nice to meet you, Harper. I'm Geneva Wallace. I'm a friend of your cousin Ellie."

Harper's lips froze to her teeth. One of the friends Logan said hadn't visited Ellie since Matthew jilted her. She shouldn't judge the woman too harshly. She didn't know the whole story. In fact, she knew next to nothing.

"It's nice to meet you, Geneva. Ellie will be happy to hear I ran into you."

Geneva dipped her head to convey sorrow, though it looked like an act to Harper. "We're all simply beside ourselves over what happened with Ellie. Please tell her how much we miss her."

Harper feigned ignorance. "Who is we?"

Geneva managed to look affronted. "Why her friends, of course. We tried to support her, but there was nothing we could do. You know how proud Ellie is. She didn't want help from anyone."

Harper didn't know how proud Ellie was, but she had to agree with Geneva's assessment. So far, it had seemed to her, too, that Ellie didn't want help. "She must've truly loved Mr. Dunleavy," she said, hoping for insight that would help her reach Ellie.

"What?" The dark-headed woman grimaced. "Yes, I suppose she did. He was…charming. Ellie was always crazy for a man who knew how to have a good time. I never dreamed, though, she'd be duped by such an obvious cad."

Harper noticed a few other parishioners slowing as they passed. She didn't want them to hear this woman talk ill of her cousin, or Mr. Dunleavy for that matter. "I don't know if I'd say she was duped."

Geneva gave her a pitying look. "Why else would a man like him get close to a woman like Ellie if not for her money?"

Harper could understand people jumping to a similar conclusion when a poor man sought out the company of a rich woman. But it was unfair to assume Ellie was so naïve. Her closest friends should know her better than that.

"I heard Mr. Lundy threatened to disinherit Ellie if she didn't stop seeing the man," Geneva said. She searched Harper's face, her gaze hopeful Harper would confirm or deny the rumor.

Harper kept her mouth shut. Even if she knew exactly where Matthew Dunleavy was and why he had gone, she wouldn't tell this gossipmonger. How dare she call herself Ellie's friend!

"Other people believe Mr. Lundy paid Dunleavy to leave town."

Harper bit her bottom lip in an effort to hide her surprise. Oh, how she hoped it wasn't true.

Geneva went on, obviously happy for the chance to air old gossip. "As soon as we realized how close the two of them had become, we tried to talk sense into her. It was too late. Ellie had fallen hard for him. It was obvious they didn't have anything in common. Obvious to everyone but Ellie, that is."

Harper thought of Logan, who seemed to love Ellie. Was he only interested in her money as well? If so, he sure was taking the long route to get at it. He had told her Ellie and Matthew had many things in common. They were both outgoing, fun-loving, and adventurous. Loved to have fun and laugh and be adventurous. Except for their financial situation, they didn't seem so different to her.

"Maybe she saw something in him the rest of you never took the time to see."

Geneva pulled back. "I'm sure I don't know what you mean."

"What I mean is I trust my cousin's judgment." She had no reason to, but she wouldn't stand here and let this woman insinuate Ellie had been played the fool by a smooth-talking charlatan only interested in her money. "I never met Matthew, but if Ellie cared so deeply for him, he must've had some redeeming qualities."

"I don't mean to imply I don't trust Ellie. But anyone can be hoodwinked by someone who knows what he's doing." Geneva pursed her lips clearly disappointed Harper wasn't forthcoming with family secrets. "Regardless of how he took his leave, Ellie wouldn't let any of us near her afterward. We tried to tell her she needn't be embarrassed over what had happened. Everybody makes mistakes. We wanted to go back to the way things were before. She wouldn't have it. Eventually we gave up."

Harper couldn't believe so-called friends could be so judgmental. "Maybe she didn't want to hear you say, 'I told you so'."

"I would never say such a thing."

"Maybe not to her face, but she must've known what you thought. It may be why she doesn't leave the house. I don't know if I could bear it either if my dearest friends considered the man I loved a mistake."

Geneva's face darkened a few shades. "I hope you haven't misunderstood me, Harper. We tried to help Ellie. We only wanted what was best for her. It soon became apparent she was beyond reason. She made her choice."

"Maybe if you had tried to understand her pain, she wouldn't have to choose."

Geneva looked past Harper and nodded at someone outside her field of vision. "It was nice meeting you, Harper. I really must go. Please give Ellie my best."

Harper didn't respond. As annoyed as she was with Ellie's former friend, she realized she hadn't been much more compassionate or understanding of Ellie's pain herself. So far, she had learned next to nothing about what Ellie was going though. Except that she was completely alone.

Chapter Ten

A few more people nodded or spoke to Harper as she exited the church, but most didn't say anything personal. Some of their curiosity could be attributed to not having seen a Lundy family member in church in years. She was nearly to the door to wish a good day to the pastor when she spotted Logan at the corner of the sanctuary. He caught her eye and smiled the first almost-friendly smile he'd ever directed at her. She looked back at the pious looking pastor talking to an elderly gentleman and pivoted on her heel to join Logan.

He saw her coming and motioned her toward the building's side exit. When she reached him, she was still breathless and warm-cheeked from her encounter with Geneva.

"I'm sure glad to see you."

His eyes widened. "You are?"

Her cheeks warmed further as she realized how her comment must've sounded to his ears. "A familiar face," she clarified, though she wasn't sure it was what she meant. "I'm not used to attending church alone. It's strange sitting in a pew when I'm not related to half the congregation."

He smiled. "You'll make friends in no time."

She thought of Geneva and nearly shuddered. Next Sunday she might pick another church.

Logan held the door for her, where a narrow staircase led to the church's side yard.

"Did Matthew attend church with you here?" she asked as she started down the stairs.

"He wasn't much for church attendance. He preferred using his Sunday mornings for sleeping in after a long Saturday night playing cards."

"That's too bad. I had hoped to talk Ellie into coming with me this morning, but she was still sound asleep when I left. Who was I kidding? I can't even talk her into finishing her breakfast."

"I can count on one hand how many times Mr. Lundy has been inside a church since I moved to Willow Wood," Logan said as they reached the bottom of the stairs. "Ellie came only a little more often."

"Where did they attend?"

"The big one on Main Street." He pointed to a dark brick spire rising above the buildings in the distance.

"Is Uncle Hugh a believer?"

Logan frowned. "I don't make it a point to judge another man's relationship with his Maker. I'll just say if he's a believer, it doesn't influence his business dealings or activities."

Harper's heart sank. Ma would be disappointed to hear it. Harper added it to the list of things she wouldn't mention in her letters home unless someone straight out asked. Was Ellie the same? From what she'd witnessed so far, a relationship with God didn't appear to be part of her life.

"I met one of Ellie's old friends today," she told Logan.

"Geneva Wallace? I saw you talking to her."

Harper followed him to the board sidewalk. She wanted to talk, to ask his opinion but wasn't sure how or where to start. "Are all of Ellie's friends so…"

"Judgmental?" he offered as she grasped for a word.

Harper lowered her head and nodded.

"I wonder sometimes if her friends' attitudes about Matthew didn't contribute to her isolation after he left. She knew they didn't approve of him. He was—both of us were—beneath them."

The pain in his face told Harper how deeply he cared for Ellie.

"I got the impression Geneva felt the same about me," Harper said.

"Probably," he replied without apology. "Do you have plans this afternoon?"

"Not really. It looked like the cook was preparing a Sunday feast when I left this morning. I thought I'd go back and enjoy it."

"A feast no one will probably eat except for you, me, and the rest of the household staff. Do you mind if I walk with you?"

"Not at all." Harper couldn't explain the way her mood lightened at the thought of spending time with him. He loved Ellie, and he didn't seem to like her at all. But his temperament was more hospitable today. She might as well enjoy it while it lasted since no one else in town had asked to walk her home.

They started down the street. Couples in buggies, families spilling out of buckboards, riders on horseback, and walking groups passed, going in all directions. Inside the gates of the Lundy estate was a different world from what Harper knew, but out here things looked like a typical Sunday afternoon in any small community.

"I hope you don't think I was speaking out of turn about your uncle," Logan said after a few moments of watching passersby. "I didn't mean to imply he isn't a good man. He gave Matthew and me a chance when we first came to town. His spiritual condition is between him and the Lord."

"I understand. I'm glad you told me. Now I know what to pray for. What about you? Should I add you to my prayer list?"

He chuckled. "I would rightly appreciate that, Miss Dixon. But don't let my soul's condition worry you. The Lord and I are good friends. My mother's parents were God-fearing people. When Ma couldn't take me, or Pa wasn't interested, they made sure my brother and I were on the church pew next to them."

She smiled, delighted at the news for reasons more selfish than she cared to admit. "I'm glad to hear it. I don't think I've missed a Sunday at church in my life. My parents wouldn't let me stay home without anything short of a terminal illness or profuse bleeding to prevent me."

He laughed again.

Harper liked the way his face crinkled at the corners of his mouth and how his turquoise eyes lit up. She imagined Ellie could put a light in those eyes if she tried.

"Hopefully you'll be a good influence on your cousin," he said. "I overheard part of what you told Geneva. Ellie needs someone to stand up for her."

Admiration shone in his eyes. Harper's cheeks warmed under the praise, though she wasn't sure how to take the compliment. The other day he had insinuated she wasn't patient or compassionate enough to help Ellie. Perhaps he had spoken out of frustration. She was frustrated too. She needed to put her irritation aside and focus on their common goal; to help and protect Ellie.

They walked in silence a few moments. Harper focused on the afternoon peace and the Creator whom she had just worshiped in church. Birdsong filled the trees. A dog barked from behind a picket fence. Two children playing in a yard stopped to watch as they passed. A woman on her porch tipped a watering can over a pot of flowers. A young man sang to a baby he bounced on his knee. On another porch, an elderly couple watched them from a swing. They waved as Harper and Logan drew abreast of their gate. Logan called out a greeting. Most of the residents of Willow Wood looked like Harper's neighbors at home. It appeared households of affluence like Uncle Hugh's were the exception, not the rule.

"I trust you're getting accustomed to Willow Wood?" Logan asked as if reading her mind.

"It's beautiful. The countryside is so different from back home, but the town seems a lot the same."

"The sheer beauty of this part of the country is what made me want to stay," he said. "Back home in Indiana, the land was wide open and flat. Beautiful in its own rite but nothing like this. Did you go through Indiana on your way here?"

She shook her head. "Not that I know of. I saw plenty of open prairie though. Sometimes I felt like I was on a ship in the ocean. I wished my sisters and brothers could've seen it too. I kept imagining the delight on their faces if they saw what I saw."

She sighed. "I'm sorry. I need to stop doing that to myself. Every time I think of home, I want to cry. I guess I shouldn't have admitted that to you either."

He smiled gently. Harper couldn't read the expression in his eyes. It was as if he were seeing her for the first time. She looked away. She didn't want to bust out crying in the middle of the street.

"It's only natural that you're homesick," he said. "I didn't have much family left in Indiana but coming west was still a hard adjustment."

Harper was thankful to get the conversation off herself. "What did you do back home? For a living, I mean."

"I worked in a cabinet factory for a while. I like working with my hands, but I prefer being in the fresh air. That's why I was thankful to get the job with your uncle. To me, any job above ground is better than the mines."

She chuckled. "My brothers would agree with you. I can't imagine one of them working in a dark mine."

"How many brothers do you have?"

"Four brothers and four sisters. There's Joan, Patrick, and Davy before me. Then after me are Billy, Doris May, Sophie, Lottie, and Little Walt. He's the baby, though he's not a baby anymore. He's nine."

"That's quite a few. I don't know how you keep them straight."

"Isn't always easy." She opened her mouth to ask about his family, but he spoke first. "I imagine the seclusion at your uncle's doesn't help with the homesickness."

If you only knew, she thought. Out loud, she said, "The quiet is the hardest thing to get used to. Just like this morning. I only had myself to get ready for church. No arguing with Lottie to get out of bed and get dressed or fussing with Doris May about taking too long in front of the mirror. Did you come from a big family?"

His footsteps slowed. She wasn't sure if it was due to the direction of the conversation or because he wanted to finish before they reached the house. "No. I had one brother. He'd already left home by the time I came here. Ma's gone too. She caught pneumonia three winter's back."

"I'm so sorry. I didn't…"

He waved away her concern. "It's all right. You couldn't have known."

"Did she pass before you came here?"

He nodded. "Right before. That's why I came west with Matthew. I had nothing left to keep me in Indiana."

What about his father? He hadn't mentioned one. The man could've died years earlier or not factored into Logan's decision to leave home. She couldn't decide which was worse; leaving the people you loved or having no one to leave behind. The stone wall separating the Lundy mansion from the street came into view. Harper hadn't noticed Logan had led her to the back side of the street so they would enter the smaller gate.

"Maybe I can talk Ellie into taking a walk with me in the garden after lunch," she said hopefully. "She hasn't been out of the house one time since I've been there. Unless she sneaks out while I'm asleep."

"I doubt she does that. Sometimes I wonder if the lack of fresh air and sunshine contributes to her unhappiness."

"I never thought of that. Ma talks about the winter blues. Maybe that's part of Ellie's problems. She just doesn't realize it's summertime. The curtains in her room are drawn all the time. It's so gloomy. If she lets me, I'll open the window and see if it makes a difference."

"It certainly couldn't hurt."

Logan held the gate open for her. She looked through the open doors of the carriage house. The bay that held Uncle Hugh's rig was still empty. It wasn't likely Ellie would join her downstairs for lunch. Mrs. Philips had the day off. She didn't want to spend the next hour alone in the kitchen, thinking of her family seated around their big, noisy table at home.

"Are you coming to the house for lunch?"

She hoped she didn't sound too hopeful.

He shook his head. "I need to take care of some things today."

She almost asked what things, and if it was something she could help with. She held her tongue. Since Ellie was squirreled away in her room as always and Uncle Hugh was out of the house for the day, Logan probably wanted to enjoy his Sunday with no demands from the family.

They parted ways in the courtyard. Harper headed to the back door while Logan went straight to the barn. It took some effort, but she didn't look back.

Chapter Eleven

Ellie didn't come downstairs for dinner that night either. Before Harper could do it for her, the Sunday cook prepared a tray and carried it upstairs.

She wished the household would stop making it so easy for Ellie to close herself off from the world. Harper had only been here five days. She was in no position to offer an opinion, or even have one. But she couldn't help thinking if Uncle Hugh would stop giving in to Ellie's destructive behavior, she might accept Matthew wasn't coming back and find her way out of her despair. If something didn't change eventually, Harper might as well go home. She couldn't be a companion to someone who barely spoke to her.

The maid's feet faded on the marble staircase above her head. Harper had intentionally delayed writing a letter home. So far, she had nothing of interest to write outside of her journey west, and she'd written most of those observations on the train. She didn't know more about Ellie than what Uncle Hugh had written in his letter. The only things she knew about Uncle Hugh was that he worked all the time and didn't attend church. She could tell the family about Mrs. Philips. Describing the house and gardens would take up several pages if she did them justice. She wasn't sure she wanted to do so just yet. She didn't want to sound like she was bragging about her new position. She wouldn't have the words to describe it anyway. She couldn't mention Logan. Her parents would think she was interested in him. Which she wasn't since he was in love with Ellie.

With a descriptive eye, she looked around the high-ceilinged foyer, taking in the dark-stained crown molding and trim. The ticking of a gigantic grandfather clock—at least two heads taller than Pa—was the only sound in the house. She had never heard a lonelier sound in her life.

With her finger, she traced the elaborate scrollwork that followed the outside of the staircase as far as she could reach. Someday when she felt more comfortable being here, she'd make a rubbing of the woodwork to send home.

Not a cobweb or speck of dust clung to her finger when she pulled it away. She imagined the miles of baseboards, stair skirts, molding, and trim throughout this house. Someone must work from daylight to dark to keep it clean and polished. It seemed like a waste of effort and resources considering how much manual labor it took to feed and clothe the Dixons at home. Still, the end result was stunning.

If Uncle Hugh wanted to employ half of Willow Wood to maintain his beautiful home, it was no concern of hers. She looked up at the magnificent chandelier above her head and turned toward the staircase. Her foot caught on the leg of a small table that held nothing but a tall, slender Oriental vase. The vase wobbled. Harper lunged for it, but her hands grabbed only empty air. She gasped aloud as the vase hit the marble floor and broke into a thousand pieces. She slapped both hands over her face. The vase probably cost more than her parents' farm.

She slowly uncovered her face, wishing she could undo what had just happened, and stared at the fragments. She fought back tears. Ma always said you mustn't cry over spilt milk. Would Uncle Hugh see it that way? She hoped so or she'd be on her way back to Kentucky—or to a debtors' prison.

She stepped around the broken pieces and hurried down the hall and past the kitchen, to the closet inside the back door where she'd seen Mrs. Philips stow cleaning supplies. She grabbed a bucket, broom, and dustpan.

Back in the foyer, she knelt and began picking up the larger pieces and placing them in the bucket. The heavy pottery even felt expensive.

"Harper?"

A sharp corner of porcelain sliced into her finger. Harper jumped up and whirled around. She pressed the injured finger into a fist and tucked it in the folds of her skirt.

"Uncle Hugh."

He looked from her face to her injured hand. "What are you doing?"

"I…um…I was going to go upstairs to write a letter and I…" Tears sprang to her eyes. She almost hoped he would send her home. She'd prefer anything over staring into the stony condemnation on his face.

"I'm so sorry. I bumped into the table."

"You're bleeding." He stepped forward and took hold of her wrist.

"Yes, sir." Blood seeped between her fingers and onto his pressed cuff.

"Let me see." Though it wasn't a request, gentleness softened his words.

Harper relaxed her fist. "I'm so sorry. I didn't mean to break it."

He took a handkerchief out of his pocket and pressed it to her hand. "It's superficial. No need to call the doctor."

"Of course not, sir. It's my fault."

He released her wrist and stepped back. "What were you doing here?"

She gulped. She couldn't tell him she was gawking at his fancy house and speculating how many people it took to keep it clean when she hooked her big clumsy foot around his table leg. "I was…uh…not watching where I was going. I'll…I'll pay you out of the money from my stipend for the—" The broken vase had just sentenced her to a life of servitude.

"No, Harper. This." He motioned to the broom and bucket. "What are you doing?"

She wrinkled her brow. Wasn't he listening? She just told him.

"I…"

"I pay a staff to clean the house. It's not necessary for you to do so."

"I wasn't cleaning. I was picking up what I knocked over. My parents raised me to clean up my mistakes." She attempted a chuckle. It came out as a croak.

He clasped his hands and rocked back on his heels. "And a fine job they did of it. But in this house, the staff takes care of menial matters."

His impenetrable expression left no room for debate. "The next time you break or spill something, summon one of the maids or tell Mrs. Philips and she'll see that it's taken care of. Housekeeping is not why I brought you here. I appreciate that you are accustomed to such tasks. It may serve you well someday, but as long as you're here, you are not required to fill your days with such activity."

Harper blushed, properly chastised. "Yes, sir."

His face softened into a smile bordering on kindness. "I'm sure you have more free time than you're used to."

"Yes, sir."

"You may have noticed the room opposite my office is our library. I have an extensive collection of the classics, American authors, science, art, and history. I even have some of the current popular novels young ladies like to read." He smiled again. "Please help yourself. If you need something you can't find, let me know and I'll order it or have Logan find it for you."

Harper couldn't imagine asking Logan to buy her a dime novel many people considered salacious or vulgar. "Yes sir. Thank you. That's very generous of you."

"Don't mention it. I enjoy seeing a young mind broadened."

The maid who had taken Ellie's dinner to her room came back down the stairs. Uncle Hugh snapped back into his employer stance. "Patty, Miss Dixon has hurt her finger. Please take her to the kitchen and see to it."

The maid hurried the rest of the way to the bottom of the stairs. "Yes, sir."

Harper clenched her fist. "No, I'm fine. I can…" She stopped talking when she realized no one was listening.

Uncle Hugh took hold of her wrist and held it out to the maid. The maid unfolded her fingers from around the handkerchief.

"I'm fine," Harper repeated.

The maid turned her hand this way and that to examine the cut.

"As soon as you're finished, send Miss Dixon to my office, and then sweep this up."

"Yes, sir."

Harper felt sick. Was she in trouble? Was he sending her home? He barely seemed to notice the broken vase, but his first priority could've been making sure she wouldn't lose her hand to gangrene. Then he'd bring the hammer down. He looked like the type to do exactly that. Before she could remind him she had planned to write a letter and didn't have time for a meeting—not that she'd have the nerve to challenge him on anything—he disappeared through a doorway she assumed led to his office.

Helplessly, she allowed the maid to lead her by the wrist to the kitchen.

Chapter Twelve

Harper wanted to apologize to the maid for creating more work for the woman through her own carelessness. She also wanted to ask her what she thought Uncle Hugh wanted in his office. The maid wasn't likely to have an opinion about either issue, so she didn't say anything. While the woman dressed the cut, which turned out to be little more than a scratch, Harper reassured herself her position here was secure. By all accounts, Uncle Hugh was a reasonable man. He hadn't liked Matthew Dunleavy, but he had kept Logan on and apparently promoted him to property manager. Mrs. Philips respected him. He had gone to a lot of trouble to help Ellie, even if Harper felt the household's pandering wasn't improving her situation.

On her way back to the front of the house, she breathed a prayer for comfort and peace. She had broken a valuable possession. She would take her punishment with dignity. If she had to work the rest of her life to pay off her debt, so be it. She was a Dixon, and Dixons paid for the consequences of their carelessness without complaint or argument.

She made a wide berth past the broken vase and crossed the foyer to Uncle Hugh's office. The door still stood open. She took that as a good sign. She tapped on the door lintel and stepped inside.

Her uncle's head was bent over a ledger, round wire glasses perched on the end of his nose. He put down his pen and removed the glasses. "All cleaned up, I see."

"Yes, sir." She swallowed, hating the tremor in her voice.

"Do you think it necessary to summon the doctor?"

"No, no. I'm fine, really." She tucked her hand behind her. The maid had wrapped a bandage between her fingers and around her knuckles, making the minor cut look like a limb was threatened.

"Well, that's good then," he said.

If she wasn't mistaken, he looked as uncomfortable as she was.

"I'm truly sorry, Uncle, for breaking the vase. It was careless of me, and I apologize. Anything I can do as restitution—"

He waved his hand dismissively, brushing aside the apology and cutting off her words. He indicated an empty leather chair on her side of the desk. Harper obediently perched on the edge of it, still not confident he wasn't mad.

A smile flitted across his stern features. "Ashes to ashes. A mere possession."

Her eyes widened at the reference. Everyone she talked to doubted her uncle's Christianity. Apparently, he had some Biblical training.

"Physical possessions are temporary. They can be replaced. What matters are the people in our lives."

Surprise at his words battled the familiar ache of homesickness that washed over her. "Yes, sir."

"I haven't properly thanked you for coming here. I realize now how inconsiderate it was of me not to meet you at the train when you arrived. You must've thought I didn't care you were coming. It's hard for me to put work aside, regardless of the personal needs of myself or my family. Sometimes I don't consider how my actions affect others."

Harper nearly fell off the edge of the chair. She had expected a dismissal, or at least a reprimand. Not an apology from one of the most powerful men in Willow Wood. In the state, from what she'd observed.

She opened her mouth to accept the apology, but he wasn't finished. "I'm sure your absence is quite a hardship on your family. I will write a letter to your mother myself and tell her how I appreciate her sacrifice."

Harper blinked in surprise. "Thank you. It will mean a lot to her."

"I will include payment for their inconvenience. They could hire someone to replace—"

"No," she practically shouted. "Don't do that."

She took a deep breath. How could she tell him her family would be mortified to receive payment for her? *Insulted* was a better word.

"It's not necessary. They were doing what they considered their Christian duty for a family member."

"If you think that's best. I just want them, and you, to realize how much your presence means to me. And Ellie. She may not show it yet, but I know my daughter. Another young woman in the house is exactly what she needs."

Harper wondered if Ellie thought she needed a companion. Uncle Hugh hadn't been home for more than twelve hours since Harper arrived, and she had yet to see the two of them interact.

"What's your opinion?" he asked. He leaned forward, his gaze hopeful. "Of Ellie. Has she spoken to you about what's bothering her?"

What did he expect? For Ellie to take one look at her and confide all her loss and pain? "No, sir. I only see her when I take her breakfast and lunch to her."

Impatience flashed across his face. Harper couldn't tell if he was annoyed with her inability to cure Ellie on sight or at Ellie for rebuffing Harper's overtures of friendship.

"I'll talk to her. You're part of our home now. She needs to accept it and make you feel welcome."

"Begging your pardon, Uncle Hugh, but I don't want to force her to accept me."

"This isn't her decision."

Harper steeled herself. She doubted many people stood up to her uncle, especially in his own home. She didn't want to offend him or insert herself where she wasn't welcome, but if Ellie wasn't his main concern she wouldn't be here. She would say what she thought and hope his desire to help his daughter was stronger than his vanity.

"If I may be frank, sir, it *is* her decision." She clutched her sweating hands together and forged ahead. "She'll talk more freely to me and accept me more readily if our relationship is allowed to develop on its own."

His steely dark eyes bored into her.

Harper kept her spine straight. She wasn't wrong. At least she prayed she wasn't.

After a tense moment, Uncle Hugh's posture softened. "I suppose you know more about what a young woman needs than I do. I have every confidence you will get through to her."

"That is my hope as well, sir."

"Ellie's been through a lot, Harper."

The pain in his voice startled her. For all his hard edges, he loved his daughter and would do anything for her.

"Her young man hurt her very deeply. Unfortunately, she was blind to his charms and couldn't see he was using her. A man in my position expects people to take advantage of him. Since Ellie was a girl, I tried to warn her that young men would attempt to get close to her in order to make life easier on themselves. I suppose it isn't a flattering notion for a young woman, especially one as beautiful and self-assured as Ellie."

He rolled the pen back and forth on the ink blotter.

"It would've been easier if her mother was here to explain such things. She said I didn't know what I was talking about. She believed I wanted to scare off every young man who came calling."

Harper figured he was successful much of the time.

"Dunleavy only cared about my money. He grew up poor, from what I gather. I have nothing against that. I started out with nothing myself. You can see the results of what hard work and determination can bring." He cast a glance around the richly appointed room's bookcases, dark paneling, and heavily draped windows. "Some men seek to profit off what others have built. They get into trouble and hope another man's labors will bail him out. I don't believe in that, Harper. I believe when a man gets into a bad situation, he has no right to ask anyone else to help him out of it."

Harper could practically hear the same words come out of Pa's mouth. At the same time, they echoed the sentiment of Geneva Wallace. She couldn't defend Matthew Dunleavy to her uncle the way she had to Geneva. Still, if Ellie was as smart and astute as everyone claimed, it wasn't likely she had fallen so completely for a charlatan.

Did Uncle Hugh and Geneva really believe only a man after the Lundy empire would give Ellie the time of day?

"Is there anything you can tell me about Ellie that might help us become friends?"

His expression warmed. "She's always been a very bright girl. She was eleven when her mother died. She took it very hard, as you can imagine. I probably gave in to her too much. Fathers should never have to raise daughters alone. I made a lot of mistakes."

A muscle in his jaw twitched. "If I had to do it over again, though, I doubt I'd change a thing."

Harper's eyes smarted at the tenderness in his voice.

"I wish I knew what she needed," he finished.

"She needs someone to listen. Not only to listen, but to actually hear what she's saying."

He nodded thoughtfully. "She wasn't always like this. A few years ago, you wouldn't have recognized the young woman upstairs in that dismal room of hers. She was a ray of sunshine on a cloudy day. Now, well…"

His fingers clenched around the pen in his hands. Harper expected it to break in two any moment.

"I want to help her, but frankly, enough is enough." He slammed the pen down on the desk. "She's wasted enough of her life on this melodrama."

He must've recognized the dismay on Harper's face. Hadn't he heard a word she said?

He let out a slow breath. "I realize I can't control how long a person nurses a broken heart. But I've been more than patient. Ellie is an intelligent young woman with plenty to offer. But if she keeps this up, she'll burn her bridges in Willow Wood. This state is ripe with ambitious, motivated, marriageable young men who would make suitable husbands for a woman of Ellie's caliber.

"I brought you here because I've tried everything I can think of, short of hogtying her and dragging her out of that room. I'm desperate, Harper. Whatever it takes, whatever it costs, I want my daughter back. If I could get my hands on that Dunleavy character, I'd…"

He growled low in his throat. He looked up in near surprise as if he'd forgotten she was in the room.

"Yes, sir." He needn't think she couldn't understand his frustration.

He dipped his head in apology. "I trust you'll excuse my outburst. It's just difficult for me to watch my daughter grieve over a piece of humanity who wasn't worth crossing the street to spit upon."

Harper wondered if that wasn't the part he hated most. Hugh Lundy controlled everything in his realm. Losing control to a man he hated must be a hard matter to swallow.

"You asked me to tell you something that would help you get closer to Ellie. She always loved to travel. She loved seeing and experiencing new things. Perhaps you can remind her of that passion. She also is quite artistic, like her mother. You might've noticed some of Mrs. Lundy's artwork around the house. Painting and sketching used to fill a lot of Ellie's free time. Do you paint?"

"No, sir."

"That could be a good thing. You could ask Ellie to give you lessons."

"With all due respect, Uncle, I fear that would be like giving singing lessons to a prairie dog. It would only frustrate both of us."

He chuckled. "Well, do think of something, won't you?"

He pushed back his chair and opened the desk's middle drawer. He pulled out a leather folder and extracted a few bills. "I am going out of town to our mine holdings in Utah. I'll be away for a few weeks. Perhaps a month."

A month? Harper wondered if it was wise to go away for such a long period with Ellie in her fragile state. It was part of running a successful company, she supposed.

Uncle Hugh held the bills out to her. "We never discussed the amount of your stipend. I trust this will suffice. If not, we can revisit the matter when I return."

Harper looked at the bills fanned out in his hand. She had never been in possession of such an amount for her own use. She wouldn't know how to spend it.

"Oh, no, Uncle. That's too much. I haven't even been here a week. I still have some of the funds you sent for my trip. I had planned to give it back to you."

His hand remained extended. "I sent for you because I want you here. I'm a man accustomed to getting what he wants, whatever the cost."

He smiled as if it were a joke, but Harper got the impression he wasn't kidding. He wouldn't be refused, no matter what he requested.

"But..."

He waved the money in his hand. "You've earned it, young lady. Or you will by the time I return. This trip can't wait another day. I put it off until your arrival. Now that's you're here, I'm assured Ellie will be in good hands while I'm gone. If necessary, you can send a telegram to the office in Utah. Logan knows how to reach me. Hopefully you won't need to."

She figured he didn't want a telegram unless the house caught fire. Even then...

"Watch over Ellie, Harper. I'm counting on you. I want my little girl back. Thank you for what you've done already. You can close the door on your way out."

Properly dismissed, Harper took the money out of his hand, totally unprepared for the weight of the job ahead of her.

Chapter Thirteen

Harper's gaze fell on the library door directly opposite Uncle Hugh's office. She loved to read but seldom had time at home or a way of getting her hands on different types of books. Her uncle had whetted her appetite when he mentioned his selection of classics. She didn't know Ellie's taste in literature, but they might find something they could read together. The art volumes might interest her and give them something to talk about.

Even with Uncle Hugh's permission to visit the library, she felt like as intruder as she pulled the heavy door open and slipped inside. The room faced north and was decidedly cooler than the rest of the house. Had she discovered it sooner, she would've come in here every day to escape the heat of the afternoons.

Someone had left a lamp burning in the corner where a large wingback chair faced the bare hearth. Bookshelves lined dark paneled walls. An intricately patterned rug done in shades of green and cream stretched from the hearth to a mahogany table in the middle of the floor. Walnut stained floorboards gleamed in the lamplight.

Harper trailed her fingers along a bookshelf as she crossed the room to the window and pulled back the heavy curtain. The early evening light filtering through the trees illuminated the nearest bookshelves. She tilted her head to read book spines as she walked the length of the shelf. She didn't want to disrupt the precise cataloging and make Uncle Hugh wish he hadn't extended an invitation.

She smiled at a copy of *Robinson Crusoe*. She pulled it off the shelf and flipped it open. She read aloud the familiar first line. "I was born in the year 1632, in the city of Kent..."

"I never would've guessed you were that old."

Harper nearly dropped the book. She spun around in time to see Logan stand and circle the wingback chair. She put her hand to her chest. "I didn't know anyone was in here."

She hoped he would blame her rapid breathing and the pink in her cheeks on him startling her. She needed to stop entertaining notions of him. He was obviously smitten with her cousin.

He smiled sheepishly. "I'm sorry. I should've made my presence known when you came in. I thought you were Ellie. She comes in now and then. Sometimes she gets a book. Usually she just stares out that window a few minutes and walks out."

He glanced toward the door as if to make sure they were alone before closing the gap between them. "I don't say anything to her when she comes in. I never know how she'll react. If she sees me, she usually ignores me. Other times she seems disturbed by the sight of me. I guess I remind her of Matthew."

Harper wondered if Ellie appreciated the irony of the situation. Logan loved her, and she didn't notice he was alive. She loved Matthew, and he had walked away with no worries over how she'd get along without him.

"It must be difficult for her if she associates you closely with Matthew," she suggested.

"I've thought the same thing, though she's never said as much."

She wanted to ask if he'd ever talked to Ellie about his feelings for her. Did he talk to her at all? Harper didn't want him to think it mattered to her whom he loved. She wagged her chin at the book in his hand. "I didn't know you were a reader."

"I always have been, though I never had much of an opportunity before I came here. About a year ago Mr. Lundy caught me in the barn with a battered copy of *Tom Sawyer* I found in an alley. He asked what I thought of the book and Mr. Twain as a storyteller. It surprised me. Until that moment I didn't think he saw me as anything other than a handyman. Right away, he offered me the use of his books. This is where you'll find me when I have a free evening."

She took hold of the corner of the book and turned it to read the cover. "*Twenty Thousand Leagues Under the Sea.*"

"I've read it before. I guess I should try something new."

"My brother Billy loves Jules Verne. I think his favorite is *Journey to the Center of the Earth.* He's read it a couple of times."

"That one's good, too, but this is my favorite." He motioned to her book. "Have you read *Crusoe* before?"

"In school. I should choose something different myself." She gazed appreciatively around the room. "I've never had this kind of selection at my disposal."

"You'll find more interesting titles than you'll ever have time to read. At least that's how it is for me."

"What about Ellie? Does she read?"

He lifted a shoulder. "Not much I'm afraid."

"Oh. I was hoping to find something we could read together."

She went back to the bookshelf and replaced *Robinson Crusoe.* "Where did you get your appreciation for reading?"

"From my ma. The only book we had at home was the Bible. She read it all the time. She studied it and read stories from it to my brother and me."

Harper turned away from the shelves to look at him, indicating he go on. He'd never spoken much about his upbringing, and she was eager to hear more. His childhood didn't sound that different from hers.

"I remember the first time Larry brought a textbook home. I came in from outside and found Ma at the table with that book in front of her. I don't remember the book's subject. It wouldn't have mattered anyway. It was the first night I remember she ever burned the beans.

"I didn't know it at the time, but she hadn't gone to school herself. Her head was like a sponge. She'd read anything we brought home. When I got old enough, I'd bring home books like *Rob Roy* or *Anna Karenina* and keep them as long as the teacher let me. Ma devoured them."

"Your teachers must've thought you had quite an eclectic reading taste."

"I doubt I was the only kid to do it. Many families in our farming community didn't have access to books except through the schools. I imagine it's how lots of parents learned to read and 'cipher. Keeping Ma's secret got harder as I got older. You should've heard my friends when they caught me sneaking *Little Women* and *Black Beauty* into my satchel."

Harper laughed. "You were a good son." She turned back to the shelves. "I should choose something with more literary merit. I don't want to disappoint Uncle Hugh."

Logan crossed the room to the opposite wall. "You needn't worry about that. He'll be happy someone is making use of his collection. When he finds me in here, he always asks what I think about whatever I'm reading and if I've read one of his favorites. Your uncle is a very interesting person. Built a powerful enterprise from the ground up. His business partner Hershel List came from the same vein. Self-made men from humble beginnings who used their brains and determination to achieve their goals. They're good examples of what's possible if a man's willing to work hard enough."

"Or woman."

He turned away from the bookshelf. "I stand corrected."

Harper slid a blue bound book with gold gilt lettering off the shelf and went to the table in the center of the room. She pulled out a chair and sat. "What about Matthew? Did Uncle Hugh leave a similar impression on him?"

"The only person inside this house who impressed Matthew was Ellie. You already know that." He selected a book of his own and joined her at the table. "After Matthew left, your uncle started keeping an eye on me. I think he worried I'd go after Ellie. I didn't want to lose my position, so I made sure to walk the straight and narrow."

She waited, hoping to hear him say he wasn't interested in Ellie, and Uncle Hugh's worries were unfounded.

When he didn't speak, she said, "Is it hard for you to stay on the straight and narrow?"

He pulled away from her in mock horror. "Me? I'm as pure as the driven snow."

"Somehow I don't believe that."

"Well, you should. "This," he indicated the room around them, "is as much adventure as I can handle."

"But not Matthew?"

He stared at the book in his hands. "No, not Matthew. He wasn't the kind to settle down. He wanted adventure. The only reason he stopped in Willow Wood was we were down to our last two nickels. He soon realized there was always a card game going on somewhere in town, so he was willing to prop his boots up a spell."

Harper clasped her hands around the book's hard binding. "And he met Ellie."

"She made him forget about leaving. At least for a while. I thought she'd be the one to change him. That he'd realize he could stop searching for whatever it was he thought he needed to find."

Now he was gone, and Ellie was the one waiting for something she may never find, Harper thought. Her heart ached for her cousin. She watched Logan's jaw work. She could tell he wanted to say more. Whether he thought her meddling or trifling, she needed answers if she hoped to help Ellie, and he might be the only one with them.

"I don't understand why he couldn't stay and be what Ellie needed."

"Matthew has a hole inside him, Harper. A hole even Ellie couldn't fill. I believe he loved her, but he was a gambler through and through. He liked any game of chance. Dice. Cards. Horses. Anything where he could put down a wager."

"Did Ellie know?"

"She knew. Everyone who knew him for more than five minutes knew. She probably didn't realize the extent of it. For a lot of people, putting money down on a card game or race is harmless fun. You win a little. You lose a little. It was much more than that to Matthew. Back home, he owed for old losses. A lot of money. More than he could ever repay."

Dread stirred in Harper's stomach.

"Matthew wasn't a big fella, and he had an innocent air about him. When he sat down at a table, the other fellas usually underestimated him. Until he whipped them, that is. He earned a good living playing cards when he found a high stakes game. Things didn't always go his way. Sometimes, even when you play a straight hand, somebody takes offense. Taking every last dime of a man's pay is a good way to make enemies."

"What are you saying?"

Logan pushed away from the table and crossed one ankle over the other. He stared at his boots for a while. "Before we came here Matthew had made a name for himself all over the southern half of Indiana. Men came from all over to watch him play. They wanted to see how he did it. Mostly, they wanted to be the one to take him out."

He ran his hand over the shadow of growth on his jaw. "The night we left Indiana Matthew had been drinking and playing cards all afternoon. By the time I finished work that evening he was in deep. I tried to talk him into folding and getting out of there while he could. He wouldn't listen. He said he'd lost too much to just get up and walk away. I didn't trust half the men at the table that night. Neither of us knew them. We figured some of the locals had brought in ringers to try to get their money back. Matthew never could back down from a challenge, even when he suspected he'd been set up. That's where the thrill lay."

Harper leaned closer and focused on every word. She wanted to ask for clarification. She wanted to know if Ellie knew the story, but she wouldn't interrupt.

"Around two in the morning I couldn't take in anymore," Logan continued. "I couldn't get Matthew out of there. I got fed up and left. About two hours later, he showed up at my family's farm. His face was busted up, and his arm had been wrenched nearly out of socket."

Harper covered her mouth with her hand. "Who did it?"

"A couple of the out-of-towners. Matthew had lost and they wanted blood. They'd already taken every nickel he had but the Confederate half dollar he kept in his pocket for luck."

He snorted. "I don't know all that happened, but he was scared. First time I'd ever seen him so jumpy. Said he was leaving town and he wasn't coming back. He said if he stayed there, the next time, they'd kill him."

Harper's eyes widened. "The next time? Do you think…is it possible those men tracked him here?"

Logan scratched the bristle on his jaw. "There was no reason for anyone to follow him all the way out here. Everybody knew he didn't have any money. You can't get blood from a turnip. But now I'm wondering all over again."

"Why didn't he ask you to go with him when he left this time the way he did before?"

"He knows I'm settled here. He wouldn't ask me to give up my life for a compulsion he couldn't control. He was too much of a gentleman for that."

But not too much of a gentleman to jilt Ellie, she thought. "Do you think that's why he didn't tell Ellie he was leaving? He wouldn't want her to give up everything she had for him."

"I think that's exactly it. If life wherever he ended up didn't turn out the way he hoped, he wouldn't want to be the reason she lost it all."

Harper's jaw tightened in anger toward a man she'd never met. What a coward. "So, not only did he leave her without an explanation, he did it because he was too spineless to take the blame if things didn't work out."

Logan's aquamarine eyes were subdued. "I know it looks that way. But Matthew loved Ellie. He didn't want to hurt her. He didn't want her following him from saloon to saloon and table to table. That's no life for anyone, especially someone like Ellie."

Harper wanted to scream. "Then why did he go?"

"He loved her, as much as he knew how, but some fellows, well…"

Harper waited a moment "Some fellows, what?"

"Some fellas can't love a girl who loves them too much."

Chapter Fourteen

Monday morning Harper picked up a breakfast tray containing a small bowl of cherries, a piece of toast, two sausage links, and a cup of coffee—all of which she would carry back downstairs nearly untouched at noon—and headed upstairs.

"Remind Ellie the doctor's coming this morning," Mrs. Philips said. "Tell her to be dressed by ten."

Harper nearly dropped the tray. "Doctor? A doctor's coming?"

Mrs. Philips looked at her like she wasn't quite right in the head. "Same as every Monday. Ellie'll pretend to be put out, but I think she looks forward to these visits. Will you be available to show the doctor in?"

Of course. What else did she have to do? "I'll be happy to."

Harper nearly floated out of the kitchen and up the grand staircase. Finally. A professional to provide insights into Ellie's bleak moods. Since Harper would escort the doctor upstairs, she hoped to stay in the room during the examination. Uncle Hugh was counting on her. So was Ellie, even if she didn't know it yet.

Most of the night she had thought of what Logan said about men who couldn't love a woman who loved them too much. When he first said it, she found it a stupid and cowardly concept. But the more she thought about it, she realized it explained Ellie's condition completely. She had loved Matthew more than he deserved, more than he loved her.

There were so many rules for love. Almost more than it was worth. She thought of Ma and Pa, or Joan and her husband Thomas. Had there been complications before they fell in love? Had Ma worried she loved Pa more than he loved her? If those concerns had been there, they wouldn't have married. Ma would've been smart enough to realize she loved a man who couldn't love her back the way she deserved and walk away. Matthew may not have been as open to Ellie. Mrs. Philips said he was a good-time Charlie, only interested in having fun, not in what he could do for Ellie. He was selfish. How could a woman—or man, for that matter—know if the one they loved was equally invested in the relationship? How did one avoid making the mistakes Ellie had obviously made in choosing Matthew?

What about Logan? He loved Ellie or he wouldn't still be here working for peanuts when he could go anywhere else and make more money. Did he love Ellie too much?

Harper's head hurt from all the pondering. She prayed God would help her keep from falling in love with a man who couldn't or wouldn't love her back.

Every time her mind went in that direction, she thought of Logan. She wasn't sure why. They seemed to have a lot in common, and she couldn't stop thinking about him. But he didn't seem to give her much thought. Was her heart setting her up to make the same mistake as Ellie by falling for a man who wouldn't love her back?

Two hours later, she sat on the settee in the foyer and tried to focus on a book she had taken from the library. She couldn't get past the first chapter. It wasn't the book's fault. She kept thinking of Logan and wishing she had an excuse to go outside to the stables to find him. If Ellie would acknowledge her, she wouldn't have so much free time to entertain notions about the only eligible man she'd met since disembarking from the train.

Promptly at ten a knock sounded on the front door. Harper was so startled she leaped to her feet and dropped the book in her haste. She looked around to make sure one of the maids hadn't seen her. They were so quiet it was easy to forget she wasn't alone in the house. She quickly stashed the book under the settee's cushion and smoothed a hand over her hair.

She swung open the door to reveal a tall, pretty woman on the other side. A dark green dress accentuated her auburn hair and hazel eyes. Harper swallowed her disappointment. The Lundys hadn't received a visitor since her arrival, and they didn't have time for one now.

She gripped the door, unsure of what to do. Should she call for a maid? The woman could be from the church they seldom attended or a civic organization seeking donations. She wasn't at liberty to answer a plea for funds or explain no one was home to receive guests.

"Good morning," the woman said and started around Harper.

Taken aback, Harper tried to square herself in the doorway. Too late. The woman was inside. Harper glanced over her shoulder toward the back of the house. "May I help you?"

"I'm here to see Ellie. You must be her cousin. I'm sorry, I don't remember your name."

Harper noticed the black bag hanging over the woman's arm. A medical bag. Was it possible? She stepped aside to allow the woman the rest of the way into the foyer. "You're the doctor? I...I'm sorry. I had no idea."

The woman's smile widened. "Yes, I'm Dr. Dutton. I should've introduced myself straight away. I thought I was expected. I have a standing appointment with Ellie every Monday."

Harper realized her mouth was hanging open. "Yes, yes, I knew you were coming. Well, I knew someone was coming. I just didn't expect...I'm sorry. I never heard of a woman doctor. Is that allowed?"

She winced and clamped her mouth shut.

"It's quite allowed. And you are..."

"Oh, yes, Harper Dixon, Ellie's cousin. But you already knew that part."

Warmth crept into her face. The woman—this lady doctor—must think her a dimwitted hayseed.

The doctor smiled charitably. "It's nice to meet you, Harper. No need to apologize. You're not the first person surprised to see me when they open the door."

Harper exhaled appreciatively. "Ellie's expecting you. She wasn't overly pleased when I reminded her you were coming."

The doctor laughed. "She never is. At least that's what she says. Yet we always have a good time."

Harper found it strange the doctor would consider examinations with any patient a good time. Especially a morose one like Ellie, who had never as much as cracked a smile in front of Harper.

"I'll show you upstairs." If the doctor came every week, she knew the way to Ellie's room, but Harper wanted to talk to her, as well as witness the examination.

"Thank you." Dr. Dutton shifted her medical bag to one hand and fell into step beside Harper. Her shawl opened. Harper's cheeks flamed at the sight of a bulge under her apron. A lady doctor, in the family way no less, performing patient examinations as if it were the most common occurrence in the world. What kind of town was this?

"How do you like Willow Wood?" the doctor asked.

Harper nearly snorted aloud. "I'm afraid I haven't seen much of it yet. The only place I've been is church yesterday."

She didn't tell the doctor no one there had welcomed her, except for Logan, and she suspected he tolerated her more than liked her.

"Where are you from, Harper?"

"Corbin County, Kentucky."

The doctor nodded, though Harper doubted she'd ever heard of it. "I'm relatively new to Willow Wood myself. I'm from St. Joseph, Missouri."

Harper wanted to ask if there were lady doctors in Missouri. If so, it was a more progressive place than Corbin County. She wanted to ask why she chose to become a lady doctor and if her parents were proud of her. She wondered what Mr. Dutton thought of having a doctor for a wife and if she would continue to see patients after her baby was born.

Those were a lot of questions for someone she'd just met so she held her tongue.

"How are you and Ellie getting along?" the doctor asked quietly when they reached the second floor and started down the hall.

Harper figured the examination had begun. "Not well," she confessed. "I take her meals to her and she barely acknowledges me."

The doctor pursed her lips as if processing the information. "I hope you don't take it personally. Ellie doesn't encounter many new people or experiences in her daily routine. As long as we show her patience and understanding, I have complete faith she'll come around."

Harper took hold of the doctor's arm and pulled her to a stop. She immediately recognized what she was doing and dropped her hand.

"Come around to what?" she whispered. "I don't understand any of this. Ellie's young man jilted her. Two years ago. At least he was thoughtful enough to do it before he married her. I would think by now she's realize she is better off."

Dr. Dutton's eyes traveled to Ellie's door and slowly back. Harper expected to see condemnation for her lack of sympathy and compassion. Instead the doctor's gaze was thoughtful, as if Harper's words had never occurred to her.

"None of us can know the depth of another's heartache or grief. I have never faced a loss like Ellie's. I pray I never do. If I should, I don't know how I would react or how long it would take me to recover."

Harper exhaled. "Nor have I. I didn't mean to sound dismissive of her pain. Uncle Hugh sent for me to help. If she had a physical ailment, I would know what to do. Or I could look it up in a book. But I don't know how to help someone sick from something only they can see."

The doctor touched her sleeve. "Sometimes pain you can't see is the hardest to cure. Especially when Ellie refuses to tell us what she needs. Just give her time."

Time was all Harper had to give. "I'll do my best."

"I know you will. My office is downtown on Second Street. You can stop anytime to talk about how best to serve your cousin. Ellie's problem is not unique, but most of us are woefully lacking when it comes to treating it. Me, most of all."

"I appreciate that, Dr. Dutton. I am in way over my head here. Would it be all right if I stayed in the room during Ellie's examination?"

"It's fine with me as long as Ellie doesn't object. She's the boss."

Dr. Dutton rapped on Ellie's door and pushed it open before Ellie could allow or reject entrance.

"Good morning, Ellie," she called out with gusto one usually reserved for an old friend she hadn't seen in years.

Harper stopped short in the doorway. She squinted at the unexpected light streaming into the room from the large window opposite the door. A gentle breeze accompanied the light, surprising her even further.

Her biggest shock came from Ellie herself. She sat at her desk, fully dressed, a sketchpad in front of her. She flipped it over at the sight of them and offered the nearest thing to a smile Harper had seen on her face. Sunlight flashed off the coppery highlights in her hair that had been washed and brushed and pulled back into a neat bun. Her complexion was still ashen, but the dark circles under her eyes weren't as noticeable.

"Good morning, Dr. Dutton. You're looking well as always. I see the baby hasn't made an appearance yet."

Harper gasped. She'd never heard anyone mention a woman's delicate condition except to their mothers and closest confidantes. Even then, the subject didn't typically come up in conversation until after the little bundle's arrival.

The doctor simply laughed. "Oh, Ellie, you are incorrigible. How are you feeling today? Have you been sleeping well?"

"No, are you? I heard women in your condition often have a hard time sleeping through the night."

Harper gasped again. "Ellie." She wagged her head in apology at the doctor.

Dr. Dutton set her bag on top of the leather tablet Ellie had been writing in. "My condition is not the topic of conversation this morning." She snapped the bag open and withdrew her stethoscope.

Despite her cousin's randy comments, Harper was heartened to see Ellie smiling and expressing an emotion other than sadness. This was the fun-loving, fiery Ellie everyone had told her about.

"I asked you how you were sleeping," Dr. Dutton repeated.

Ellie didn't respond until the doctor stopped moving the stethoscope over her chest and back. "I sleep the way I always do. Sometimes good. Sometimes not at all."

"Why do you think that is?"

"It's hard to relax when I know I'll be quizzed about it every Monday morning."

"How is the new medicine working?" the doctor asked without rising to Ellie's bait. "Does it help with your bleak moods?"

"Do you mean does it keep me comatose so I feel nothing? Because that's what it does."

Dr. Dutton slipped the stethoscope off her neck and put it back in her bag. She pulled the stool away from the vanity table and sat down next to Ellie. "I don't want you comatose. I want you comfortable enough to resume activities that bring you satisfaction and contentment."

"I don't think you have a drug for that."

"Nothing will help without some effort on your part."

Ellie threw her hands into the air in feigned outrage. "I wondered how long it would take you to launch into a lecture."

"I don't mean to lecture. Believe it or not, I'm here to help. As is Harper."

"Harper?" Ellie pinned Harper with a shocked gaze. "How can she help? I don't know a thing about her. She never speaks to me. She comes in, drops off my meals, and rushes out the door like a scared rabbit."

"I'm not afraid..." Blood rushed to Harper's face. Ellie was right. She hadn't made an honest effort to get to know her. Ellie never ordered her out of the room or refused her admittance. It was Harper who rushed out as soon at the first sign of resistance. She had never encouraged interaction.

Ellie and the doctor stared at her.

"Harper, do you think Ellie doesn't want your company?"

Harper wouldn't have come into the room if she'd known she was going to become an active participant. "I...I'm a guest here. I didn't want to overstep my bounds."

Dr. Dutton grunted. "It sounds like we have a lack of communication. Harper, it appears Ellie has been waiting for you to extend a hand of friendship. And, Ellie, Harper didn't want to thrust her friendship upon you if you didn't want it. She doesn't know what you need. Does that sound right?"

"Yes," Harper murmured, inwardly kicking herself for looking like a scared chicken to Ellie.

"All I need is to be left alone," Ellie snapped. This time, the stubborn set in her jaw was not for dramatic effect.

"We all know that isn't going to happen," Dr. Dutton said. "Too many people care for you." She turned on her stool to face Harper. "Harper, Ellie doesn't know anything about you. Tell us something about yourself."

"I have four brothers and four sisters."

"I already know that." Ellie looked petulant. "Papa told me."

"All right. Harper, tell us something else."

Harper looked from Ellie to the doctor. What did they want to hear? The doctor looked interested. Ellie's gaze challenged.

"It was hard for me to come here," she finally managed. "I've never been out of Corbin County in my life. I miss my family very much."

"Now, Ellie, you tell us something about you we don't know."

Ellie's lips pursed. Her jaw clenched. Harper held her breath, not expecting her to comply.

"I always wished I had a sister."

Ellie's words hung in the air. The simple sentiment revealed more about her than Harper thought she would ever know.

"I always wanted a sister, too," Dr. Dutton said after a few moments. "Looks like Harper took the lion's share."

Harper smiled. Even Ellie's lips twitched in amusement.

The doctor turned her attention back to Ellie. "Now that Harper's here, you can see what you missed by not having a sister. Harper, spending time with Ellie might take the sting out of missing home."

Ellie studied a broken nail. "I didn't ask her to come."

"Perhaps not, but she's here, so you can both make the best of it."

Ellie's lips tightened. Harper tensed. Ellie was withdrawing into herself again.

Dr. Dutton looked down at the leather tablet on the desk. "I see you have your sketchpad out. Is there anything you'd like to share with Harper or me?"

Ellie pulled the sketchpad out from under the doctor's medical bag and put it into a drawer. "No."

"Fair enough. Ellie's mother was quite the artist," Dr. Dutton told Harper. "You've probably noticed some of her work around the house."

Harper opened her mouth to respond.

"She wasn't an artist," Ellie interjected. "It was just a hobby. Papa says so all the time." Her eyes narrowed.

"Hobby or not, her talent was exceptional. Harper, I've been fortunate to visit some of the finest art museums in the country, as has Ellie. Her mother was very talented, and she gave that talent to Ellie. Perhaps Ellie can show you some of her favorite paintings."

Ellie waved her hand. "She can see them anytime she wants. She'll see Papa is right."

"Speaking of your father," the doctor said without missing a beat, "have you spoken to him about some of the things you and I talked about?"

"Do you mean if I'm crazy or not? I haven't had the chance. He's never here."

Dr. Dutton laughed again. Harper wondered how she could find amusement in Ellie's caustic comments. "I never said you were crazy. Your father doesn't think you are either. He wants to help you. You're his chief concern."

Ellie barked out a humorless laugh. "That's what you know. Ask Harper. The only thing he cares about is money."

"It may seem that way, given his success, but he loves you very much. If he wasn't worried about you, he wouldn't have me come every week. He wouldn't have sent for Harper."

"He only wants someone watching over me like I'm a child."

"I'm sure Harper doesn't want that role any more than I do."

"I would love to see your sketches," Harper burst out. She blushed when both women turned to look at her. "When you're ready to share them."

"Yes, whenever you're ready," Dr. Dutton said. "If sketching is only a hobby, it won't be so intimidating to share with your cousin."

Ellie stared at the wall.

Dr. Dutton watched her for a moment before gathering her things into her bag. "The weather has been lovely of late, Ellie. I want you to go outside and enjoy it. That's my prescription for this week. Take Harper for a walk. Even if it's only to the garden.

Show her around. Take your sketchbook. Maybe you'll find something worth capturing with your pen."

Harper held her breath. Was that all it took? A simple request to walk outside.

Ellie glanced at Harper. She got up and went to the window, signaling the end of the examination. Though a disappointing ending, Harper considered it a success. Ellie hadn't ousted her from the room the moment the doctor arrived.

She wished, though, the doctor had mentioned the root of Ellie's malaise. Matthew Dunleavy. If no one ever brought him up, she doubted Ellie would ever recover.

Chapter Fifteen

Logan watched Lisette Dutton's buggy disappear through the large wooden gate. Calvin, one of the young stable hands, usually closed it, but he was running errands today. Mr. Lundy wanted the large gate kept closed at all times if company wasn't expected—which was all the time except for Monday mornings when Dr. Dutton was due.

Logan couldn't understand why a man would spend so much time and money building the most beautiful mansion in this part of the state only to hide it behind a stone wall. Mr. Lundy wasn't even home to enjoy it more than a few days a month, and Ellie didn't appear to enjoy it at all.

Mr. Lundy's prolonged absences worked out well for Logan. Not only was he well suited for his position as groundskeeper, maintaining the Lundy estate afforded him the free time he needed to build up his own farm. It wasn't his farm yet. The small ranch outside of town belonged to Hiram Campbell for as long as the old man lived or until Logan paid off the debt. Considering how much farther he had to go, Mr. Campbell would probably pass to Glory first.

Working at the mines or the railyard wouldn't have afforded him a spare moment or ounce of energy to give to Mr. Campbell. When Mr. Lundy worked out of town there wasn't much for Logan and the stable hands to do at the estate. He finished his work in the mornings and headed to the farm. Each week brought him closer to achieving the dream he'd been working toward since nearly the day he arrived in Willow Wood. His first priority was starting a simple cabin on his farm since Mr. Campbell's dwelling had seen better days. While he wasn't envious of the Lundy mansion's luxury—which no one seemed to appreciate but him—he sometimes grew discouraged just looking at it.

He crossed the drive to the large gate. Occasionally, if he or Calvin left the gate untended for too long, some bold boys from town would sneak onto the grounds to take a look around. They'd pick a rose from the garden or snitch a stone from the path to prove to their buddies they'd been here. Logan didn't fault their curiosity. If he didn't work on this side of the wall, he'd be tempted to sneak in himself.

Whenever it happened, he scared the trespassers off before Mr. Lundy discovered the lawbreakers. Fortunately for their young hides, the owner of the estate missed a lot of what happened around here, including the seduction of his lovely daughter.

Matthew and Ellie would never have had the chance to get to know one another if Mr. Lundy had come home from work every night. Had he paid closer attention to what was happening under his nose, Matthew would've been sent to Utah to work instead of remaining on the estate grounds to fall in love with the charismatic Lundy daughter.

After two years Logan still missed his friend. He missed Ellie. He missed the good times the three of them had. He had often been the third wheel of the group as they raced mounts across the countryside or swam in the wide pool at the creek. Sometimes he'd watch Ellie and Matthew and wonder if there was a girl out there for him.

It didn't take long to dismiss the thought every time it jolted through his head. He had more pressing matters consuming the space between his ears. He didn't have the time or energy to think about love. No girl in town captured his attention enough to pursue her anyway.

Until now.

Lately, the thought of owning and operating a farm had lost some of its shine. What was the point of owning and building a property into a profitable enterprise if he had no one to share it with and no one to leave it to after he was gone?

Such thoughts hadn't bothered him before. Mr. Campbell seemed content enough working the farm alone for the last twenty years. The dismal state of the house didn't bother him. The barn and meadows were immaculate, and his herd was thriving from the good water supply and ample grazing.

In the beginning, Logan planned to work on the Lundy estate until he took over the farm. Recently Mr. Campbell began to talk of Logan moving into the small shed they'd erected a few months ago. The shed was tight and warm and would provide a solid roof over his head until he moved into the house. Mr. Campbell liked having him around, and work went faster if Logan didn't have to divide his time between the farm and the estate.

But he couldn't leave the mansion. Not after he promised Matthew he'd watch over Ellie. He wasn't sure how long that would take if she continued to show no signs of improvement. He was beginning to doubt she'd ever be well enough for him to leave.

After two years she still hadn't faced the fact Matthew was gone and not likely to come back. She wandered around the big house as if she expected him to walk through the door any minute.

Logan hadn't faced the fact either. He still couldn't fathom how Matthew would leave without telling him. Without telling Ellie. Unless things had gotten out of control the way they had in Indiana, leaving him no time to warn Logan.

The night Matthew came to him in Indiana and said he needed to go Logan had no reason to question him. He had tied his few belongings into a rag, mounted his horse, and they lit out. Ma was gone. Pa spent his time looking for answers to life's problems in the bottom of a whiskey bottle. Within an hour of Matthew walking through his door, they were kicking up dust with no thought about what they were leaving behind.

Matthew knew Logan wouldn't just pick up and go this time as he had that night. For the first time in his life he was working toward something on which to build a life. Something too good to leave behind.

The front door opened, and Harper Dixon stepped onto the porch. Logan's breath caught. He swallowed hard.

He had nearly convinced himself it was Harper's questions about what happened to Matthew that made him uncomfortable every time he saw her on a bench in the garden or walking past the stable doors or he caught a whiff of her vanilla scented soap.

Seeing her now on the porch above him, a soft breeze rippling her skirt around her legs, he knew it wasn't her questions that bothered him. It was her. She, with her soft blond hair, deep blue eyes, and lilting voice that tormented him as he tried to fall sleep in the loft above the stable.

He shoved the heavy gate closed and strode across the drive to the marble steps leading to the veranda. The sun's glare was in her eyes, and he doubted she could see him from where she stood. He took the opportunity to study her.

She wore a pale blue dress with short sleeves and scooped neckline. Even from the distance, he saw the dress was faded, and the cuffs and hem were worn.

The late morning rays splashed her face with color and created a halo of light around her honey-blond hair. Her hair was piled loosely on top of her head with a braid wrapped around the pile, looking like it held the whole thing in place. Logan marveled at how a woman could hold back such a mass of hair with one skinny braid.

From the moment he saw her step off the train, he'd looked for evidence she was trying to worm her way into the Lundys' good graces. So far, he'd seen nothing to substantiate his suspicions. Harper seemed genuinely concerned for her cousin. He wanted to believe in her, but he wasn't ready to let his guard down yet.

She must've heard his footsteps in the loose gravel. She turned her head in his direction. She lifted her hand to shield her eyes from the sun. Her easy smile warmed him all the way to his toes.

"Logan, I didn't see you there."

"I didn't think so. I thought about sneaking right up on you."

"And what would you have done when you got here? Put a frog down my back?"

"You sound like someone who had that trick pulled on her."

"Several times. Don't forget, I'm sandwiched between two brothers. They were always pulling pranks like that on me."

He reached the top of the stairs. "Like what?"

"Where to begin," she said with a laugh. "I've had frogs put down my back. Nightcrawlers in my shoes. A box turtle in the cook pot. The worst was when they put a washtub over me and wouldn't let me out."

"How did they manage that?"

"I was really little, about four or five, I think. I was sitting on the ground, and they sneaked up behind me, slammed that washtub over top of me, and sat on it. It was dreadfully hot that day, just like today. I screamed and cried and threatened for all I was worth. They thought it was a grand time until they realized how much trouble they'd be in once I got out. Before they got off the tub, they made me promise not to tell Ma."

"Did you tell?"

"I couldn't. I promised."

Logan laughed as he imagined a tiny Harper trapped under a washtub, begging her rotten brothers to let her out.

He stopped laughing and wiped his eyes. "I like to think I would've grabbed those little rapscallions by the ears and dragged them off the washtub. I hate to admit it, though, I'd have been the one to think up the scheme."

"Huh. That's what I thought. You seem like that kind of brother."

They moved to a shady spot on the veranda. Harper perched on the stone railing. Logan leaned a shoulder against a porch column.

"I'm sure you and your brother got into trouble all the time."

Logan crossed his arms over his chest. "You'd be right about that. Larry was two years older than me. It was probably good we didn't have a sister to torment. We got into enough trouble as it was."

She leveled a look at him. "Why do you talk about him in the past tense? Did something happen?"

"Life, I guess. He's not dead that I know of, if that's what you mean. He took off when he was about seventeen. Things were hard at home. My parents fought a lot. Pa drank, and Ma didn't take it well. There was never enough money, which made matters worse. Ma favored Larry. She had big dreams for him. I think he was afraid if he stayed, he'd become like them. It was easier to take off than to risk disappointing Ma."

"What about you?"

He felt pinned by those big blue eyes and helpless to move.

"Were you afraid of disappointing anyone?"

He didn't want to tell her. He didn't want to say anything that would encourage more uncomfortable questions he'd rather not think about.

"You can't disappoint someone who doesn't know you're alive."

A little mew of sympathy escaped her full lips. Suddenly, Logan couldn't think of anything else but putting his hand behind her head, pulling her against him, and kissing her. Long and soft and gentle. He hadn't kissed a girl in.... Well, long enough he'd never admit it to a friend. But that wasn't why he wanted to kiss Harper. He didn't want to kiss just any girl. He wanted to kiss *her.*

He shifted his weight against the column and looked past the trees and over the wall. From here, they could see the rooftops of their neighbors' houses. Sometimes it was easy to forget anyone existed on the other side of those high stone walls.

"I didn't tell you so you'd feel sorry for me," he said. "It's just the way things were. Life isn't always easy. I'm sure you know that."

"Is that why it was easy to leave Indiana?"

He started at the tenderness in her voice.

"You said there was nothing keeping you at home when Matthew asked you to come west," she reminded him.

"Pretty much. It was just me and Pa by then, and he was distracted to say the least. If not for the cows not getting milked, he probably still wouldn't have noticed I'm not there."

She reached over and brushed her fingertips against his arm. A shiver ran through him. He hoped it didn't show on his face.

"I'm sure he misses you. Just like your brother, wherever he is. He probably thinks about you and all the poor neighborhood girls you used to pester."

He smiled appreciatively. "It's nice to think so. I do miss him. He was the only friend I had. Before Matthew, that is."

His brows slid together as he studied her. What was she doing here? Was she as innocent and genuine as she appeared? Or was it all an act? He hated to think she had nefarious intentions toward Ellie. More than that, he didn't want to believe his fool head would be turned by such a woman.

He remembered his initial reason for coming over to talk to her. "How was the visit with the doc?"

"Very well, I think. Ellie interacts with Dr. Dutton like nothing I expected. She actually teased her about..." Her cheeks colored. "She seemed to enjoy the examination at first. Then the doctor told her to go outside and enjoy the gardens this week and she clammed up. More than once, she said she didn't want me here."

She glanced over her shoulder toward the house. She slid a few inches along the porch railing to close the gap between them.

"Do you think she's improving? She barely talks to me."

Her voice was low and hoarse, her breath soft on his skin. It took Logan a moment to focus on her words.

"Don't be too hard on yourself. You haven't been here a full week. She hasn't talked to the rest of us for two years. You can't expect her to open up to you overnight."

"I suppose. I'm trying not to get impatient with the situation, I really am."

She looked out over the treetops. Suddenly she gasped and turned an accusatory gaze back to him. "Why didn't anyone tell me Dr. Dutton was a woman? I thought she was applying for a cleaning woman's position. I very nearly put my foot in my mouth."

Logan laughed, as much at her expression as what she said. "We knew you'd figure it out."

"I did, no thanks to you. We don't have women doctors in Kentucky. If there are, I've never heard of one."

"I never had either until Dr. Dutton came to town. Folk are still getting used to her. It became easier after she married one of Willow Wood's most prominent citizens."

"Well, I was very impressed by her ability to get Ellie to talk. I think she impresses Ellie too."

"I hope so. No one else has gotten through to her."

After a few moments, Harper said, "Ellie told the doctor she didn't talk to me because I haven't been talking to her. I thought I was giving her what she wanted by keeping my mouth shut."

"It seems like what she wants is to keep feeling sorry for herself and missing Matthew. I thought you came to change that."

She lifted her chin. "You're right, I did. I just wish I knew what I was doing. The doctor made it look so easy."

"Ellie's smart. If you truly care for her, she'll recognize it and accept your friendship. If you don't, well, you'll never get anywhere."

She looked sharply at him. "What do you mean, if I don't? Of course I care for her."

Logan's gaze bored into her. "Then you don't have anything to worry about."

Her blue eyes darkened. He couldn't tell if he had offended her or hurt her feelings. He hadn't meant to do either, but he had to know if she could be trusted.

"I never give anything less than my best," she said around a tight mouth. With her proud chin in the air, she went inside.

Logan flinched at the sound of the door slamming behind her. No question about it. He had insulted her. But he still didn't know if she was here for Ellie or herself.

Chapter Sixteen

What an insufferable man!

Just when Harper thought she and Logan were getting to know each other, and even becoming friends, he went and insinuated she didn't care about Ellie. Why did he think she had come here if not to help her cousin?

His apparent disdain for her would be easier to stomach if she didn't like him so much. She hadn't realized how much she needed an ally in this cold, strange place until he openly rebuffed her. For the life of her, she couldn't figure out what she'd done to make him dislike her. Where she came from people liked you first and only dismissed you after you gave them a reason to. She had half a mind to march out to the stable and tell him so. But she wouldn't give him the satisfaction. Telling him his rude behavior had offended her would prove to him she cared what he thought. Well, she didn't. Not one bit. A man who would judge another based on preconceived notions was beneath contempt and not worth her time.

She spent the rest of the day trying to read the novel she had taken from the library. It was nearly bedtime when she gave up on the storyline—Blast Logan for stealing into her thoughts and making it impossible to concentrate—and took it back to the library. Fortunately, he wasn't there. She wasn't sure what she'd have done if she found him sitting in the wingback chair, smiling that lopsided smile and teasing her with more questions about her ornery brothers. At the same time, she almost wished he would be there so she could stick her nose in the air to show how perturbed she still was by his rude behavior.

He wasn't, so her imagined scenarios of passive vengeance were for naught.

She chose another novel she hoped would appeal to Ellie that they could read together and went upstairs.

Ellie had told Dr. Dutton that Harper hadn't tried to make friends. She'd change that tonight. Before she could talk herself of it, she rapped on Ellie's bedroom door and pushed it open without waiting for a reply the same as the doctor had done. With a huge grin plastered on her face, she held up the book.

Ellie stood at the window staring out at the moonlight. She glanced over her shoulder. "Ah, it's you."

Harper remained at the door, clutching the book and wishing she had the nerve to march across the room and demand Ellie tell her who she was seeing through the trees. But she already knew.

She crossed the gleaming wood floor to join Ellie. She couldn't see much of anything through the trees except for a few lighted windows down below in Willow Wood. She trained her gaze toward the night sky.

"What a beautiful night. On nights like this back home the whole family would sit on the porch and watch the little ones playing in the yard. Pa and my brother Patrick would play the guitar and the mandolin. We would sing and laugh, and Ma would tell stories from the Bible or from when she and Pa were young."

Harper sighed wistfully. This was the first time she thought so much about home without crying. She found Ellie's reflection in the glass and smiled gently.

Ellie made an effort to smile back. "I never realized how important family is until Mother passed away. Papa did the best he could." She lifted her narrow shoulders. "I meant it when I told you and the doctor I wished I had a sister. So many times over the last fourteen years I've thought how much easier her loss might've been if I hadn't been alone."

"I'm here now. Not exactly a sister but still family. With all the Dixons in Kentucky, you have more relatives than you'll know what to do with."

A genuine smile played across Ellie's lips. Harper doubted she knew how pretty she was when she smiled. With a little color in her cheeks and without the dark smudges under her eyes, she'd be downright beautiful.

Ellie went to her desk and motioned Harper to the chintz occasional chair next to it. "Tell me about them. You said your papa and your brother play musical instruments. Do you play? Do any of you sing?"

Harper's pulse quickened. How nice to have a real conversation. If it continued, she'd get to know Ellie in no time. She settled into the chair.

"The only places most of us sing are at church and around the house. I wouldn't say any of us are very good. It doesn't matter though. We're singing for the Lord and our own ears. He only cares about our hearts, not our pitch. Ma sings all the time while she does her chores. We children learned to walk to the music in her voice."

Tears tickled her nose. She sniffed them back. "Pa's family is musically inclined. Patrick, he's my oldest brother, he takes after Pa the most. Even when he was little, if you put an instrument in his hand, he'd figure out how to make it sing. Doris May and Sophie, they're the sisters closest to my age, they aren't the best singers you'll ever hear, but they make up for it in enthusiasm. They've sung solos in church since they were wee things. Neither of them have a shy bone in her body. Not like me. The only singing I do is when the rest of the crowd will drown me out. What about you? Do you sing?"

"In grammar school we had recitals or presentations for the parents every year. I almost always got the solo."

"You must be good."

"Not at all. I was the richest girl in school, and I had the nicest dresses. Papa employed most of the town, so I guess the teachers wanted to stay on his good side."

Harper wasn't sure what to say. Back home children of the more prominent citizens were often favored at school. She supposed some things were the same no matter where you went.

"I didn't mind it at the time," Ellie said. "All the kids liked me. Or I thought they did. They always wanted to sit next to me or play the games I wanted to play. They laughed at my jokes and thought I was smart."

She pulled her legs into the chair and set her chin on her knees the way Harper used to do when she was a kid. "After a while I realized it wasn't me they liked as much as my last name. *Lundy* carries a lot of weight in this part of the country. But people expect a lot out of me too. Especially Papa."

She dropped her feet to the floor and turned in the chair to face the mirror.

"Your papa wants the best for you," Harper said hopefully. "He wants you to be happy."

Ellie lifted a bony shoulder as she stared at both their reflections.

"That's why he has Dr. Dutton come see you. They both want to help. So do I."

"By drugging me?"

"That's only to help you sleep," Harper said, though she wondered if medication was the best idea. She thought it was better for Ellie to face her melancholy instead of sleeping it away. But what did she know?

"I don't know what will happen once Dr. Dutton has her baby," Ellie mused. "Mrs. Philips said she heard another doctor was moving to town. A man." She wrinkled her pert nose. "I hope Papa isn't thinking about sending him into this room." Her face hardened, reminding Harper of Uncle Hugh. "That won't happen."

"Maybe Dr. Dutton can bring her baby to your appointments. Wouldn't that be fun? I haven't cuddled a baby since Little Walt was born."

"I've never even held a baby. I don't think I'd know how."

"It's easy. Babies can feel the love in your arms, and they settle right in and go to sleep. It's the best feeling in the world."

"Well, I'll never know. Babies are for other women, not me. But I do like Dr. Dutton. If she stops coming after her baby's born, I won't talk to another doctor. Certainly not a pompous man who thinks he knows what I'm going through."

"I'm sure not all men are pompous."

"Ha. You must not know many of them. Regardless, Dr. Dutton is the only person who doesn't treat me like an invalid. Or like I'm crazy."

"I don't think you're crazy."

Mischief shone in Ellie's eyes. "That's because you don't know me very well."

Harper chuckled. "I can't believe the way you talked to Dr. Dutton about her condition."

"She knows she's going to have a baby. Why pretend I haven't noticed?"

"You have a point."

"Of course I do. She's easy to talk to. I like teasing her. As I'm sure you've noticed she isn't as young as most brides. She's nearly thirty and she only got married a little over a year ago. This is her first baby."

Harper gasped. "How do you know?"

"I asked her."

Harper gasped again, louder. "Ellie. That's not polite conversation outside the family. Especially with a doctor."

Ellie spun away from the mirror. "Oh, pooh. Who cares about polite conversation? It isn't like we don't all know where babies come from." Her face turned grave, though the mischief shone brighter in her eyes. "You do know, don't you, Harper? If you don't, I'll tell you."

Heat rushed to Harper's face. "Of course I know. I'm a farm girl. I just...um..."

Ellie laughed heartily. "Oh, Harper, you're so funny. This is nice. I think I'll like having you around."

"Really? I didn't think you even noticed I was here."

"I noticed. Believe me. I just don't like the way you tiptoe around me like you're afraid I'll break. Enough people already treat me like that. We'll get along fine as long as you don't try to force me to tell you things I don't want to talk about."

"I'd never do that."

"All right. Then I'll tell you something I've never told anyone except Papa. When I was a girl I wanted to be a schoolteacher."

"You did?"

Ellie nodded. "I wanted to move to a remote community and teach children in a one-room schoolhouse." She pursed her lips. "When I told Papa, he got so mad. He said teaching school was for poor girls who couldn't find husbands. It wasn't for me. I never talked about it again."

Harper breathed a silent prayer of thanks for her parents, who would never squelch her dreams, no matter how impractical or impossible.

"I'm sorry."

Ellie sighed. "He was probably right, but I still liked thinking about it. What about you? What's your dream?"

Harper tilted her head and considered the question. Since learning she was coming to Willow Wood, she hadn't thought beyond her arrival. "What every woman wants. To fall in love. Have children. I thought it would happen in Kentucky, but God had other plans."

She realized how insensitive her words must sound to Ellie who had been jilted by the man she dreamed of marrying.

"Whatever I do, wherever I end up, I want to make a difference to someone. I'm not sure what that means or how it will happen. I didn't go to a university. I've never traveled or seen anything of the world, except for coming here. But I want to make an impact, something grand that could change the world."

She inwardly winced at how vain the words sounded. "It would be God changing the world, not me. I just want Him to use me, whatever that is."

Ellie began taking pins out of her hair and lining them up on her dressing table like tiny soldiers. ""I think anything you do, Harper, will be grand. Not like me. My dreams have always been selfish. I never thought about doing anything for someone else."

"Yes, you did. You dreamed of teaching school. That's about the most selfless profession there is, next to motherhood."

She glanced at Harper's reflection in the mirror. "It was just a childhood dream. I wouldn't have actually done it."

She removed the last pin and combed her fingers through her hair.

Harper stared in surprise. "Ellie, you remind me of my sister Sophie with your hair down like that. I never saw the resemblance before. The first time I saw your pa I thought he looked like my Grandpa Ferguson."

"Grandpa? Is he still alive?"

Harper shook her head. "No, he died about eight years ago."

Ellie's shoulders sank. "Oh. I never had a grandpa."

She covered a yawn with her hand. She stood and went to the bed and pulled back the covers, signaling the end of the conversation.

Harper got up and smoothed the wrinkles out of her skirt. Time to get ready for bed herself. But talking with Ellie and getting to know her better had been the best thing to happen since she arrived in Willow Wood. She went to the lamp and turned down the wick.

Ellie's bed creaked as she snuggled into the covers. "Do you ever dream about, you know, other things?"

Harper turned back from the door. "What things?"

"Babies." She stared at Harper, her eyes brown luminous orbs in the moonlight. "Men. Getting married. Having a family of your own."

Logan flashed through Harper's mind. She was glad the lights were dim so Ellie wouldn't see.

"No."

Ellie sat up on one elbow. "That was an awfully strong protestation for something you've never dreamed about."

"All right, so maybe I've thought about it. But I've never been in love. I think you're supposed to do that first."

"Not always." Ellie giggled.

Harper grinned, though Ellie's words scandalized her more than anything she'd ever heard. "Do you think about it?" she asked.

She heard a heavy sigh. "I can't. It hurts too much." Ellie rolled over to face the wall.

•••

In the dream, Harper was on the porch with her sisters and little brother. Everyone sang and laughed and clapped their hands in time to the music Pa and Patrick played. Billy and Davy jumped up on the porch and stood on either side of Harper. They clapped and stomped their feet so loud Harper could barely hear the music. Harder and harder they stomped until Harper couldn't hear anything else. She glared at them, but they only grinned and stomped harder. She yelled at them to stop, but she couldn't hear her own voice.

She looked around the circle of faces. No one else noticed. Pa and Patrick continued to play. Ma turned her face toward heaven the way she often did when she sang. Harper couldn't hear a word.

Suddenly everything went quiet. Harper was alone inside the house. The darkness was so thick, it seemed to reach out for her. Though she couldn't see, she knew she was in the main room of the cabin Pa had built and added on to as his family expanded.

Harper turned in the direction of the front door. She couldn't see it in the darkness. Something scratched the wood from the other side. She reached toward the sound, but her bare feet remained rooted to the smooth boards. Cold air wrapped around her legs. The scratching grew louder.

A shiver slithered up her spine. She listened for Ma and Pa in their bedroom next door. All was quiet. Where was everyone? Her home was never completely quiet, even in the dead of night. Someone was always stirring or murmuring in his or her sleep.

She pivoted her head to the four corners of the large room. No fire burned in the hearth. Not even one red coal glowed to give her a point of reference. She turned back to the scratching sound. She strained to listen as another sound separated itself from the scratching. Someone was crying. Or whimpering. Not in pain but despair. Or fear.

She reached again for the door. She wanted to help, but her feet wouldn't move. The whimpering grew louder, the scratching more insistent. It didn't sound like a person. It sounded like an animal. A wounded animal trying to get inside.

Fear pushed at the back of her throat, but she couldn't scream. She needed to keep the evil thing outside. She strained to reach the bar to drop across the door. She opened her mouth to call out. Where was everyone? She needed help. She couldn't do it alone.

A loud bang jerked her upright.

Harper gasped aloud and blinked rapidly to get her bearings. She wasn't in the cabin. She was in her room in Uncle Hugh's house, her heart pounding in her chest.

Banging in the next room sounded again.

Ellie.

She freed her legs from the tangled sheets and grabbed her dressing gown. She slid her arms into the sleeves as she hurried next door.

When she went into Ellie's room, she found Ellie kneeling in the corner of the room in front of her armoire. One of the heavy oak drawers sat upended behind her. She was struggling to free the other from the drawer guide. Its contents were strewn on the floor around her.

Harper hurried across the room. "Ellie, what are you doing?" She lowered her voice in case Uncle Hugh had come home and might hear them. "What are you looking for?"

Ellie stopped jerking on the drawer and looked up at her. Her eyes were wild and red-rimmed. Her brown hair shone in the moonlight spilling through the window and lay in ragged swirls around her face and shoulders. "Can't you hear it?" she hissed. "We have to find it."

"Find what?"

"The baby. Help me."

Harper's heart lurched in her chest. Ellie was dreaming. She was sleepwalking. Harper knelt in front of her and gingerly grasped her hands. "Ellie, it's all right. Everything's fine."

Ellie jerked her hands free. "We have to find it. Can't you hear it? Don't just stand there. Help me."

Harper wasn't sure what to do. Ellie looked awake. She acted awake, but her words didn't make sense. Had the sleeping tablets Dr. Dutton mentioned given her nightmares? If so, it explained why she never got a good night's sleep.

She reached again for Ellie's hands. "I don't hear it now. The baby stopped crying."

Ellie didn't pull her hands free. She cocked her head and listened as she looked in all directions. The only sound was her ragged breathing. "I heard it," she whispered insistently. "It woke me up."

"I know." Harper straightened the nightdress that had slipped off her shoulder. "It's quiet. We can go back to sleep now." She helped Ellie to her feet.

Ellie looked at the mess around them. "What happened? I heard the baby. I tried to find it."

Harper shivered in the warm room. How odd that they had such vivid nightmares at the same time. "Let's go to bed. We'll clean this up in the morning." *Before the maid finds it,* she added to herself.

Ellie didn't resist as Harper led her to the bed. "I couldn't let it cry, Harper. She was cold. She needed me. I only wanted to help…"

Harper pulled the blankets up around her shoulders. "Of course, you did."

Ellie smoothed her tangled hair out of her face. Her eyes were clear and alert. "You believe me, don't you, Harper? I'm not crazy. Papa thinks I am. My old friends think I am." Her chin tightened in resolve. "But I couldn't let her cry without doing something."

"I know."

Ellie settled into the blankets. "As long as you believe me."

"I believe you heard the baby. But it's all right now. Go back to sleep."

Ellie squeezed her hand. "I'm glad you're here. I don't want to be alone anymore."

"You're not alone. You've never been alone."

Dread dogged Harper's steps all the way back to her room. She shouldn't have talked about babies and family and a grandfather Ellie didn't know so close to bedtime. Maybe sometime this week, she'd go to Dr. Dutton's office and ask for advice on suitable topics of conversation that wouldn't add to Ellie's malady. Tomorrow she would try to interest her in reading a novel together. A make-believe world was surely safer than the one in Ellie's head.

Chapter Seventeen

arper didn't see Logan the rest of the week, except at a distance as he hurried about his work, and only for a minute or two before he disappeared again. Every time she stepped outside, she listened for his voice calling to her across the wide yard. At the same time, she didn't want to see him. She had nothing to say to the man. He had made it plain he didn't trust her to help Ellie, and he liked her even less.

The morning after her and Ellie's bad dreams, she talked Ellie into walking through the garden with her. They sat quietly on benches and shared the morning breeze. The next day Ellie showed her a loose brick in the wall where she used to stash pretty pebbles or notes to her dolls. Before lunch she pulled Harper inside the stables to see the horses. Harper held her breath the whole time, hoping to see Logan but dreading it at the same time. Ellie was astute; she would see Harper's emotions on her face if they ran into him.

Every morning for the next two weeks, Ellie was awake when Harper took her breakfast to her room and anxious to begin the day. They finished reading *The Portrait of a Lady* by Henry James and began *A Connecticut Yankee in King Arthur's Court.* Ellie had read them before and was eager to share them with Harper.

They ate dinner every evening in the kitchen with Mrs. Philips. The first night Mrs. Philips couldn't contain her tears of joy when Ellie sat down at the table. Ellie had laughed and hugged her and told her to stop acting like she'd seen a ghost.

After dinner each night, Ellie immediately retired to her room to take a cool bath. July had blown in, hot and humid, and the house drew heat throughout the day.

Loneliness got the better of Harper after Ellie went to bed. She tried to think of an innocuous way to ask Mrs. Philips where Logan had been for nearly two weeks. She told herself she only cared because he reminded her of home and not because he stirred any feelings in her.

She had grown accustomed to the lonely creaks and echoes of the massive house. It was harder getting used to the lack of physical activity, sleeping alone in a bed, and eating food she didn't have to dig out of the garden herself. Despite Uncle Hugh's instructions not to do anything he paid servants to do, she tidied her room every day. She didn't speak about it to the maids, but after a few days they stopped going into her room to dust and change the linens. They had enough to do without picking up after her.

Friday morning, she breezed into Ellie's room and found her cousin still in her nightclothes, staring out the window. Her stomach sank. What happened? Everything had been going so well the last ten days.

"I brought breakfast," she sang out.

Ellie barely glanced at her. "I'm not hungry."

Harper recognized the signs. "Why not? Didn't you sleep well?"

"My sleep has nothing to do with it. I don't do enough to work up an appetite."

"And who's fault is that?" Harper exclaimed before she could stop herself. She set the tray on the table but didn't uncover the food. "I'm sorry. I just can't abide waste. You should've seen some of the meager meals in my house over the years."

Ellie nodded at the tray. "You're welcome to send that to them."

Harper's mouth dropped open.

Ellie stared at her a moment. Harper stared back. Finally, Ellie dropped her gaze. "I'm sorry. That was unfair and unnecessary. I'm just feeling maudlin today."

"No, it's my fault. I shouldn't have lectured you about what you eat. Remember, I have three little sisters. Bossing people around is in my nature."

"I noticed."

Harper laughed at the dry smile tugging the corners of Ellie's mouth. "It's beautiful outside today. I have a wonderful idea." She moved to the wardrobe and threw open the double doors. "How about putting on something suitable for a ride? We'll have Burt saddle some horses and we can go riding out of town before it gets too hot."

The blood drained from Ellie's face. "Off the grounds?"

"Where else? We've done the trails here plenty of times. The horses are itching to feel some real earth under their hooves." She pulled a mint green summer dress out of the wardrobe. She held the dress in front of her and swayed back and forth. The lightweight fabric rustled against her plain cotton dress.

She stopped swaying and focused on Ellie. "We could go shopping if you're not up to a ride." She thought of the money Uncle Hugh had given her. She hadn't yet spent a cent of it. She wondered what it would be like to walk into a store and buy whatever she wanted without a care over the things she had to have.

Ellie wrapped her arms around her middle and lifted her chin. "I'm not going for a ride. And I don't want to shop." At Harper's sigh, her face softened. "Don't be mad, Harper. I just can't do it. I can't bear everyone staring at me."

Harper set aside the green dress and went to Ellie. "Who cares what anyone thinks? You can't stay locked up in this house the rest of your life. God gave us a beautiful day. It's ungrateful not to enjoy it. We can ride straight through town and take the road out to the old grist mill. We won't stop and talk to anyone."

"You don't understand. You don't know what it's like to have everyone in town whispering about you behind your back. They know Matthew left me. They know the doctor visits every week. She wouldn't come here if I wasn't crazy. I can't do it. Please don't badger me into it."

Harper wanted to tell her she did know what it was like to have people whispering about her behind her back. She had heard the snickers when she and her sisters walked past in their hand-me-down, oft-mended dresses. She understood the hushed innuendoes about Ma and Pa carelessly bringing more children into the world than they could feed and clothe. But this wasn't about her. It was about Ellie. Her friends had abandoned her because she didn't recover from losing Matthew the way they thought she should. She needed a friend who would support her and take her side, even if Harper thought she knew best.

"You're right. I'm sorry."

She hung the dress back in the wardrobe. "I'll try to stop lecturing you about what you eat and where you go. You'll just have to remember I've been doing it for years to my little sisters. I might not stop overnight."

"I'm older than you," Ellie exclaimed.

Harper put her hand on her hip. "Well, don't start thinking you can boss me around. Just let me say as a friend, not a bossy sister, you can't hide in this room forever."

Ellie smiled appreciatively. "I don't want to keep hiding. I promise you I'll go out soon. Just not today."

Harper squeezed her hand. "Don't do it for me, do it for yourself."

"I'm not crazy, Harper."

"Of course not. I'm sorry if I made you think I believed you were."

"I'm not sad either. I'm just waiting. I wish people could see that. Matthew is coming back, and I plan to be right here when he does."

Harper exhaled. "I understand," she lied.

"What would you think if you went home and no one noticed you'd been gone? Well, I can't do that to Matthew. No one else cares about him. No one believes in him. But I do. No matter how long he takes, I'll wait."

She spoke with such passion, Harper nearly expected to hear his boots on the stairs. "Tell me about him. What kind of man is he?"

Ellie turned hopeful eyes on her. She probably hadn't heard anyone speak about him in the present tense in a long time.

"Is he serious?" Harper prompted. "Is he ambitious? Is he smart? Does he love art the way you do?" She kept her face impassive. She believed what Logan had already told her about Matthew. She believed a lot of what Mrs. Philips and Uncle Hugh said. But she wanted to hear about the other side of Matthew from the woman who loved him.

"He's a lot like you, Harper."

Harper nearly fell over. She hadn't expected that. "How do you mean?"

"He's kind and warm. And generous. He doesn't care about money. He would give you the shirt off his back. The best thing is how he makes me laugh." Her face warmed the more she talked. "Out of the blue, he would say or do something, and I'd laugh and laugh. He was so much fun. Everything with Matthew was easy."

Her eyes darkened. She snagged her bottom lip with her teeth. "See? I'm doing it myself. I'm talking about him as if he's gone for good." Tears sparkled in her eyes. "I don't want to give up on him, Harper. I'll wait no matter how long it takes. I owe him that much."

Harper wanted to tell her she didn't owe him anything. He didn't deserve her loyalty. If he had left to stay ahead of gambling debts, she was better off without him. Even if he left simply to chase adventure, she deserved better than a man who would abandon her without a word of explanation.

"Why do you think you owe him?"

"Because I'm the reason he left. It's all my fault."

Chapter Eighteen

Harper didn't know what she was doing wrong. She and Ellie had a great couple of weeks together. Ellie had been lively and engaging. She was inquisitive about Harper's life in Kentucky and equally revealing about growing up in Willow Wood and traveling with Uncle Hugh. The only topic they hadn't discussed until this morning was Matthew Dunleavy.

And when they did talk about him, Ellie fell apart.

Harper went back to her room feeling nearly as gloomy as Ellie. After two weeks of walking and riding through the gardens, making each other laugh with silly stories, and sharing moments of their lives, it was strange to have an entire day stretching ahead of her with nothing to do.

Back home, she never had a complete day to herself. Whether her birthday, Christmas, a baptism or wedding, chores and children still clamored for her attention. Here was nothing but a wide open calendar that revolved around Ellie's whims and moods.

She looked out her window into the beautiful July sunshine and decided she wasn't going to waste her day wandering around this big house waiting for something to do. She hadn't spent any of the money Uncle Hugh gave her except for the coins she dropped into the offering plates as whichever church she attended on Sundays.

Ellie may not be ready to venture outside the estate's wall, but Harper was. She hadn't visited any of Willow Wood's shops. She needed some writing paper and a new pen. She wouldn't mind a pretty lace handkerchief that wasn't faded from a thousand washings. Maybe even a reticule. She'd never owned one that wasn't handed down from an aunt, cousin, or neighbor. It seemed almost a sin to buy one when there were starving children in the world—probably right here in Willow Wood—and everything she carried fit easily into her pocket. But there was no harm in looking. She shivered in anticipation. Yes, she was going shopping. She folded one of the bills Uncle Hugh had given her into her handkerchief and tucked it into her pocket. She pinned her wide straw hat in place and headed downstairs.

She hurried past the kitchen to avoid Mrs. Philips. She didn't want to explain why Ellie wasn't with her and set the older woman to worrying.

In the courtyard, she headed for the side gate, which was easier to navigate than the imposing ten-foot one at the front of the house. Logan stepped out of the stable leading a roan mare. "Where are you off to this morning?" he called out.

Harper considered shouting a greeting back and continuing on her way. The last time she saw him he had suggested she didn't care about Ellie. Why should she give him the time of day? At the same time, her pulse still quickened at the sight of him. They hadn't spoken in nearly two weeks, and she realized with a start, she missed him. If she walked by without stopping, she would torture herself all day wondering what he wanted or if she had misinterpreted his words the last time they talked.

She dipped her head so the brim of her hat concealed any flush on her cheeks. She certainly didn't want him to think she harbored romantic notions about him or that his face was the one she saw when she closed her eyes at night to dream.

"Good morning," she said when they were within speaking distance. "I'm going for a walk." No need to tell him she'd never owned a new reticule and she was considering rectifying the situation.

"Then I'm glad I caught you. I was about to come looking for you."

She tried to look disinterested. "I'm not hard to find." *Unlike you,* she added to herself.

"Instead of going for a walk, how about a ride?"

She studied the roan for the first time and nearly clapped her hands in delight. "A ride? Do you mean off the grounds?"

The roan lifted its head and snorted. She burst out laughing.

Logan tightened his grip on the reins. "Of course, off the grounds. The other day you asked me why I didn't go with Matthew when he took off. I'd like to show you why."

"Show me?"

"Yeah. I thought I'd saddle this roan for you if you think you can handle her."

She tilted her head at his teasing. "I can handle any horse in this stable with one hand tied behind my back."

He laughed. "I guess I'll take your word for it. I'll finish saddling the mounts. You go inside and ask Mrs. Philips to pack us a lunch basket."

"Lunch? How far are we going?"

"It's a fair piece, unless you can't keep up."

"Oh, I can keep up."

"Well, go on, then. We'll head out in about ten minutes. Don't keep me waiting."

She wanted to throw one last barb at him, but she was too excited. She turned and headed inside as fast as decorum and her long skirt allowed. She stuck her hand in her pocket and shoved the money down as far as it would go. She could shop for a reticule any old day. Today she was going riding. With Logan.

•••

Logan had to hand it to her. She wasn't a complainer. She hadn't stopped smiling since she threw her leg over the roan back at the house. He was happy to see she hadn't been exaggerating when she said she knew how to handle a mount. They had ridden for nearly an hour, cantering some, walking some, a pleasurable pace since the sun was hot. He also wasn't in a hurry to arrive at their destination. He usually made the trip to the farm in less than thirty minutes. He knew the cuts in the hills and the breaks in the tree where he wouldn't lose his hat to overgrowth or low-hanging branches.

He drew Mr. Lundy's big bay up next to Harper's roan. Mr. Lundy wasn't home long enough to properly exercise his mounts, so the job was left to Logan and the stable hands. The bay was Logan's favorite, and he rode it as often as time and other duties allowed.

"You're holding up pretty well, Miss Dixon."

"Why wouldn't I?" A mischievous gleam shone in her bottomless blue eyes. "It's been too long since I've been on horseback. Reminds me of home." Her gaze slid past his shoulder to the ridge in the distance, her eyes sparkling.

Their horses stood so close the wind rustled her skirt against his leg. Logan wanted to reach out and touch her cheek. To let her know he understood. To remind her she wasn't alone.

When she looked back, her faraway expression was gone. "I tried to talk Ellie into going for a ride today. She's been in good spirits the last two weeks. This morning when I went to her room, she wasn't even dressed. She told me she was the reason Matthew left. Do you know what she might've meant by that?"

Logan thought he knew what Ellie meant, but he wasn't sure how much to tell Harper. "You already know Mr. Lundy didn't care for Matthew. Ellie wanted to marry him, but she wasn't willing to leave her father. Even though I knew Matthew would never follow through with marrying her, they argued about it. He said she needed to choose between him and her pa."

"If he wasn't going to marry her, why would he give her such an ultimatum?"

Logan blew out a puff of air. Harper sure was naïve about the ways of men. "He didn't plan to marry her, but it was easier on him if she thought her attachment to her pa was the reason instead of his own restless feet."

Harper drew up in her saddle. "That's not fair. You should tell her the truth. She's torturing herself over this. Tell her he used Uncle Hugh's dislike for him as an excuse to leave her."

He searched for a way to tell her in which she would understand. "What do you think a woman in love wants to hear? That her man can't marry her because of her narrow-minded pa, or that the fella doesn't love her enough to marry her?"

She opened her mouth to respond, and then slowly closed it back. "Okay, I get it."

He brushed his hand across her elbow. "Ellie didn't do anything wrong. She accepted Matthew the way he was. He was blessed to have her. It's a shame he never saw it."

She nodded. He nudged his mount forward, and she followed suit.

"Where does that road go?" she asked, pointing.

"The mines. Your uncle stays at the settlement there when he's working in the area."

"Is that where we're going?"

"No." He pointed past the Y in the road. "We're going over that ridge over yonder." He smiled as her eyes bulged.

She removed her hat and wiped her forehead with the back of her arm. Logan held out the canteen. She smiled her thanks and drank deeply. He watched a drop of water slide down her throat and into her neckline. He forced his gaze away and took the canteen from her.

"We better get moving," she said when he lowered the canteen from his lips. She kicked the roan into a gallop.

"Hey." He replaced the cap on the canteen and shoved it into his vest.

After a quarter mile, Harper allowed her mount to slow. Logan caught up with her and indicated a line of trees with his chin.

Under the canopy of trees, he found the trail that cut back and forth on its way up the mountain. The trail had been sufficiently cleared, but it was rough travel. He glanced over his shoulder now and then to check her progress on the narrow as they ascended. Her face was obscured by her hat as she kept her eyes on the ground. Logan watched her slim fingers deftly guide the horse. Her arms and hands displayed strength from hard work, but her touch was gentle.

"Have I misjudged her all this time, Lord?" he prayed. Her compassion and sincerity were evident in everything she said and did. She hadn't come to Willow Wood to take advantage of her cousin. He was sure of it now. He didn't know much, but he knew that. She was a beautiful woman, inside and out. And he…

He reined in his thoughts before he could admit his feelings for her to himself.

At the top of the ridge he stepped aside to give her room on the flat ground to join him. Her gaze swept the valley below. Her lips parted and her blue eyes sparkled in amazement. The sun had nearly reached its zenith. Her face was warm and flushed from the heat and exertion from the trail. Her dress clung to her, accentuating her trim figure. Logan appreciated her feminine form a few moments before looking away.

A hot wind kicked up and tossed a swirl of sand and grit over them. The horses snorted and stamped their feet. Harper pulled her hat down over her face. Logan held onto his own hat and watched her through squinted eyes. The dirt devil passed, leaving strands of golden hair stuck to her cheek. Before his muddled brain could tell him to resist, he reached out and brushed the hair away. Her breath caught at the contact of his calloused fingers on her warm skin.

He fixed his gaze on her throat as she swallowed. He imagined trailing his hand along her throat to the back of her neck and pulling her against him. The horses were only separated by a few inches on the narrow shelf. He could easily lean close enough to cup his hand behind her head. Would she accept the contact? Would she pull away in disgust? He would understand if she wondered if he had brought her here away from the watchful eye of the household to steal a kiss. And maybe more.

His face warmed at the thought. He wasn't that kind of man. He was the kind of man whose kisses she would never accept. He was her uncle's hired hand. A servant. He could never hope she would see him as anything more.

Chapter Nineteen

Harper turned her gaze back to the vista. Anything to keep her eyes off Logan. She couldn't understand a thing she saw in those dangerously blue, aquamarine eyes.

Why had he invited her here? At first, she had been flattered to think he wanted to show her the reason he didn't leave town with Matthew. If he didn't want to spend time with her, he could've told her instead of going to all this trouble. For a few glorious moments she thought her growing attraction for him wasn't one-sided.

After the wind subsided, he looked like he had wanted to kiss her. When he brushed his hand across her cheek, she thought—

Then he turned away.

When she saw the intent on his face, her breath had stilled. She had tensed in the saddle and nearly leaned forward to wait for his parted lips to meet hers. Fortunately, the moment passed before she went as far as closing her eyes and offering her lips to his. Humiliation flamed her cheeks. How could she be so wrong? This trip was nothing more than an excuse to avoid chores at the house while Uncle Hugh was out of town. Logan only invited her for a ride because Ellie would've turned him down.

She wished for another drink from the canteen so she could trust her voice before she spoke. "It's beautiful here. Is this the reason you chose to stay in Willow Wood?"

It was a redundant question. She already knew the reason he stayed. Ellie.

"Let's go down into that canyon. Then I'll show you."

Her gaze followed his pointing finger. Below them, among clumps of trees and a meandering stream, she saw a small cabin and a few cows munching on lush green grass that reminded her of the blue grasses of home.

"Maybe we're not welcome."

"Everybody's welcome in Willow Wood," he said as he started down the mountainside.

She fell into line behind him. This side of the ridge was rockier. A wide trail had been beaten through the rocks, sand, and scrub growth. She gratefully focused her attention on reaching the bottom safely instead of her complete misreading of Logan's intentions for bringing her here.

They reached the bottom in less than half the time it had taken to come up the other side. Without a word or a glance in her direction, Logan started across the gently rolling pasture into a box canyon. A solid square barn stood about a half mile in front of them. The sun and wind had bleached the boards a pale gray. A corral circled the back of the barn. A lean-to and rough-sided shed lined an irregular path to the small cabin. The cabin had been built from sawed lumber next to a stand of trees that offered shade and a windbreak. It was small and simple with a covered porch barely wider than a man's stride. But it looked tight and solid with no gaps for letting in the winter's chill.

Chickens scratched the yard. A gray-muzzled hound lifted its head to watch their approach.

"It's so quiet," Harper observed. "Where is everyone?"

Instead of answering, Logan motioned to the hills surrounding them. "The bluffs provide a natural pen for the stock. There's water past that dip and plenty of pasture. A man could support five hundred head here. Easy." He indicated a square rock foundation. The dirt around it was freshly turned, and a pile of cut rock suggested the builder was just getting started.

"There's the site of a new barn. The old one was the only thing standing when Hiram Campbell bought this property twenty or so years ago from a miner who hit a vein of ore and gave up farming. Hiram made a good living selling chickens, eggs, and beef to the miners while he built up the rest of it."

"This is a big property for one man."

"Too big. It's a lot for Hiram to keep up, especially now that he's getting older. He's hired a few hands over the years, but mostly it's been him after his family died."

"His whole family?"

"Yeah, he lost two little ones when a fever went through. His wife died a couple years after that. His last son was killed in a farming accident about twelve years ago. Since then, he's been on his own."

"How sad."

"It happens. Here maybe more than other places."

"I suppose. Are you kin to Mr. Campbell?"

"Just a friend." They reached the barnyard. Logan dismounted and looped the horse's reins through a fence slat. Harper did the same.

The old dog left the porch and ambled over to them. Logan leaned forward and scratched the dog behind its ears. "Howdy, Dog."

The dog went to Harper and leaned against her leg. She scratched obediently. "Does it have a name?"

"I just said it. Dog. Hiram couldn't think of a better one."

"Poor dog."

The hound swiveled its head up to look at her. She laughed. Even if Logan had brought her here as a replacement for Ellie, she was having a good time. Any day on horseback was a good day in her book. She'd never ridden as good a mount as the roan. It didn't hurt that she was with Logan, even if she very nearly embarrassed herself up on the ridge.

She looked toward the cabin, feeling a bit like a trespasser. "Where is Mr. Campbell?"

"I don't rightly know. His oxen are missing along with his flatbed wagon. Probably rode over to the quarry for more stone. I'd feel better if he'd waited on me."

"Why should he wait on you?"

"Like I said, he's getting up in years. A job like that goes easier with two backs. Knowing him, he'll try to unload it on his own, too."

"You're a good friend, Logan."

"I appreciate that, but friendship doesn't have much to do with it. This is part of our arrangement. I help with the barn and do whatever other work I can since someday it'll be mine."

"The barn?"

"No, the whole place." His chest expanded inside his shirt.

"I don't understand."

He leaned against the fence slats and gazed around the barnyard. Contentment shone on his face. "The first afternoon Matthew and I had off from work after moving to Willow Wood, he went searching for a card game. I got on my horse and ended up on that ridge over yonder. Mr. Campbell was in the field behind a plow. I needed water and it looked like he needed someone to push the plow a turn or two. We spent the rest of the afternoon talking and working the field. He told me he'd been looking for someone who might be interested in striking a business arrangement."

He turned his back to the fence and rested his elbows on the top rail. "I always dreamed of owning a place of my own. I never thought it would happen. Especially in Indiana. All the good land back there's already taken. Unless you've got a gold mine to spend, which I don't. Goes to show how little faith I had in how the Lord can work things out for my good."

Harper tilted her head while she watched him talk. Pride was evident on his face. This hunk of land obviously meant the world to him. And he was sharing it with her. But why? Her heart filled. Did she dare hope that showing her this farm—his future—meant more than simply sharing why he hadn't gone with Matthew?

Or was he thinking of Ellie? Harper couldn't imagine her cousin herding cattle or setting stones for a barn's foundation. But what did she know about what Ellie wanted once she got Matthew Dunleavy out of her system? What did she know about Logan? Except that he set her heart to racing when he brushed her hair out of her face.

"I come out here and work for Hiram as often as I can. The value of my labor goes toward the price of the property. Mr. Campbell doesn't have anyone to leave it to. I could never earn enough to buy it outright in three lifetimes. This way works for both of us."

Harper wondered if this was why he didn't work at the mines or in the railyard. But if he didn't love Ellie and want to be near her, he could stop working at the estate and move out here to work all the time.

Logan freed his horse's reins. "There's a nice shady spot by the creek where we can eat."

Harper mounted without comment. She gazed around the nicely kept farm as they walked. The cabin was rough but well built, the yard tidy. She could imagine life in a place like this. Raising tomatoes and raising babies. Watching the edge of the fields for her man to come home after a hard day's work.

Logan.

She stole a glance at him as the horse's started down a low embankment to a gurgling creek. She needed to stop torturing herself with dreams that would never come true. Ma had been right. The love of her life was here in Willow Wood. But she wouldn't waste her life like Ellie, loving a man who would never love her back.

They stopped the horses in the shade at the water's edge and dismounted. Logan untied a blanket from behind his saddle. Harper took it from him and moved a dozen or so paces from the horses to spread it on the ground. He unpacked their food from the saddlebags and set it on the blanket.

Harper dropped to her knees. "Everything looks delicious. I often miss Ma's cooking, but Mrs. Philips sure makes the missing easier."

He chuckled. "I never ate like this in my life. Ma meant well, God rest her soul, but I never ate this good until I put my feet under Mrs. Philips' table."

"Ma could create a feast out of the most basic ingredients," Harper told him. "I can only imagine the meals she would've made from Uncle Hugh's pantry." Her voice cracked. She arranged the food on the blanket though it wasn't necessary.

Logan covered her hand with his, effectively stopping her fidgeting. "Sometimes I forget how much of a sacrifice it was for you to come here."

She stared at his hand on hers. "Not a sacrifice. Just something I had to do."

She sat back and met his gaze. He was staring at her as if waiting for her to go on. She wouldn't. There was no point in telling him she was here because Ellie needed her, and Ma and Pa couldn't afford to keep her. It was just the way things were. Like he had said, it was how life worked out sometimes.

He must've realized she wasn't going to go on. He handed her a plate and blessed the food.

After he filled his own plate he sat back. "Mrs. Philips told me Ellie comes to the kitchen for dinner most nights."

Harper was glad he diverted the conversation away from her. "Almost every night since Uncle Hugh's been gone. She and I have gotten to know each other better, too. That's why it worried me so much this morning when she didn't want to get dressed."

He chewed thoughtfully on a roast beef sandwich Mrs. Philips had packed. Harper pinched a piece of beef from her sandwich and nibbled on it.

After a moment he tapped her knuckles. "Try not to worry overly much about it. Ellie's been closed off inside herself a long time. She won't throw those doors open overnight."

She looked up sharply. "I like that analogy. Her heart has been like a closed door."

He nodded. "It's been hard for her. If Matthew had been man enough to leave the right way, some of the suffering she's endured could've been avoided. I put all the blame on him. But..." He raised a finger for emphasis, "it's time she picks herself up and dust herself off. She's strong. I know she can do it. I don't mean to sound indifferent to what she's going through, but it's time she stopped waiting for what she's lost and open her eyes to someone who can give her what she needs."

Harper's mouth went dry. Someone who could give her what she needs. Someone like him.

With shaking fingers, she wrapped the remainder of her sandwich in the napkin.

"Aren't you hungry?" he asked around a big bite of his own sandwich.

"Not as much as I thought."

"Well, I am. You don't mind if I finish, do you?"

"Of course not." She clambered to her feet and brushed the crumbs off her skirt. "I'm going to watch the water for a bit." She hurried away, barely able to keep her tears in check.

Logan loved Ellie. Even with today's setback, Ellie was slowly clawing her way out of the mire that had buried her. It could take a year or two, but she'd eventually be ready to let someone else in her heart, and Logan would be there waiting. What would Harper do then? She wasn't a selfish person. She believed God had brought her to Willow Wood for a reason. But she didn't know if she could endure it if God's plan was for her to help Ellie recover so she could marry the man Harper had dreamed of her whole life.

Chapter Twenty

After Logan finished eating they packed up the remainder of their lunch and got back on the horses. He pointed out features of the farm as they rode. Harper tried to muster the appropriate enthusiasm. She wasn't sure why he was sharing any of it with her, unless he hoped she could convince Ellie to trade her palatial estate for a simple country farm.

The longer they rode, the worse Harper's heart ached. This farm was Logan's dream. The farm and Ellie. Ellie's dream was for Matthew to return. Harper didn't factor into anyone's dreams.

Ma always told her she was a dreamer. She was destined for greater things than what she'd find at home in Kentucky. Ma would be disappointed if she knew how petty and small Harper was feeling now. Since coming to Willow Wood, her dream had been Logan. She wanted to help her cousin rebuild her life. She wanted to please God. But all she cared about was herself.

Help me, Lord, she prayed. *I'm becoming a selfish person who only thinks of herself. Help me remember why I came here. It's not to fall in love. It's for Ellie.*

"Did you hear me?"

She jerked her head in Logan's direction. He stared at her from under the brim of his Stetson.

"Oh, I'm sorry. I was just…enjoying the sunshine. What did you say?"

"I said, I've been thinking of Ellie."

Of course you are, she thought.

"I want to help her realize she shouldn't waste another day waiting for Matthew. The other day I ran into a lady at Endicott's General Store who might be able to help. She may know something about where Matthew went."

Harper pushed aside her petty jealousies. "Really?"

"Freda Bannock's nephew owns The Pick and Shovel. It's a saloon in town. Now, don't worry, I'm not taking you to a saloon. Your uncle would have my hide if I did, but Matthew spent most of his free time playing cards there. Freda cooks food in the back. Matthew thought a lot of her and would often talk to her between hands. I think he almost thought of her as a ma. If he had secrets he didn't tell anyone else, he might've confided in Freda."

Harper sat up straighter in her saddle. Learning what became of Matthew was probably the only thing that would pull Ellie out of her melancholy. "Do you think she'll talk to us?"

"I'm sure of it. Freda's a nice lady. Even the miners respect her. She can settle them down when they're getting rowdy and about to bust up the place."

"I want to go with you when you talk to her."

"I figured as much. That's why I brought it up."

Even if Ellie's recovery meant she would end up with Logan, Harper was willing to do her part to restore her cousin to complete health.

Lord, give me the courage and compassion to see Your will fulfilled, whatever that is, she prayed as she followed Logan back up the trail to town.

•••

The July heat shimmered in waves above Willow Wood's streets as Harper and Logan rode through town. Few people were outside, which suited Harper just fine. They turned onto a narrow street where tiny, rundown shacks leaned dangerously toward the street. From Harper's bedroom window in her uncle's house, she had no idea these kinds of neighborhoods existed in Willow Wood.

A bleached, hand painted sign nailed to a skinny tree at the end of the street read; Pine Street. There wasn't a pine tree in sight. Harper wondered if they'd all been cut down to build the derelict shacks. Two barefoot children playing in the gutter stopped to watch the horses pass. Their clothes were worn and too short for growing bodies, but their faces were clean. She admired the unseen parents who managed to keep their children clean and respectable under such conditions.

The horses picked their way through the debris-strewn street. Harper tucked her chin to her chest and took shallow breaths to avoid the stench of waste clogging the gutters. Logan continued forward until they reached the last house that butted up against a ravine. He looked back. "Are you all right?"

She gave a brief nod in response as she slid off her mount. He needn't worry this scene would unsettle her. She'd experienced poverty and desperation herself.

They looped the reins over a hitching rail that seemed to support the structure. The front door creaked open before they stepped onto the sloping boards that served as a porch.

"Well, look who's here." The woman peering out at them wore a warm smile that filled her faded brown eyes. Straight fingers and a straight back intimated a woman possibly in her forties, but her wrinkled face and thinning, steel gray hair made her look closer to sixty.

Logan's warm smile matched hers. "Good afternoon, Freda. I wasn't sure I'd find you here this time of day."

"Lunch is over at the saloon, and folks wantin' dinner won't show up for another hour or so."

The stoop wasn't big enough for the three of them, so she remained in the doorway. Her gaze swept up Harper's faded green dress to her face. "Who'd ya bring with ya?"

"This is my friend, Harper Dixon. She's Mr. Lundy's niece. Harper, this is Freda Bannock. She helped Matthew and me get work with your uncle when we first came to town. If Freda doesn't know a person in Willow Wood, they're probably not worth knowing."

Freda's smile warmed further. "Well, now, I don't know about that. You boys would've found work eventually. I could see right away you were hard workers and it wouldn't hurt my reputation none by puttin' in a good word for you."

"I'll be forever in your debt," Logan said.

Harper pursed her lips. Naturally he would think highly of this woman since she was responsible for him meeting Ellie.

Freda reached for Harper's hands. Harper offered them, and the woman clasped them firmly.

"How do you do?" Harper said.

"I do right fine. You come on inside, girl." Still holding Harper's hands, she pulled her into the tiny house. It looked like it consisted of two small rooms. A kitchen area filled the back wall of the main room with a stove, sink, and scarred table barely big enough for two. The floor sloped toward the west wall. Daylight showed around the window casing and back door. Layers of newspaper plastered the wall above the sink. Harper's family had used the same method over the years to insulate against drafts. Despite the lack of material goods, the house was clean and swept and the short counter spotless. The only dish out of place was a half-filled coffee cup on the table.

Freda studied Harper with a keen eye. "You ain't from around here, are ya, girl?"

"No, ma'am. I'm from Kentucky."

Freda cracked a wide smile, revealing a blank spot where a canine tooth had been. "That's what I thought. I'm from Berea."

The tension slid out of Harper's shoulders. "Berea, Kentucky? I'm from Corbin County."

"Well, if that don't beat all." Freda dropped Harper's hands and motioned her toward a faded, sagging sofa. "You two have a seat then and tell me what brung ya."

Harper perched on the edge of the sofa, afraid it wouldn't support hers and Logan's weight. Logan must've worried the same thing. He sat gingerly next to her. The dilapidated davenport was barely wide enough, and his shoulder brushed hers.

"Could I get either of ya a cup of coffee?" Freda asked.

Logan answered first. "We really don't have time, Freda. Like I told you at the general store the other day, I wanted to talk to you about Matthew and his state of mind right before he went away."

She settled into the rocking chair opposite them and folded her hands in her thin lap. "Well, now, I been pondering that ever since you brung it up to me. I don't know how much I can tell ya that ya don't already know." She looked at Harper. "How's your cousin gettin' along?"

Now wasn't the time to sugarcoat the truth. "Not well, ma'am. Not well at all. That's why we're here. I believe the only thing that will help her move past the grief of losing Matthew is finding out where he went and if he's coming back."

Freda clicked her tongue. "That poor, poor girl. Young women's heads get turned by a handsome face and an easy smile. That was Matthew. My, how he could make a body laugh and forget her troubles." She sighed. Her gaze slid toward the door. "But a light heart don't always make for a good husband. Matthew had wanderin' feet. I'm sorry your cousin didn't recognize it before it was too late. His kind is off to find adventure ever' time the wind blows. I thought a lot of him, but Ellie is better off with him gone."

Harper wanted to tell her she couldn't agree more. Ellie's problem was reconciling in her heart what she probably already knew in her head.

"The boy was always looking for somethin' he couldn't find," Freda went on. "I tried to talk to him ever chance I got. Sometimes he'd come into the kitchen while I was fixin' dinner for the miners. We'd talk about home since we was both from somewhere else. You might not believe it, Logan, but he missed his kin. It sorrowed him something awful that he'd never see them again. He knew he couldn't go back."

"Did he ever mention a place he thought about going?" Harper asked. "West, perhaps? California?"

Freda snorted. "I don't expect he knew where he'd go until he woke up already there. If he didn't tell you, Logan, I'm sure he wouldn't have told me."

The sofa was too short for a man. Logan rested his elbows on his knees and leaned forward. "Matthew thought a lot of you, Freda. I hoped he might've confided in you about what was on his mind that he'd have been too proud to tell me."

"Well, now, I expect he did do that a time or two. As you know he had a rough go of it growin' up. He knew he disappointed ever'one he cared about. You was the only one left, Logan, who believed he was worth savin'. He told me that time and time again."

Harper watched Logan's jaw clench. She could nearly read his mind. If Matthew cared so much for her, why had he left without a word of explanation?

She'd heard enough pity for Matthew Dunleavy to last her a lifetime. From what she could see, his own behavior was the root of his problems. He couldn't blame a bad childhood for the choices he made.

"What about Ellie? He had *her*. She loved him, yet he walked away. She's the one suffering."

She took a deep breath to rein in her irritation. None of Ellie's pain was the fault of the woman in front of her. But she wanted someone to understand she was here to help Ellie. She wasn't interested in wasting a drop of pity on the man who broke her heart.

Compassion and understanding softened Freda's faded brown eyes. "He loved that girl. I could see it in his eyes. He just wasn't strong enough to do right by her. Try not to think ill of him. but his guilt over disappointin' her too was more than he could face."

"What guilt? How did he disappoint her?"

Freda's gray brows slid together. She studied Harper and then Logan. "Oh, dear, I thought you knew. Your cousin was goin' to have a baby."

Chapter Twenty-One

Harper gasped. "A baby? But how?" She stopped talking. She knew the how behind the creation of a baby. What she didn't understand was what had become of it and how this was the first she'd heard about it. What other secrets was Ellie keeping from her?

She looked accusingly at Logan, but he appeared as blindsided as she was.

A baby explained Ellie's level of sadness and her confidence Matthew would return even when all logic indicated he would not. She remembered Ellie's dream of a baby crying. At the time she thought the dream was brought on by Dr. Dutton's condition. Had Ellie been looking for her own baby?

"What happened to it?"

"She never had the baby. She lost it."

"Oh, no." She looked again at Logan. He ran his hand over his jaw and stared into space. "Did Uncle Hugh know?" she asked.

Freda shook her head. "I doubt it. As far as I can tell no one in town knew. Not that I've asked around or anything. I would never do that to a young woman hoping to cover her indiscretion."

"Then how did you know?" Harper didn't want to call the woman a liar, but she was practically a stranger to Ellie. How did she know something Ellie and Matthew had obviously gone to great lengths to keep hidden from everyone else?

"Ellie came to one of the girls in the saloon for help."

Harper winced. "What kind of help?"

Once a baby was on its way, there was nothing a body could do about it except let nature take its course. Oh, she'd heard stories of desperate women who chewed on roots or drank castor oil to stimulate an early birth. She hated to think such practices existed or that her cousin would engage in them. Impossible. Ellie wouldn't go to a saloon to ask a soiled dove what to do about an unwanted child.

Freda stared unflinchingly at her. "Ellie was scared. Matthew told her about the girls at The Pick and Shovel. She came in one night as white as a sheet. She told Carlotta what happened. Carlotta brought her to me."

"What about the doctor? She must've…"

"Not necessarily," Freda put in. "Things like this often happen at home and a doctor is never called, especially with the young people aren't married."

"How did Matthew react?"

Freda arched her thin eyebrows. "You don't see him around here, do ya? I expect a baby was enough of a scare to send him down the pike for good."

Harper sat back in her chair and processed what she'd heard. "Is that what happened to the baby? Carlotta told her how to..." She couldn't say the words. She couldn't even form them inside her head.

"No. Carlotta and I just listened to her that night. Like I said, she was scared out of her mind. She was afraid to tell Matthew, but she believed he'd do right by her. She couldn't imagine tellin' her papa. She was more worried about him than anything else."

"She's always worried about disappointing him," Logan said.

Harper flinched at the sound of his voice. She had nearly forgotten he was beside her. Ordinarily she would never talk about an unborn baby in front of a man. Especially in front of the man who loved Ellie. Did this revelation change his feelings? Not likely. He wasn't that kind.

"Did she lose the baby before or after Matthew left?" she asked Freda

Freda rocked back in her chair. "I can't say. Carlotta told me she saw Ellie a little while after Matthew took off and she didn't appear to be carryin' a little one. It wasn't likely she'd've gone out in public if she was."

Tears stung Harper's eyes. "No wonder she can't get over losing him. I can't believe he'd do that to her." She wasn't sure what made her angrier. Matthew putting her with child or abandoning her after he did.

She turned to Logan. "Did you know anything about this?"

He shook his head. "I had my suspicions, but Matthew never said for sure."

"What else don't I know?"

"That's why we're here." He turned to Freda. "Ellie has her good days, but she doesn't show much sign of coming out of her depression. She hasn't left the house in months. Like Harper said, if we knew something about where Matthew ended up, maybe Ellie'd stop fretting over him and waiting for him to come back. Have you heard any rumors on the wind about what may have happened?"

"I believe I just told you all you need to know. Some men can't take the pressure a little one brings. Especially knowin' how her pa felt about him."

"Did Uncle Hugh know about the baby?"

"Nobody knows, but in my mind, that's why Matthew left. Of course, there's always the chance it had to do with the miner that was killed."

Harper nearly fell off the sofa. "What miner?"

"There was a card game that turned ugly the night Matthew left. I don't know what really happened. Ever'body there had a different story. Only thing we know for sure is the miner wound up dead."

Harper felt the blood drain from her face. "What did Matthew say about it?"

It was Logan's turn to answer. "He didn't say anything. By the time the sheriff got there, Matthew was gone."

•••

"Why didn't you tell me?"

Logan didn't need to ask Harper what she was talking about. He was surprised she managed to keep her questions inside long enough to ride up Pine Street and head back to the more refined neighborhoods of Willow Wood.

"I didn't know about a baby."

"But you had your suspicions. You knew Matthew left the very night the miner was killed. That seems like an even bigger reason than a baby for a man to disappear. "

"Matthew may have been irresponsible and selfish, but I'll never believe he was a killer."

She exhaled so loudly he heard it from atop his horse. "It seems to me there's a lot about him you don't know."

He clenched the pommel. He wanted to defend himself, but he could see her point. He thought he knew Matthew like a brother. It turned out he didn't know the half of it.

They rode in silence a few moments, stewing in their own thoughts. "Was Matthew the kind of man who'd leave a woman carrying his child?"

He didn't want to answer. Worse, he didn't want to admit he wasn't sure. "I never thought so. Now I don't know."

Harper's face went white. She clenched her jaw so tightly he thought it might pop.

He reined his horse a little closer to hers. "He wasn't always this way. I think it was the gambling. It was a sickness to him. He loved doing it even when he was losing. He couldn't control himself. I think it affected every decision he made."

She swung her head around and glared at him. She didn't speak. She only clenched her jaw tighter.

"I'm not making excuses for him," he said quickly. "I'm just telling you what I think. I know you don't want to just know where he is, but the why behind it. Ellie will want to know, too."

Harper finally pried her clenched jaws apart enough to speak. "What about the miner? Are you going to tell her about him?"

"I believe we'll have to by the time this is said and done. But whatever happened, and for whatever reason Matthew used to justify his behavior, I want the whole story."

"So do I."

He studied her face, stark white against her dark blond hair and deep blue eyes. "Are you sure? You sound like you've already made up your mind about what happened."

He wanted to remind her everyone made mistakes, often when they were in love as Ellie and Matthew had been. He was asking himself the same questions reflected in her eyes. The Matthew he'd known his whole life wouldn't leave a woman with a child on the way alone to face her father and an unforgiving society.

There was a chance he hadn't. Ellie might've lost the baby before Matthew left. They might've planned to tell Mr. Lundy, but the baby died first. Matthew's departure revealed a lot of things about his character, but it didn't prove he had run away from his paternal responsibilities.

"I told you Matthew had made enemies in Indiana. We were just one step ahead of a group of men who wanted his head."

"Because he owed more than he could pay."

"Yes, but that was only part of it. The night he came to my cabin to tell me he was leaving home, the bruises on his face told me what he wouldn't say. Matthew was good at pretending anything could roll off his back. It wasn't the first night he'd taken a beating, but that time shook him up more than I ever saw. He owed some important people money, and they weren't going to sit around and wait for him to make it square.

"He laughed and joked all the way across the prairie. But when he didn't think I was watching he kept an eye out over his shoulder. He knew he had gone too far. I don't believe he cheated anybody. He didn't have to; he was that good. But once somebody puts the thought in people's heads, they'll believe it. Nobody wants to think they were honestly bested."

Harper kept her eyes on her horse. He could tell she was listening intently.

"They wanted blood. They may have come here to get it."

Chapter Twenty-Two

For the first time since coming to Willow Wood Harper was thankful Ellie was sequestered in her room. She opened her desk drawer and removed the letter she'd received from home yesterday. She read it twice last night and had been thinking about a reply. Knowing what she knew now, she didn't know where to begin. How could she tell Ma Ellie may have had a baby? Or that Uncle Hugh didn't go to church and expressed no interest in his spiritual wellbeing? How would she tell her highly moral family that Ellie's beau was a gambler and owed money to everyone from here to Indiana, and one of them may have come after him to collect? They would never understand. They could even demand she come home before the influence of the Lundy mansion could corrupt her beyond redemption.

She stared at the letter a moment before tucking it back into the narrow desk drawer. She was too distracted and unnerved to write a letter home. She had begun keeping lots of secrets from her parents since coming here.

Thinking of secrets, she hadn't told them about Logan either. There was nothing really to tell. He loved Ellie. They'd figure it out soon enough anyway after Ellie and Logan's wedding and Uncle Hugh sent her back to Kentucky.

A soft knock sounded at the door. She pulled it open to find Ellie on the other side, looking pale and thin and vulnerable. Harper immediately regretted her self-pity. Ellie deserved to be happy, no matter who it was with.

"I wondered if you were home," Ellie said. "I haven't seen you all day."

Harper nearly apologized until she remembered she had asked Ellie to go out with her.

"Logan and I went for a ride." She searched Ellie's face for interest or jealousy. She found neither. "Did you have a nice day?"

Ellie shrugged her thin shoulders. The smudges under her eyes that had been nearly erased after her days in the sun were back.

"It was fine. Are you hungry? I waited for you to come home before I went to the kitchen."

Harper felt even guiltier. "I'm actually famished." She didn't tell her she had only nibbled on her lunch after Logan told her he hoped Ellie would open her eyes to the possibility of love standing right in front of her.

In the kitchen Ellie ate ravenously. Harper tried to put Freda's words out of her head. She could only imagine how Ellie would react to inquiries about a baby. In her fragile mental state, such a question might set her back a hundred paces from the progress they'd made. The night she dreamed about a lost baby crying for her, she had been completely confused by it. She hadn't realized—or hadn't hinted at realizing—the baby in her dream was hers. Harper wouldn't bring up the subject until she had a chance to discuss it with Dr. Dutton.

Was it ethical to mention Ellie's baby to the doctor? If the doctor didn't know, it wasn't Harper's place to tell her. And if she did know Ellie had given birth, she wasn't free to discuss it with Harper.

Could she believe Freda Bannock? The story could've been rumor or conjecture. No one actually saw Ellie in the family way. Ellie may have been wrong about a pregnancy when she talked to Freda and the girl at the saloon. She may have suspected Matthew was preparing to leave, and she made up the story of a baby to trick him into staying. Ellie said it was her fault Matthew left. Was that what she meant?

Harper didn't know what to think. If there had been a baby it seemed unlikely Mrs. Philips or one of the maids wouldn't notice, even if Uncle Hugh and Logan didn't recognize the signs another woman would see.

After they ate Harper disregarded Uncle Hugh's orders to leave menial tasks for the servants and began clearing the table. She smiled to herself when Ellie joined in, though it readily became apparent she had never washed a dish in her life.

Within minutes they were on their way back upstairs.

"I worked on a sketch today."

Harper's heart soared. If Ellie was drawing, that meant she was improving. It also meant she was one step closer to realizing Logan loved her. Harper wouldn't torture herself with those thoughts tonight. "Is it something I can see?"

Color crept into Ellie's face. She was still terribly thin, but with color from the sun on her cheeks and a smile on her face, Harper could see the beautiful vivacious woman inside.

She followed Ellie into the large bedroom and across the floor to the desk. Ellie flipped the sketchpad over and studied the drawing a moment before handing it over. She snagged her bottom lip in her teeth while she waited for Harper's reaction.

Harper gasped aloud. She had expected a likeness of Matthew. Instead, her own image smiled up at her. Besides her physical appearance, Ellie had somehow captured her personality. An inner strength and peace she wasn't sure she possessed shone out of her blue eyes. "Ellie, it's beautiful. I mean, not that I'm beautiful...."

Ellie laughed out loud and clasped her hands, reminding Harper of a child eager to please a parent. "You are beautiful, Harper, on the inside and out."

Harper studied the sketch through a veil of tears. "I...I don't know what to say. I don't know how you did it, but you made me look so wise. So strong."

"You are strong, Harper. And brave."

"I don't know about that."

Ellie grabbed her free hand, her grip strong and her eyes earnest. "Well, I do. You're the bravest person I ever met. You make me think I can do anything too."

"I do?"

"You're a good friend to me, Harper. You put my needs before your own even though I've been a dreadful trial the whole time you've been here."

Harper opened her mouth to deny it. She stopped. She didn't believe in false humility, and Ellie would see through it anyway.

"You have been a trial, Ellie," she said with a smile. "But I love you."

"Do you mean it?"

"I wouldn't have said it if I didn't mean it. You're like a sister to me."

Ellie's eyes sparkled. "I never thought you'd want another sister. You have so many."

Harper laughed. "I can always use another sister. And I'm glad it's you."

Ellie threw her arms around Harper's neck. In shock, Harper hugged her back. Ellie had never been demonstrative. She claimed she didn't want Harper here, but it looked like all that had finally changed.

They drew apart. Ellie dabbed the corner of her eyes. She carefully tore the drawing out of the sketchpad and pushed it into Harper's hands. "I want you to have it."

Harper looked down at the drawing. "Oh, I couldn't. You put so much work into it."

"I did it for you."

"Are you sure? It's the most thoughtful thing anyone's ever done for me." She studied the drawing for a moment. "Would you mind terribly if I sent it to my ma? I would love to show off your talent to my family, and this will keep them from forgetting me."

Ellie touched her hand. "You silly thing. You don't really think they'll forget you, do you?"

Harper shrugged off a wave of homesickness. "I don't know. Sometimes."

"No one who met you would ever forget you. You're a special person. I'm glad you came."

"I'm glad I'm here too."

Ellie dropped into the chair at her desk. "Do you remember when I told Dr. Dutton I didn't ask you to come? I didn't want you here because I figured Papa was using you to make me forget Matthew."

"None of us are trying to make you forget. We just want you to focus on the life you have, not something you wish you had."

Ellie stared thoughtfully at the blank page in her sketchbook. "I don't know if I can. I've lost everything that means anything to me."

Harper thought of the baby. She wondered if Ellie was too. She took Ellie's hand. "It may seem like that today, but you have a lot of living left to do. You'll never forget Matthew or all the joy he brought to your life. That doesn't mean you can't love again. I don't think you can do it on your own, but God can help you. He can ease your pain."

"I don't know, Harper. I always figured God thinks of me the same way Papa does. That I've disappointed Him, too."

Harper squeezed her hand. "Ellie, no. You haven't disappointed God. He loves you more than you'll ever know. Nothing you may have done has surprised Him. He doesn't approve of sin, and He won't ignore it. But He's quick and merciful to forgive when we ask Him."

Ellie pulled her hands free. "You don't know what I've done, Harper."

Harper tensed. Was Ellie about to tell her about the baby? Would she be able to look like she didn't already know? Did Ellie even remember, or was she still in denial the way she'd been the night she had the dream?

"No, I don't," she said, "but I know what God did. He sent his Son to die on a cross to save us from our sins. No sin is too big for Him to cleanse us from."

Ellie stood and went to the window. She looked out. Harper could see her stricken face in the reflection from the gathering dusk outside.

"Papa can't forgive me. He can barely look at me."

Harper wanted to tell her God was perfect and her father most certainly was not. But it wasn't what she needed to hear at the moment. She joined her at the window but kept a few feet of space between them.

"Your papa loves you so much. Look at all the trouble and expense he went to to bring me here."

Ellie shrugged. "He brought you here to keep an eye on me so he could go back to work."

Harper wouldn't insult Ellie by denying it. Uncle Hugh told her he had put off his business trip until she came.

Ellie turned to face her. "He may have loved me in the past, but I don't think he has in a long time.

"Oh, Ellie, you know that isn't true."

"Papa is motivated and driven. To him, giving into grief is a sign of weakness. I never saw him shed a tear when Mother died. He got up the next morning and went to work. I needed him here with me, but he let Mrs. Philips console me. He had no patience for when I cried."

"He knew he couldn't take your pain away, so he ran from it. He didn't mean to abandon you. He just couldn't shoulder your pain and his as well."

Ellie lifted her chin. "He could've tried instead of leaving a little girl alone while he chased the almighty dollar."

Harper wasn't sure it was welcome, but she pulled Ellie back into her arms. "I'm sorry you felt alone, Ellie, but your papa loved you then and he loves you now."

"He's tired of me. He's tired of my melancholy. He's tired of me moping around the house. He never thought Matthew was good enough for me."

Harper didn't tell her she already knew what Uncle Hugh thought.

"He wanted me to marry a man of distinction. There were a few men in town he hoped I would fall in love with. None of them were like Matthew. They were stuffy and stodgy and so...upright."

She wrinkled her nose and gave Harper a small smile. "They were too much like Papa. Matthew was nothing like him. That's what I liked about him best."

She went back to her chair. Harper followed. This was the first Ellie had talked about Matthew without looking like she was moments from bursting into tears.

"All Papa ever cared about was making money. Don't get me wrong. I have nothing against success. I respect hard work and ambition as much as the next person. I just never wanted a man who loved wealth and power more than me."

Harper listened to Ellie talk without interruption. Matthew may not have loved wealth and power, but he seemed to love gambling more. Was that why he'd gone? Had he been involved in the miner's death or had someone else driven him out of town? Or had he run from the responsibility a wife and baby would demand of him?

She couldn't ask Ellie any of the questions bothering her. She would let her remember Matthew however she wanted. But someday she would have to face the truth that he wasn't coming back.

Chapter Twenty-Three

Logan finished his work at the Lundy estate every day by early afternoon and spent the rest of the day working with Hiram Campbell on the farm. Mr. Lundy wouldn't stay away forever so he wanted to take advantage of the lighter workload.

In the two weeks following his trip to the farm with Harper, he and Hiram had set the foundation and walls of the new barn. Hiram said they'd have to hire help to put up the trusses Logan built and set the roof. Logan wished they could manage on their own, but he recognized their limitations, as unwanted as they were. Every dollar spent hiring help meant more time required to achieve his dream. At times like this when there was more work that needed done than hours in the day to complete it, he thought about quitting his position at the Lundy estate and living here fulltime. He slept in the shed they had built last year when he had a few days away from the estate. He could move into it fulltime and save himself the trouble of riding back and forth to town.

Whenever his mind went in that direction, he thought of how he couldn't leave Ellie. Lately, though, instead of Ellie, his mind went to Harper. If he quit his position at the estate, he'd never see her again. He knew it would happen eventually. She already admitted she was here out of obligation rather than by choice. Once her obligation was met and Ellie recovered, she'd be on the first train back to the Kentucky hills she missed so much. She'd be out of his life forever.

Every time he pictured her sweet face and imagined her full lips, he kicked himself for not kissing her on the ridge when he had the chance. What an idiot he'd been. At the time he figured she wouldn't be interested in a stable hand whose biggest dream was owning a farm that would never make him rich or powerful. Why settle for him when her uncle could introduce her to the most successful men in Idaho the way he hoped to do for Ellie?

No matter, Logan should've taken the chance before it slipped away. The worst she would've done was spurred her horse down the hill to get away from him. The best she'd would've done…

Well, those thoughts kept him awake most nights.

"Easy there," Mr. Campbell called over the ringing of Logan's hammer. "That nail don't need to go no further in unless you plan to drive it out the other side."

Logan looked down at the scar on the board his hammer had left. He smiled sheepishly. "I don't want it working its way out during a high wind."

Mr. Campbell smirked. "No chance of that."

Logan put another handful of nails in his mouth and moved down the length of wood.

"Don't suppose that sad sack look you're wearing has anything to do with the little filly you brung out here a couple weeks ago."

Logan's arm froze mid-swing. He brought the hammer down and tried to look like the words hadn't nettled him.

He removed the nails from between his lips. "I thought you went to the quarry that day."

Mr. Campbell's cheeks pulled into a grin. "You don't think word gets around even out there? A fella told me he saw you and a purty little blonde riding this way. Didn't take much ponderin' to figure out what you was up to."

Logan shrugged. "I wasn't up to nothing. It was a nice day for a ride. She hasn't been away from the estate since she got here. Figured she'd like to see some countryside."

"So you brung her all the way out here? Long way for a hot day."

Logan knew the old man was hunting for gossip. He got lonely with only the cows to talk to, and he'd gotten nosy in his later years. "Good a place as any."

Mr. Campbell's gaze searched Logan's face. "I reckon so. Especially if a young fella's wanting to get the approval of the gal who caught his fancy."

"I didn't say anyone's caught my fancy…" Logan's words tapered off as he realized Mr.

219 - TERESA SLACK

Campbell was baiting him. An innocent man wouldn't work so hard to defend himself. He put the handful of nails on the board and removed his hat to comb his fingers through his sweaty hair. "Ain't no harm in taking a nice long ride with a pretty gal. Doesn't have to mean anything."

Mr. Campbell laughed as Logan knew he would. "It don't at that. I sometimes miss those days myself." He studied Logan again for a long minute. Logan tried not to squirm. With one deft tap he set another nail in place, mindful not to drive it too deeply into the wood.

Mr. Campbell continued to study him. "I guess after we finish this barn, our next project'll be to get started on a new cabin." He gave the existing one a critical glance. "I can't let you move a bride into that old shack. The fellas at the quarry would never let me live it down."

Logan brought the hammer down on his thumb. He bit down hard on a protest of pain. "Who said anything about a bride? Unless you've got one in mind for yourself."

Mr. Campbell slapped his leg with his hat and whooped with laughter. "Well, now, wouldn't that be a sight." He wiped his eyes and replaced his hat. "But we're not talking about me, and you know it. I was a young man once. I'm not so old that I forgot how a fella's mind works when his eyes take note of a pretty gal. I've been waiting for nearly three years for you to find the young lady who'd join you out here. I can't abide the idea that we're doing all this work so you can turn into a crusty old bachelor with no little 'uns to set around his table."

Logan slowly exhaled. He didn't want to snap or speak harshly to the old man. He didn't want to continue the conversation either. "I'll marry if it's the Lord's will. If not, I'll make this place prosperous on my own the same way you have. I won't make you sorry for selling to me."

The mirth slid from Mr. Campbell's wizened features. He closed the gap between them. "You'll never make me sorry, Logan. I have every confidence in you, and the good Lord for that matter. I just hate to think of you out here alone for the next fifty years. I had my heart set on a mess a' young'uns playing under that tree again." He wagged his chin toward the oak tree near the cabin door.

Logan looked despite his insistence he'd leave his marrying to the Lord. He envisioned a trio of sandy-haired children running and chasing each other around the tree's trunk. His gaze moved to the door. In his mind's eye, Harper stood there on the dog run watching them play.

He blinked to clear the image. He could never offer Harper the life she'd find with one of the men her uncle could introduce her to. He didn't expect her to forego a comfortable life in town for hard work and uncertainty with him. He took hold of another nail. "We'll let the Lord see to it."

Mr. Campbell waited until he drove the nail home. "The Lord might have plans, but He expects a fella to get off his backside and put some work into the process."

Logan waved the hammer. "That's what I'm trying to do. I'd get a lot more work done if you'd stop clucking like an old hen."

He grinned and bent back over the board hopeful Hiram wouldn't see how hard he was trying not to think about Harper Dixon.

He had imagined sharing this farm with her from the moment he saw her step off the train last month. There were plenty of pretty girls in Willow Wood that would make a man a good wife. But none of them had ever affected him the way she did.

She didn't know how he felt about her, and he had no idea how to fix it. From the moment she showed up, he made no secret that he didn't trust her. Now he knew she wasn't the person he believed her to be. He'd been wrong, but what could he do about it now? It wouldn't benefit either of them if he tried to straighten things out now. She could go back to her life in Kentucky—whatever that was—and he'd...

He glanced toward the stack of trusses he'd hammered together. He had the farm. He had Ellie to protect in case his fears were right and someone from Matthew's past came after her for vengeance. That was enough. It would have to be.

But Harper had worked so hard to find the truth. Harder than anyone before her and harder than anyone would after. Logan had thought of one more place to ask questions about the night Matthew left. He should've thought of it sooner. Without Harper's determination to help Ellie, he might never have. He owed it to her to include her in this last attempt to get the whole story about why Matthew left, and maybe even where he went.

Once they had their answers, she could get on with her life—whatever that looked like—and he could get her out of his head once and for all.

Chapter Twenty-Four

Logan threw the saddle over the horse. "It's a long ride. You sure you're up to it?"

Harper put her foot in the stirrup and swung onto the horse in response. "Must we have this conversation every time I climb onto a horse?"

Logan laughed. "Don't say I didn't warn you."

She merely smiled. Hugh had returned home from Utah last night. When Logan asked her to join him on a fact-finding mission, he warned her not to tell her uncle. He hadn't provided many details, which of itself told her they were embarking on a search for some of Matthew's old friends. Since he told her it was a long ride, she knew they weren't going to the saloon. The only remaining logical location was the mining camp where the miner had been killed the night Matthew left town.

223 - TERESA SLACK

As the horses began an easy walk down the hill
toward Willow Wood's main thoroughfare, her mind
raced about what they might discover. Neither Ellie
nor Logan had said anything to make her think
Matthew possessed a violent bone in his body. But
desperate men had been known to do desperate things.
If Matthew was involved in the miner's death, how
would she tell Ellie? *Should* she tell her? It was bad
enough he was a gambler willing to lose every penny
he had and possibly every penny she had. If she found
out he was a cold-blooded killer she may never
recover.

She looked at Logan. Anxiety showed in his jaw
under the shade of his battered hat. How would the
truth about Matthew affect him? They had grown up
like brothers. She was sure he'd prefer to go on
thinking Matthew had left town in search of adventure
than to discover he'd been involved in a murder. She
almost regretted her dogged resolve to find out what
became of him. Would the truth actually help anyone?
If she had been more patient, she might have helped
Ellie out of her melancholy without needing to dig
into Matthew's past.

The only thing that could come from her pursuit
of the truth was making herself unnecessary to her
cousin.

She no longer worried that Uncle Hugh would
turn her out when Ellie didn't need her anymore. He
would let her remain at the mansion like an indigent
spinster aunt. He would keep her in new hats and
pretty dresses and all the books she could read. She
would never want for a thing again. Except love.

She stole another peek at Logan. Why had she fallen in love with a man who wouldn't love her back? She shook the thoughts out of her head. Logan wasn't hers. He loved Ellie, and after Matthew was out of her system, Ellie might realize Logan was the one she loved all along. Harper would never stand in the way of her cousin's happiness. She needed to banish the dream of Logan from her heart and figure out what to do with the rest of her life.

But she couldn't worry about any of it until they learned what happened to Matthew.

At the edge of town, she and Logan stopped the horses at a row of water troughs. "Are we going to the camps?" she asked.

Logan didn't look surprised that she'd figured it out. "They knew Matthew there better than anywhere. If a game didn't come to town, he'd go to the game."

They watched the horses drink until they had their fill. As they moved on, Harper said, "You seem so different from Matthew. What kept your friendship strong?"

He didn't answer right away. He studied the landscape in front of them as the horses plodded along. "I know you've heard he had a rough time growing up. That doesn't begin to describe it. Both our pas were poor providers. They had a taste for the bottle. That's why I don't touch the stuff myself. Matthew's pa didn't know when to stop. Sometimes when he came home with a little in his belly, somebody was gonna get hurt.

"He was one of those fellas who liked being mean for the sake of it. Liked throwing his weight around." Logan's hands tightened on the reins. "Matthew didn't like to fight. He'd rather settle a dispute by making you laugh and forget you were mad. His pa took it upon himself to drive what he saw as a weakness outta him. Matthew wasn't big enough to fight back so his best defense was staying out of the old man's way.

"Whenever I'd see the situation getting to him, I'd get him away from there. I'd get a group of boys together and we'd go fishing or looking for mischief like spying on girls at the swimming hole. I couldn't bear to see his pa tear him down. That's how we got so close."

Harper's heart ached for them. Her upbringing had been difficult, but she always knew she was loved, and she never had to steer clear of a drunk man's fists.

They rode in silence, Harper thinking of how growing up under a hard man could shape a person.

"How did he get into the card playing?" she asked at length.

"His uncle Cy was as rough as Matthew's pa, but he liked Matthew. Cy went to horse races and card games and let Matthew tag along. Maybe, like me, he wanted to help Matthew stay out of his pa's way. Matthew told me they'd let him sit at the tables when he was only six years old. Had a gift for it. My ma always said card playing was the devil's game. I never understood what she meant. I thought it was harmless fun. But as we got older and I saw the trouble it brought Matthew, I started to think she was right. Sometimes he'd come to my house with his pockets full of money. We'd have us a good time those nights. He wasn't interested in saving any or spending it on something useful. Oh, no. He just wanted to have fun and show his friends a good time. 'Money's for spending,' he'd say.

"Other nights he'd come to my place with a black eye or empty pockets without enough to buy a bite of food. I worried about him, whether he was winning or losing."

"He was blessed to have a friend like you, Logan."

"I don't know about that. If I'd 'a been a better one, he might still be here."

Harper heard sounds of the mining camp a half mile before they crested a ridge and it came into view. Despite the late afternoon heat, most of the men were still hard at work. They reminded her of ants on a hillside. There was apparently a method to the frenetic activity, even if she couldn't tell exactly what was happening.

Dark clouds scudded across the sky in the distance. She supposed they wanted to finish as much as they could before the storm arrived.

Logan pointed to a tree near a dingy tent where a small group was preparing a meal. She wondered if the miners took turns with kitchen duty or if the same crew prepared all the food. Logan reined in that direction.

A few workers stopped to watch their progress. Harper's mouth went dry. She wanted to find out what happened to Matthew, but she wondered about the wisdom behind this trip. Uncle Hugh would have forbidden her from coming, but she would feel better if he knew where she was in case there was trouble.

They drew closer and stopped the horses a few feet from where a stewpot hung on a metal rod suspended over a fire.

"Something smells good," Logan observed. To Harper's surprise, he was right.

A heavyset, unshaven man wearing an apron that looked like it hadn't been washed in months folded his arms over his stomach. "Don't go getting no ideas. This here food's for working men."

Logan laughed. "Guess that means I'll go hungry." He swung his leg over his horse and dismounted. Harper stayed astride the horse. The big man laughed and strode toward Logan.

"Don't look like you're missing many meals in town," The man said as he grasped Logan's hand and pumped it hard.

"Life's good in town, Jed, but the money's not as good."

Jed sucked air around a missing front tooth. "That's why I'm here." He squinted up at Harper. She looked around and realized most of the men were openly gawking at her. She kept her spine stiff and resisted the urge to pull her bonnet lower over her face.

"Who's she?" Jed said without taking his eyes off her.

"The boss man's niece," Logan said loud enough for the closer men to hear. Harper didn't think she was in danger, but she appreciated having Uncle Hugh's name to protect her. She imagined every worker here feared him a little.

Jed tore his gaze away from her. "What's she doing here? What're either of you doing here?"

Logan rocked back on his heels in a relaxed stance as he surveyed the camp. "Got any card games going on tonight?"

A man dumped an armload of wood on the fire, shooting sparks up around the pot. Logan's mount started and shuffled against Harper's. She tightened her hands on the reins to settle her roan.

Jed took a big ladle and stirred the bubbling pot. "Ever'body knows you're no card player," he told Logan. He and the man who'd dropped the wood chuckled.

"Losing a week's wages took the fun out of it for me."

The big man sniffed in acknowledgement. Logan looped his reins around the back of a chair. "What I'm really interested in is the miner that took a bullet for cheating at cards about two years back."

Jed didn't stop stirring. "Lot of miners take lead when they get stupid enough to cheat in the saloons."

"Wasn't at the saloons. It happened right here. It was the night Matthew Dunleavy disappeared."

Jed's eyes narrowed. He cast a quick glance to Harper still astride the horse. "I'm sorry about your friend. He shouldn't have been here. These fellas would just as soon cut you as look at you if they draw a bad hand. Dunleavy wasn't that way."

A shiver went up Harper's spine. Had something more happened to Matthew than getting run out of town?

Logan nodded solemnly. "That's what I tried to tell him. He wouldn't listen. We didn't come to talk about him though. We want to find out more about the miner who got killed that night."

"Smoke Henshaw."

"Yeah, that's the one. I hate to spread rumors, but I think he's the one who liked spending time with another gent's wife."

Chuckles came from a few men at the edge of the crowd. "That was Smoke all right," someone said.

Logan's lips flattened. Harper could tell he didn't want to speculate about a man who wasn't here to defend himself, but it seemed to be the only way they'd find out where Matthew went.

Jeb sucked air again through the gap in his teeth. "Yeah, Smoke had a reputation for liking the ladies."

"And cheating at cards?" Logan put in.

Jeb nodded gravely. "That's how the fool ended up with a bullet in his belly."

"Any of the fellows from that night still around?"

Jed looked dubiously at Logan. "Don't know what good it'd do to talk to one of them after all this time."

"Maybe none, but I need to talk to somebody anyway. I remember a man named Lefty. He still around?"

"Lefty's dead," the other man spoke up.

Logan looked up at Harper from under the brim of his hat. She couldn't read his expression, but she supposed he was as unnerved as she was.

"Took hold of a rattling cough last winter," the man continued noncommittally as if discussing a splinter in his thumb. "Couldn't shake it. Didn't make it til spring."

"Pity." Logan's voice was purposefully devoid of emotion. "Anybody else?"

A third man detached himself from the small group watching from the tables set up for chow. "I can answer any questions you got. I was there that night. Told everything I knew to the sheriff. Wasn't no secret what happened. Smoke cheated and he didn't make it outta camp. That's the way it goes. Sheriff knows it as well as we do."

Harper glanced around the growing crowd. Unease sent a trickle of sweat down her back. A strong breeze blew down from the mountain, proceeding the coming storm. Conversation ceased among the clusters of men. More drifted near the tables as if to eat, but she knew they were more interested in the discussion. Were she and Logan safe? Whatever they discovered today would be known among all the miners. If a guilty man was in their midst, would he do whatever was necessary to keep them quiet?

Logan didn't appear to share her concerns. He turned to the newcomer. "Was Dunleavy in the game when they caught Smoke cheating?"

The man came closer. He pushed his hat back on his head with a dirty thumb. He stared at Logan for a moment. Harper held her breath. She was nearly afraid her trembling legs would cause her horse to bolt.

"Name's JW. I remember your friend there that night. Always smiling. When I first met him, I didn't think he was serious enough to be a cardplayer. I soon figured out that was his cover. He could handle himself just fine."

"Were you at the table too?"

"For a spell. Run out of money so I just watched. Your friend didn't last much longer."

"I thought he played all night."

"Nah. He folded pretty early. The cards weren't in his favor. All he had left was a worthless Confederate half dollar."

Logan took a step toward the man. "How'd you know about that half dollar?"

"He told me, that's how. Made a joke about having nothing else left in his pocket."

"And he showed it to you?"

JW's eyes narrowed. "I didn't take it from him if that's what you're getting at. He didn't want to show me. Said he never showed it to anybody. But I hadn't seen one since I was a boy, so I sorta pestered him about it until he showed me. He looked around to make sure nobody was watching and showed me right quick. Said it was his good luck piece and he wouldn't part with it for nothing. Said it wasn't worth nothing in money, but to him, it meant everything."

Logan seemed to think hard on it. "How long did he hang around after that?"

JW shook his head. "Wasn't long. I would've offered him a coin for that half dollar if'n I had one. I wouldn't mind having one to take out and show folks. Sure wasn't bringing him luck that night."

Two large men at the corner of the group caught Harper's attention. They rested their shoulders against opposite sides of a crooked tree, their postures mirroring each other with broad arms crossed over wide chests as they watched the exchange. Now their eyes narrowed, and they leaned in to listen intently.

Harper had heard enough talk of a Confederate half dollar. She raised her voice to be heard over the men. "What about the man who shot the gambler? Was anyone apprehended? Were there eyewitnesses?"

She watched the two men out of the corner of her eye. Their expressions tightened further.

Jed gazed up at her, his expression measured. "There may have been. Dolph...er...Smith or something."

"Swisshelm," the cook provided.

"Yeah, that's him. Dolph Swisshelm. The sheriff wanted to question him, but nobody could find him."

Harper started to speak, but Logan beat her to it. "Why was the sheriff suspicious of him? Did someone see the shooting?"

Jed stepped between Logan and JW. It looked to Harper like he was warning JW not to speak. "Weren't no witnesses. Dolph caught his wife with Smoke a week or two earlier is all. It was an ugly scene, but they seemed to get past it. Of course, could'a been an act since Smoke took lead."

"Where's Dolph now?" Harper asked from atop the horse.

Knowing glances moved from man to man. She looked around the group as the silence lengthened. At last her gaze landed on Logan. He locked eyes with her.

JW stepped forward and took hold of her horse's bridle. He smiled, making the move look benign, but a chill ran through her. Logan stiffened. Jed slapped his hand on JW's shoulder. JW released the bridle, but his expression didn't change.

Logan edged between JW and Harper's mount. "Ain't nobody seen Dolph since that night," Jed told them.

"Did anybody look for him?" Logan demanded.

Jed managed to look offended. "Like I told you, men disappear around here all the time. The sheriff sent out word." He shrugged. "Wasn't much he could do beyond that."

"So that was the end of it?" Harper said in exasperation.

JW and Jed gazed up at her. Jed smiled, but his eyes were hard. "Dolph wasn't the only one who had a beef with Smoke. I doubt your friend shed a tear when Smoke was killed."

"What do you mean by that?" Logan asked.

"Dunleavy owed Smoke money. He owed purt near ever'body, I reckon. Smoke was an easy-going fella ordinarily, but when he heard Dunleavy was down to that useless half dollar, he got real mad. Said he was tired of waiting for what was owed him. If Dunleavy didn't come up with money quick, he was going to find himself staring down a gun barrel."

Harper gasped. "Smoke threatened him?"

"You could say that. Don't know what come of it though. Maybe Dunleavy found enough money to pacify him."

Over Jed's shoulder Harper saw the one of the large men elbow the other. They shuffled off. One kept his head down while the other looked directly at her. She wanted to flinch and look away, but she stared right back.

"None of us think Dunleavy had anything to do with what happened to Smoke," JW was saying. "He lived a reckless life. Makes sense that he'd die that way."

"Stew's ready," the cook called out. "I reckon we can spare a couple bowls if'n you wanna stay for supper."

Logan loosened his reins and mounted the horse. "Maybe next time. We gotta head back to town before the rain comes."

They turned as one and headed out of the site, ignoring the curious stares.

Harper dipped her head and surveyed the camp as they rode, looking in vain for the two big men. When they reached the road, she asked Logan, "Who do you suppose JW was talking about when he said, 'he lived a reckless life'? Matthew or Smoke?"

Logan stared straight ahead. "Both I guess. He isn't wrong."

Chapter Twenty-Five

Harper glanced behind her. Most of the men had moved close to the chow wagon to get their grub before the rain arrived to douse the fire. A few continued to watch them.

"Are we safe?" she asked Logan, speaking just loud enough for him to hear over the creaking of their saddles.

"I reckon so. Everybody knows your uncle. It wouldn't do them good for something to happen to you."

She gulped. "Is that meant to comfort me?"

He didn't answer. They rode over the rise. She breathed a little easier after the mining camp fell out of sight.

"If Dolph was the one who shot Smoke for messing with his wife, and Dolph is gone, there's no reason for anyone to get their back up about us asking questions."

Logan processed her words for a moment. "If that's what happened. They seemed itching to make us believe Dolph shot Smoke and then took off. If that's the whole story, it doesn't explain what happened to Matthew."

Harper swallowed a lump in her throat. She still felt like the eyes of the camp were upon them. She didn't look back since she couldn't see the camp any longer anyway.

She looked at Logan and found him staring at her. "Until you came, I thought Matthew just took off. If there was nothing more to it, we wouldn't have attracted so much attention. Did you notice those big fellas under the walnut tree? They seemed to worry we might hear something they didn't want us to."

Harper exhaled. "I saw them. Do you know who they are?"

"Never saw them before, but like Jed said, men come and go so fast, it's hard to keep them straight."

"They sure acted like they knew something."

Logan frowned. "That's the impression I got. The problem is, we didn't get any information we don't already know."

"Maybe we learned something and don't realize it yet. "Is there a chance Matthew and the miner who was shot, Smoke, fought and Matthew…"

She couldn't say the rest out loud.

Logan jerked his head around to stare at her, his blue eyes icy. "No way. Matthew wouldn't shoot anyone, if that's what you're asking. He wasn't that person. He isn't that person," he amended.

Harper pressed on. "It could've been an accident. Maybe the other man went after him to get his money and Matthew shot him in self defense."

Logan shook his head again. "If that had been a possibility, somebody back there would've said it. The most likely explanation is usually the right one. Dolph Swisshelm shot Smoke, either because Smoke was cheating with his wife or cheating at the table."

"Or it's very important to them for us to believe that's what happened."

Logan pointed off the road toward the ridge. "If we go that way, we should beat the storm home."

Harper reined her mount in that direction. She chewed her lip as she rode, puzzling over everything they'd heard, and the possibilities of what they hadn't heard.

Logan was obviously puzzling over the same things. "I don't know why anyone would care what we think."

"Jed said Matthew owed everyone money, just like you said he did back in Indiana. If they ran him out of town back there, it isn't hard to imagine the same thing would happen here."

The horses began the assent to the top of the ridge that cut across to Willow Wood. The sun had dropped behind the mountains, and the vague trail was shrouded in shadows. She pictured the two big men again. Had someone back there been responsible for chasing Matthew out of Willow Wood, or had something more ominous kept him from leaving the camp that night?

So many accidents could happen to a rider out here, and no one would know. Mrs. Philips didn't know where they were headed when they left the estate. Uncle Hugh didn't even know they were off the property. She wished Logan would go back to the road. They would save nearly an hour by crossing the ridge, but she didn't like the idea of being cornered under the trees with a storm approaching.

At the crest of the ridge Logan stopped to let his mount catch its breath. Harper stopped beside him.

"Why did you ask JW about the Confederate half dollar? You acted surprised that he'd seen it."

"Matthew's uncle Cy gave it to him. I think it was the only thing anyone ever gave him without expecting something in return. He never took it out of his pocket for fear he'd lose it or someone would try to talk him out of it. It meant a lot to him."

"Maybe that night he did a lot of things he wouldn't normally do."

"Maybe, but not that. Not killing someone either. Even if Smoke would've come at him with a knife or a pistol, Matthew would've done everything in his power to diffuse the situation. You heard 'em back there. He didn't have it in him. He was harmless. The only person his behavior hurt was himself."

"And Ellie," she couldn't resist adding.

Logan urged his horse forward down the incline. The trail was plenty wide enough for Harper to ride beside him. "You're right. He hurt her. But I'll never accept he was a killer. A gambler, yes. Reckless, yes. Sometimes stupid, yes. Even a man with the poor character to carnally know a woman outside of marriage. But a killer? I won't accept it, Harper."

She didn't want to accept it either. Nor did she want to badger Logan into believing something he knew couldn't be true. He knew Matthew better than she ever would. If he didn't think Matthew possessed the ability to hurt someone, he was probably right.

"What if…" She stared at the trail in front of them, unable to put her suspicions into words.

Logan looked at her. "What if what?"

"What if something happened to Smoke that didn't involve Dolph Swisshelm? Dolph may have just left town. If he was having trouble with his wife. He might've left to get away from her. It may have had nothing to do with Smoke's murder."

"What would that have to do with Matthew taking off?"

She gnawed her top lip. "Maybe Matthew saw something. A robbery. Or Dolph's murder. Maybe someone at the mining camp had to keep him from telling what he knew. And now they'll want to keep us from telling."

"We don't know anything. We don't even know if there's something to tell." Despite his words of doubt, Logan cast a glance over his shoulder.

Harper looked too. The trail was empty. She didn't want there to be a conspiracy behind Matthew's disappearance. She may not have a high opinion of the man, but she wanted him safe in California, or maybe Alaska, panning for gold and waiting for the next card game, not to be the victim of a murder that was never meant to be discovered.

They reached the bottom of the hill where they could ride without studying the ground so closely. The trees grew closer together, blocking out the fading daylight. Harper knew the trail would take them back to the road and into Willow Wood. She hoped the light would last long enough to reach it. It was easy to lose her sense of direction in the gathering darkness. If she veered off the trail without Logan, she wasn't sure she'd find her way back to town.

Logan laid a hand over hers resting on the saddle's pommel. "I had hoped to get some definitive answers at the camp. Something to comfort Ellie and close this book for her for good. Sadly, we may never know what happened. Whether chasing excitement or running from the responsibility of a family, Matthew isn't likely coming back."

Harper looked down at his hand on hers. He slowed his horse. Hers slowed along with it. Her pulse accelerated. She couldn't see Logan's expression in the dim light under the trees. But she sensed he was thinking of something other than Matthew.

"What will we tell her?" she asked, her voice barely above a whisper.

"We'll tell her we aren't giving up. We'll keep looking. But we need to convince her she can't keep waiting. He's gone."

She tried not to focus on the heat from his hand on hers. What did he mean by keeping it there?

"She loves him."

"He didn't love her the way a man should love a woman."

Her stomach dropped. Just as she thought. Matthew never loved Ellie the way Logan did.

"A woman should never wonder how important she is to the man who loves her."

His fingers slid entwined with hers. "Ellie will find a man like that someday."

Harper tried to clear her head. What was he saying? *Someday?* Didn't he love her now?

Logan released her hand and touched the side of her face. He stroked her cheek with his thumb. "I'm sorry for what he did. If I could take away her suffering I would. At the same time, I feel a little guilty. If Matthew hadn't left, you wouldn't be here."

She parted her lips to say something, but her mouth went dry. Her brain couldn't form a thought anyway with his hand cupping her face.

He leaned closer. Without realizing it, she moved toward him until she found herself against him. The horses shifted under them. Harper's leg wedged between the horses, but she didn't mind. Logan's mouth met hers. Her breath caught in her throat as their lips touched, warm and sweet. Logan moved closer, and the kiss deepened. A tiny sound erupted from Harper's lips. She leaned even closer.

A horse's hoof scratched the loose soil above them on the trail. Logan jerked back and whirled toward the sound. Harper tried to catch her breath. Her horse turned after its stable mate with no command from her. She swallowed hard and tried to still the wild beating of her heart. Over the rushing of blood in her ears, she heard a horse's movement, heavy with the weight of a rider. She caught the snatch of a word spoken by a masculine voice meant to settle the animal. Logan grabbed her horse's bridle and directed both horses off the trail and under a heavy copse of trees.

"Stay here," he whispered. "I'm going to see who's back there."

She thought of the two men at the camp. "No. You don't know who it is?"

"I plan to find out."

She stiffened. "I'll go with you."

"I'm just going to see who's there. You stay under the trees where he can't see you. If it's safe, I'll call for you."

Harper understood the words he didn't say. Under the trees she made a less discernible target. She wanted to ask Logan how much danger they were in. She wanted to tell him to stay. But she knew they couldn't venture farther into the woods without first knowing if they were in danger.

Logan moved his horse to the edge of the trail where the soft shoulder would muffle its hoofbeats. The man at the top would hear him eventually. What would happen when the two men met?

"Dear Lord, let whoever's up there be a friend, not a foe." She prayed under her breath. She listened intently. Within moments, she couldn't distinguish which hoofbeats were Logan's and which belonged to the man moving down the hill.

She heard more shuffling above her head. "Hey," Logan called out. A horse whinnied and galloped in the opposite direction.

She urged her mount onto the trail. Through the closely growing trees along the skyline, she saw flashes of dark brown horseflesh moving along the ridge.

For an instant she had a clear view of Logan's mount as it reached the ridge before he disappeared among the trees. She nearly called out in alarm, but she didn't want to endanger him.

She moved toward the base of the hill. She couldn't see anything from there either. It was getting dark fast. Within moments, she couldn't distinguish the top of the ridge. She looked behind her. She probably wasn't more than a few miles from town. Should she go for help? Could she find the road alone in the dark? The horse could probably find the way home without her, but she prayed it wouldn't be necessary.

Thunder rumbled in the distance. She put her hand to her mouth, still warm from Logan's kiss. Why had he kissed her? What had it meant when he said Ellie would find someone someday? Didn't he love her? If he did, Harper didn't think he would've kissed her the way he had.

Thunder rumbled again. Closer this time. The roan tossed its head and shifted under her. Hoofbeats from one horse sounded on the trail. She couldn't see. Was it Logan? She edged into the trees. Her horse whinnied. The other reached the bottom of the hill and whinnied in return. Harper exhaled aloud in relief. It recognized its stablemate. She moved onto the trail as Logan came into view.

"What happened? Who was it?" She didn't try to keep her voice down. It wasn't likely the other rider was near enough to hear, especially over the thunder and increasing wind.

"I don't know. All I could see was a big man on a big horse. We've got to get out of here. The storm'll be on us any minute."

"Do you think he—"

"I don't know," he repeated. "I just know at this moment the storm is a graver danger than any man."

She hoped he was right. They turned and headed toward town, too fast for her to ask more about the man or about the kiss and what either of them meant.

Chapter Twenty-Six

Black clouds swirled overhead by the time Logan and Harper reached the stone wall that surrounded the estate. The horses slowed to a walk as they started up the hill. Rainwater from an earlier storm that had hit Willow Wood in their absence overflowed the gutters.

"Looks like we missed a lot of rain and wind." Logan indicated the top of the wall. A good-sized tree limb had broken out of a tree and hung over the wall. Smaller limbs and large sticks littered the street around them.

Harper didn't speak. She kept her eyes on the street as the horse picked its way around the storm damage. Tension rose in Logan's gut. His mind had reeled since they left the countryside with questions raised by what they'd heard. The greatest cause of torment, though, was Harper and her sweet lips on his. He wanted to pull her back into his arms even now. Even the man he had chased up the mountainside couldn't keep his mind off her for long.

He wanted to apologize for misjudging her for so long with no evidence that she only wanted to get her hands on the Lundys' money. He had not treated her fairly when she first came. Instead of simply asking what he wanted to know or getting to know her better first, he had let his suspicions create a story for her. It wasn't a very Christian way to conduct himself. She had never been after money or status or a comfortable situation in her uncle's estate. She hadn't come to pursue a personal dream. Only to help her cousin. He would apologize even if she hadn't known the thoughts stirring in his head. He just didn't know where to start.

"Harper..." he started and immediately ran out of words.

"Logan," she said back in that lilting voice that turned his insides to mush. Her lips quirked upward in a teasing smile, reminding him of how much he wanted to kiss her again.

The best thing to do was just get it out. Confess every ill thought and suspicion he'd harbored.

"I'm sorry for the way I treated you when you first came. I had no right—"

"Oh, no," she exclaimed.

He hadn't even gotten to the rotten stuff yet.

She pointed up the hill. He turned to look. The west wall's gate had come into view. A large tree limb had fallen across it, partially blocking their entry. His apology fell out of his head at the sight of the damage.

He urged his horse to pick up its pace. Harper's followed suit. Parts of the limb were tangled in the bars at the top of the gate. Bottom limbs brushed the ground, obscuring the left-hand side of the entry. Logan dismounted and absently handed Harper his horse's reins. The gate's top hinge, just above his eye level, had been bent out of shape from the impact of the large limb.

He opened the right side of the gate to allow Harper and the horses to pass through. "I'll need an axe and some rope." He got back on the horse and they rode up the drive, leaving the gate standing open. "I doubt Burt's still here."

"I can help," she said eagerly.

He laughed. "I've never met anyone who missed blisters and splinters as much as you."

"I miss any kind of work," she said with a musical trill in her voice. "God didn't make me a sitting-around girl. He made me a get-your-hands-dirty girl."

Logan opened his mouth to tell her she better not let her uncle catch her with dirty hands. He stopped as the wind rushed out of him like someone punched him in the gut. He'd known for some time she was the girl he waited for his whole life. The girl with whom he wanted to watch the sun crest over the ridge. The girl who'd get her hands dirty right next to him. The girl he wanted to marry.

They reached the barn. Her pale brows had gone together in confusion as if to decipher his sudden silence. Thunder rumbled in the distance. One half of the stable doors stood open. Burt was gone already, but he had left the stable door open for ventilation and for Logan and Harper. Logan picked up his pace and ducked inside.

He dismounted at the forge. "Can you put the horses away? I need to chop down that limb before the storm hits."

"It'll go faster if you let me help," she said again. She looked down at him from atop her horse. Her expression was earnest and warm. He fought the urge to take her hand, pull her off the horse, and wrap his arms around her.

He looked away to get the image out of his head. "It'll be a bigger help for you to take care of the horses. I need to straighten out that hinge as best I can so it'll withstand the winds tonight. If the storm tears it out of the wall, I'll go from having a small job to fix now to a big job to fix tomorrow."

She dismounted and took the reins of both horses and led them toward their stalls, leaving him to stare after her for a moment and wonder where she'd come from and if she'd ever agree to be part of his life.

•••

Mrs. Philips was tying her bonnet strings under her chin when Harper stepped inside the kitchen door. "That storm's about to turn into a real gulley washer," the housekeeper said. "I feel it in my bones. Soup's on the stove. I took Ellie a bowl up. She's already retired. These nights make her blue. Your uncle's still at the office in town."

Harper exhaled in relief, glad he hadn't looked out and seen her brushing down the horses and giving them fodder. "Is he coming home tonight?"

"More than likely. When he does, he can serve himself from the soup. You don't need to worry about him, child. You just have yourself a good evening."

"I will. Be careful at the gate. There's a limb down."

The housekeeper waved and ducked out the door. Harper hurried after her and pushed the door shut as rain and leaves blew inside. She returned to the stove and dished out a big bowl of soup. She inhaled deeply of the spicy mixture. She still missed Ma's cooking but not as much as she had when she first got here. A basket of warm rolls sat in the center of the table wrapped in a towel. She took a large one off the top of the pile and sat down to eat.

Conjecture swirled in her head. Logan was probably right. They may never know what happened to Matthew, short of him walking through the door and explaining where he'd been all this time. She prayed they'd learn something definite for Ellie's sake. But Ellie was strong. Harper had every confidence she would recover from her grief and move on with her life.

She swallowed a mouthful of soup, a flutter of anxiety killing her appetite. Logan would be busy the rest of the night securing the gate. She wouldn't have a chance to talk to him again until tomorrow. For now, she would have to satisfy herself with the memory of his lips on hers. What had his kiss meant? Who was he talking about when he said a woman should never wonder how important she was to the man who loved her? Was he talking about himself and Ellie? Or…

If he'd been talking about Ellie, she couldn't believe he would've kissed her so passionately.

She forced herself to finish the soup and rinsed out her bowl and spoon and put them away. With her mind on Logan and the kiss, it was difficult to focus on what she'd heard and seen at the camp. She needed to write down exactly who said what while the details were fresh in her mind. She'd sort them out later. Ellie could be helpful as well if she was up to it. Harper needed to stop treating her like a fragile flower. If Ellie honestly wanted to know what happened to Matthew, there was no reason she shouldn't put in some of the work. Like Logan, she wouldn't believe Matthew was capable of murder. Harper admitted they were probably right. But doubts would remain until they exhausted all means to reach the truth.

She pushed open the library door. A small fire crackled in the grate. Now that she regularly used the library, the maids kept it tidy and warm on days like today when clouds hid the sun and chilled the cavernous room.

She went to the fireplace and stoked the flames and added a chunk of coal. Two gas wall sconces bathed the room in a pleasant light but weren't bright enough to write by. Harper didn't bother opening the curtains. Because of the brewing storm, it was full dark outside even though it wasn't quite eight o'clock. She lit the lamp on the desk instead and slid open the center drawer where writing paper was kept.

She took out a tablet and stared down at the blank page. She wasn't sure if this exercise would accomplish anything, but she worked out problems better in her head when she wrote them out.

She quickly wrote everything the men had said about Matthew and the miner whose wife had cheated with the dead man. Dolph, whose wife had been seeing Smoke, had the strongest motive for killing him. But he was gone. Or so everyone believed. Had Matthew been involved in Dolph's disappearance or Dolph in his? Was it simply a coincidence that both men disappeared at the same time a miner was shot? A miner who had an unfaithful wife and to whom Matthew owed money?

In no time Harper filled half the page with scribblings and observations that would probably amount to nothing when she discussed them with Logan and Ellie. She stopped writing and stared at the page. Instead of the words, she saw Logan's face coming toward her, his lips parted, his eyes soft and…

Filled with love? Yearning? She wasn't sure. Was it all wishful thinking on her part?

The front door opened. Determined footfalls sounded in the foyer. Uncle Hugh was home. She pushed her thoughts of Logan aside and took up her pen again. She listened to her uncle shake the rain out of his coat and hang it on the hall tree. His footsteps echoed across the marble floor. Harper carefully turned the paper over so the ink wouldn't smudge. She wouldn't deny it if he asked, but she hoped he wouldn't find out she had gone to the camp tonight. She might not get in trouble, but Logan would.

"Harper?"

She stood and faced him. "Yes, Uncle."

"I thought Ellie might be in here." He glanced at the desk behind her.

"No, sir. She's retired for the evening. Mrs. Philips left soup for you on the stove."

He smiled. "Yes, I smelled it as soon as I opened the door."

"Would you like me to serve some up for you?"

"No, no, I'll take care of it. Hot soup is exactly what a man needs on a night like tonight."

"How was Utah?"

"Productive. But it's nice to be home."

She wasn't surprised that he would only think of his trip in terms of business without considering the things he'd seen or the people he'd met.

"Ellie is doing much better, sir."

He lowered the stack of mail he'd been leafing through and gave her his full attention.

"We spent nearly every afternoon in the gardens or riding the horses while you were gone."

His eyes widened. "You don't say."

"Not off the property," she clarified. She didn't want to get his hopes up. "She's drawing again too. She drew a sketch for me the other day. It was quite good."

She hoped he wouldn't ask to see it. She looked forward to sending it to Ma, and she didn't want Uncle Hugh to want to keep it for himself.

The big man's eyes moistened. Or it could've been the lamplight reflecting off the rain streaked windows.

"She inherited her talent from her mother." Harper had already heard the sentiment, but this time his voice grew soft and distant. "Through her artwork, it was as if part of her mother was still alive. When she stopped—after Dunleavy left her—it was like losing Rebekah all over again."

No one in the house talked much about Mrs. Lundy. Harper had never even heard the woman's first name before. She understood their pain, but it wasn't healthy to act almost as though she never existed.

Words of comfort and compassion failed her. What would Ma say if she were here?

"Ellie and I are getting closer every day," she said. "Sometimes we stay up and talk half the night."

"Mrs. Philips told me. I'm glad. I'm thankful for all you've done, Harper. I couldn't reach Ellie on my own. Besides paying the doctor to look in on her every week, I didn't know what to do. I suppose I still don't."

"Most of all, she needs patience and understanding." *And the truth,* she wanted to add. She didn't think he would appreciate it.

His lips flattened. He looked past her to the window. "That's the rub, isn't it? I've never been a patient man. I'm used to men doing what I want when I want it done. It never worked that way with my daughter. Mrs. Lundy said Ellie got her stubborn streak from me."

Harper believed the same thing, but she doubted telling him so would help the situation.

"We've always been like two buck elk butting heads. Then she fell in love with that gambling skunk. Nothing I said could make her see reason."

He looked at Harper as if challenging her to take Ellie's side. She wouldn't dream of it. Not out loud.

"I thought after Dunleavy went away our lives would get back to normal. Ellie would realize she was better off without him and find a more suitable husband. I wanted to send her on a holiday. She and I used to travel a lot. Did she tell you that?"

"Yes, she did. She showed me paintings and sketches she's done of different cities."

He smiled and nodded. "She loved doing that. When I'd go to meetings, she'd stay at the hotel or walk to a park and draw all day. Her talent amazed me. With study, I believe she could become more skilled than her mother."

His gaze hardened again. "But she wouldn't consider it. Once Dunleavy jilted her, she stayed upstairs in her room, growing thinner and paler with each passing day while he..." his jaw clenched. "...walked away without accepting responsibility for what he'd done."

Harper's stomach clenched. Had he heard the rumors that Ellie carried a baby? She certainly couldn't ask. Whether true or not, he would probably pick her up and throw her through the window if she mentioned Ellie having a baby.

"He might not have left on his own accord," she said.

He drew back in surprise like she'd thrown cold water in his face. "What do you mean?"

She almost wished she hadn't brought it up. But Logan didn't know what happened. If the miners knew, they weren't talking. Perhaps Uncle Hugh had insight into what could've happened that she could pass on to Ellie. He was around the miners all the time. He might have heard something and not realized its significance.

"You know he gambled. He owed everyone money, including a miner who was killed the night he disappeared. Whoever shot the miner might've wanted something out of Matthew too."

She couldn't tell him she wondered if Matthew was involved in the miner's death.

Uncle Hugh shook his head. "I wouldn't worry about what became of Dunleavy if I were you. All that matters is Ellie is better off without him. With your help, it appears she's finally begun to accept it."

"That's my prayer."

"We're all better with him gone. He was trash, Harper. As worthless as that Confederate half dollar he carried in his pocket."

The fire popped, and a spark hit the screen over the grate. Harper jerked her head in that direction.

A Confederate half dollar.

When she looked back at her uncle, he was studying her closely. Dread filled her heart. He knew about the half dollar Matthew kept in his pocket; the coin Logan said he never mentioned to anyone.

How could he? They weren't friends. They hated each other. Matthew never would've shown it to him. Unless…

She looked past Uncle Hugh's imposing frame to the doorway. A few lights flickered intermittently along the hallway, but the foyer was quiet and cloaked in darkness. Everyone was gone for the evening, except for Ellie, who had probably taken one of the sleeping tablets Dr. Dutton prescribed to calm her.

Without turning around Uncle Hugh reached behind him and pushed the door shut. He advanced toward her. Harper backed away until the desk stopped her. He picked up the paper she'd been writing on. He glanced at it and then looked back at her and exhaled.

"Young men disappear out here all the time, Harper. No one asks any questions." He crumpled the paper and tossed it on the floor. "You shouldn't have either."

Chapter Twenty-Seven

Harper's mind raced. She thought of every person she'd encountered inside this house since the moment she arrived. None of them were here to come to her aid. Logan was forging a new hinge for the gate. It wasn't likely he'd come to the kitchen for dinner when he finished. The storm would keep him inside his apartment above the stables. Mrs. Philips and the maids were warm and dry in their own homes. Only Ellie remained inside the house, and she was probably sound asleep.

She cast her eyes around the room, desperately seeking an escape or distraction.

"I…uh…only want to help Ellie."

Uncle Hugh tensed as if to slap her. Harper froze. This wasn't happening. She wasn't in danger. This man was her mother's cousin. The family respected him. He surely had kind feelings toward them. Toward her. It was a misunderstanding, that's all. He would explain how he knew about the half dollar, and she would apologize for thinking the worst.

With a visible effort, he pulled himself together. He straightened but kept her pinned against the desk. She couldn't get around him. The look in his eyes told her she hadn't misunderstood.

She needed to think, to make sense of what was happening. She needed Ellie to come downstairs or for one of the maids to come back for something she forgot. Who was she kidding? She couldn't stall or wait for someone to save her. Hugh Lundy was not a stupid man. She wouldn't fool him for more than a minute anyway.

"Why did you kill Matthew?"

He didn't pretend he didn't know what she was talking about. "He owed everyone money, even me. I bailed him out on previous occasions. He came to me again. I knew he would never stop." His gaze slid away from her.

Harper stiffened against the desk and prepared to vault away if he moved as much as an inch. Lightning flashed, filling the room with bright light that illuminated the pain in her uncle's eyes. Rain pounded against the window. No one would hear her over the sound of the storm, no matter what she did.

"He came to me at my office at the mines and said he was in trouble," Uncle Hugh continued. "He owed a thousand dollars to some men who wouldn't hesitate to tear him apart if he didn't pay." He sneered. "How could a person be so stupid, Harper? To wager more money than he'd earn in his entire miserable life?

259 – TERESA SLACK

"But he did it, and he needed me to pay. He said if I paid the debts and gave him a little extra to get out of town, I'd never see him again."

He shifted and allowed a sliver of cool air to pass between them. Harper exhaled carefully to make him think she was hanging on every word.

"Like a fool, I gave him the money. I handed over fifteen hundred dollars and thanked the Lord the little worm was out of our lives. But he didn't go. I vowed then he would never cheat me out of another dollar.

"A few weeks later, I heard around town he was back in debt. He had no intention of leaving town. He never would as long as he had my daughter to play the cash cow. I brought him here and offered to pay him to leave. A lot more this time. He smirked and said he loved Ellie and she loved him. He said he was through with gambling and he'd pay me back the fifteen hundred dollars I'd given him."

He leaned around Harper and cleared the desk with a swipe of a strong arm. Harper cried out. Her entire body trembled.

"He didn't know I already knew he was in debt again. He thought he could keep taking advantage of me because he had Ellie hoodwinked."

He slammed a big fist down on the desk. "I told him, 'Over my dead body'. He wasn't getting what I worked so hard for."

"Of course, you couldn't let him do that," Harper said in a small voice. "You couldn't let him hurt Ellie."

"He had hurt her, Harper. I'll never forget how she cried when…"

His voice tapered off. He stared at her as if deciding how much to reveal.

"It wasn't long after he...after he went away that I caught sight of Ellie as she was turning up the stairs. She was apparently trying to hide her condition from me, but I saw the widening of her hips and thickening around her waist." He growled in his throat as a muscle twitched in his jaw. "She said she loved him. They were going to marry as soon as he came back."

He snorted. "Back then, she expected him back any day. I tried to make her see we were all better off with him gone. Her present condition proved that, even if his gambling and extortion didn't."

He exhaled in defeat and brokenness and took a full step away from her. Harper sagged with relief. She couldn't act quickly. She needed to plan her escape.

"She wouldn't believe he had come to me for money. She said he wasn't interested in anything I had. He loved her." He barked out a laugh that made Harper flinch. "Could you imagine that bloodsucker getting his claws into everything I've built? I couldn't let it happen. He'd destroy everything without affording me the dignity of dying first. After I was gone, well... My daughter and that man's spawn would be left with nothing but poverty and ridicule."

Harper shuddered in realization. The more he talked and the more she learned, the less likely she'd get out of this room alive.

"What happened to the baby?"

He exhaled painfully. "We were at the top of the stairs. Ellie was screaming. I told her to stop being stupid. He wasn't worth her tears. She lunged at me.

She's always been a fighter, especially when she thought she was wronged. She fell…"

"And the baby…"

"She started hemorrhaging," he said, matter of fact. "No one was here but she and I. I carried her to her room. She was delirious for two days. I kept everyone out. The town didn't have a doctor then. I wouldn't have called on one if I could. I took care of things myself the way I've always done.

"I convinced her not to tell anyone. Not Mrs. Philips or anyone else. With Matthew gone, she was so distraught anyway. I was able to convince her there had never been a baby. Her memories of it were a product of grief and wishful thinking. I buried it in the flower garden outside that window."

Harper looked over her shoulder to the big window. "But she does remember. She comes in here sometimes and stares into the garden. She hasn't forgotten."

Doubt clouded his face.

"You may have confused her, but she remembers. One day she'll remember everything."

Anger flashed afresh in his eyes. She could see Hugh Lundy did not like to hear he wasn't successful in something he'd worked to do.

"I had to protect her, Harper. That meant exterminating the parasite who took advantage of her and threatened everything I've built. Now I have to save her from you."

Harper shrank against the desk. "You don't need to. I understand why you killed him. I know you were only protecting Ellie."

He wagged his head from side to side. "I care deeply for you, Harper. Having you here has been good for Ellie. Soon, I'll have my beautiful daughter back completely. But not if you stay. I can't let you jeopardize that."

"I'm not like Matthew," she exclaimed. "I have people who love me, people who'll never stop looking for me."

A sad smile softened his expression. "It isn't only young men who disappear around here. Your dear mother doesn't have the means to launch a search after you're gone. She'll believe whatever yarn I spin. I'll tell her you fell in love with a local man and left town with stars in your eyes and a dream of building a life together in your heart. She'll be happy for you. I'm sure you've written to her about Ellie's problems. She'll have no reason to doubt me when I tell her you grew weary of waiting for Ellie to come to her senses."

Harper's heart sank lower and lower with each word.

"No one will look for you. They wouldn't know where to start if they tried. Your mother will wait for a letter that will never come. Eventually she'll stop waiting. She'll assume you died in childbirth or succumbed to an epidemic or met with calamity, and there was no one who knew how to send word home."

Harper nearly cried out. That was exactly what would happen. There was nothing or no one to stop him from what he planned to do.

She slid one hand along the edge of the desk until her fingers reached the narrow drawer. Inside was a slim letter opener. It wasn't much of a weapon against someone as big and strong as Hugh Lundy, but it was her only chancc of getting out of here. She scooted her hips a fraction of an inch toward the center of the desk to conceal her hands.

"You can't do this, Uncle Hugh. You can't murder me in cold blood. I haven't done anything to you."

"Ellie is my only daughter. She is the most important thing in the world to me. I can't risk you taking her from me."

"Think about what it will do to my mother if you take *me* away from *her*." She opened the drawer wide enough to slide her fingers inside.

"Your mother has a large family to console her. All I have in this world is Ellie."

"Liar!" she screamed. Her hand closed around the letter opener.

Uncle Hugh drew back in surprise at the venom in her voice.

"You're not protecting Ellie," she cried as shrill as she dared. "You're protecting your wealth. You're protecting your name in this state. You don't care about anybody but yourself."

She saw the slap coming and was able to partially get out of the way. His massive hand caught her on the side of the head and knocked her off balance. She used the momentum to right herself and hurl her body at him, the letter opener aimed at his face.

At the last moment Hugh saw her hand coming and whipped his head away from her. The letter opener sliced across his cheek, drawing a perfect line. His cheek split open, and blood streamed down his face.

He roared in pain and pushed back at her before she could recover from the swing. He pinned her arms against her body and swung her in a circle. Her legs crashed into the desk. She screamed again, this time in pain as her right leg took a direct hit against the side of the desk.

Uncle Hugh released his hold on her. She toppled across the desk. She tried to slide all the way across to the shelter on the other side, but he caught her and pulled her back against him.

Harper screamed and kicked the blotter and a few books onto the floor. The lamp crashed to the floor, but the oil immediately extinguished the small flame.

She bucked her body against his and managed another scream before he threw her against the desk, sufficiently knocking the wind out of her. She didn't have time to catch her breath before his ham-sized hands wrapped around her throat.

Harper's eyes bulged in shock. She stared into her uncle's rage-ravaged face. He couldn't be bent on killing her. He loved his daughter. He was highly respected. She kicked against the desk, with the heels of her pointed-toe shoes. She couldn't kick him with her legs pinned against the desk. She couldn't pray. She couldn't scream. She couldn't fight back. Her kicks began to weaken. She clutched at his hands, but her efforts were useless. His grip only tightened.

She twisted her body in a last effort to escape. A glint of broken glass from the lamp shade sparkled in another flash of lightning. If she could reach it, she could drive it into his leg or hand or eye. Anything to make the pressure on her windpipe lessen.

265 - TERESA SLACK

Bright dots flashed before her eyes. Her nose filled with the scent of coal from the stove. Something was burning. The house. She'd be dead soon. She smelled something sweet. It reminded her of Ma's cornbread. She hadn't tasted it in so long. Her mind was playing tricks on her. She had to break free. She gathered her strength and bucked under him. If she could ram his nose with her head, she'd have a chance to lessen the pressure. She didn't care about getting away anymore. She only wanted a breath of precious air.

Light flashed again. Not from the window this time. It came from the other side of the room. A scream. A crash.

Uncle Hugh's hands fell away. He stumbled and fell to his knees. Harper dropped to the floor, banging the side of her head against the desk on her way down. Another flash of light, and everything went black.

Chapter Twenty-Eight

"Harper? Harper?"

She became aware of someone calling her name.

She tried to reach toward the voice. She needed help. *Hurry,* she cried inside her head. *Get me out of here before he kills me.*

Her head hurt so much. Her throat. She couldn't swallow. Her throat convulsed as she struggled to catch a breath.

"Papa. You killed her."

Harper gasped hard for breath and jerked herself to consciousness. She tried to shake her head to tell Ellie, no, she wasn't dead. She opened her mouth to speak, but the effort of trying to make a sound was too painful. Her eyes fluttered open.

Hugh was on his hands and knees beside her, one hand gripping the side of his head, the other holding onto the corner of the desk. Harper screamed. No sound came out of her mouth. She couldn't roll away from him. Her right leg throbbed in pain. She felt a large goose egg pressing against the skin on the side of her head where she'd hit the desk.

With great effort she turned her head to look past Hugh's form to Ellie. Ellie stood over him holding the handle of a broken pitcher. Heavy shards of glass scattered around the hem of her shift.

Ellie noticed Harper watching her. She let loose of the pitcher handle, and it clattered to the floor and broke in half. The glass crunched under her feet as she reached down to help Harper up.

"Oh, Harper, I'm so sorry. Be careful of the glass. What happened?" She looked past Harper to her father. "Why?"

"He…" Harper rasped. She winced in pain and put her hands to her throat. Her head spun. She couldn't make the words go from her brain to her mouth.

"Papa?"

Hugh came to his senses. Harper grasped Ellie's arm to pull her toward the door as Hugh lumbered to his feet. He pulled his hand away from his head. It was soaked with blood. The wound on his cheek had stopped bleeding, and his face was caked with blood.

"Ellie," he said, weariness and pain in his voice. "I was trying to protect you."

"No," Harper tried to scream. Again, nothing came out. She pulled Ellie's arm, but Ellie stood fast.

"From Harper?" Ellie asked her father incredulously.

Harper pulled against her. "He…" she tried again to no avail. Her throat ached, inside and out. She needed water. Her legs were so weak she could barely stand.

Uncle Hugh's face was ashen from the loss of blood. Regardless, he focused on Ellie. "It was all for you, sweetheart. I was trying to save you."

"I don't need saving." She clasped Harper's hand. They stepped away from him. "We're going to the sheriff, Papa."

"I can't let you do that."

She dropped Harper's hand and reached into the pocket of her dressing gown. She pulled out a gun and leveled it at him. "You killed Matthew and you tried to kill Harper. You won't get away with it."

"Ellie." He took a step toward her.

Ellie flinched but raised the gun and pointed it directly at his chest. "Don't come any closer, Papa. We're going to go out and lock you in here. You can explain everything to the sheriff when he gets here."

"I'm not waiting around for that buffoon."

"You don't have a choice."

"You must see everything I've ever done is for you."

"Stop saying that. I loved Matthew, and you took him away. I was going to marry him."

Hugh's face darkened, despite the loss of blood. "I couldn't let you do that."

"You hated him so much, you killed our baby."

Harper gasped. It was the first she'd heard Ellie mention the baby. From the look on Uncle Hugh's face, it was the first he'd heard it too.

"I didn't kill a baby. You fell."

"You pushed me."

He shook his head. "I'm not a monster."

"No," she screamed, "you're insane! What did you do with Matthew? Where is he?"

"I already told you. I was trying to protect you. He came here for money. Again."

"It's a lie."

Harper watched her uncle tense. He had edged a little closer to them. She doubted Ellie noticed.

"I paid off his debts once, but he wanted more. I knew it would never end. He would keep coming to me for money every time there was another coyote nipping at his heels. Until I was in my grave and he could help himself anytime he wanted. You'd be ruined inside of a year if you'd married that scum. I had to end it."

Tears spilled down Ellie's cheeks. She lowered the gun and wiped her face with her free hand. "He loved me. He didn't care about your money."

Uncle Hugh barked out a laugh. "Girl, I thought I raised you smarter than that. He may have loved you, but he loved my money more."

"It isn't true." Ellie jerked the gun up with both hands and fired twice. The first bullet hit the wall over the fireplace. The second shot hit her father's shoulder and spun him over the desk as it slammed into the wall behind them. A wall sconce crashed to the floor.

Harper's scream came out as a hoarse gurgle. Ellie shrieked in surprise and nearly dropped the gun. She stared at it as if to determine why it had fired.

The bullet had only grazed the top of Uncle Hugh's shoulder. He glared at Ellie, pain and anger flashing in his eyes.

"For goodness sake, Ellie, put that gun down, before you kill yourself." He grabbed a handkerchief from his pocket and clamped it over the wound.

She inhaled shakily. "No." She leveled the gun again. "Not until you tell me the truth. Where's Matthew?"

"He came here threatening me. He said he was marrying you, and he'd have all the access to my money he ever wanted. I told him to get out. Once I realized he had given you his..." he gestured toward her stomach. "....his issue, I knew I had done the right thing."

Ellie put a hand over her stomach. "My baby?"

He leaned his hip against the desk, pain and blood loss getting to him. "Sometimes a parent has to make the hard decisions. I made it and I'd do it again. When he realized I wasn't handing over more money, he attacked me. I was only defending myself."

"I don't believe you. Matthew wouldn't attack anyone. Even you." She raised the gun again. "Where is he? What did you do with him?

Lightning flashed across the sky and illuminated the window. In the brief reflection, Harper saw movement. She nearly turned her head to look over Uncle Hugh's shoulder to confirm what she'd seen. She kept her gaze straight ahead. Logan had entered the room through the small door off the dining room.

He must've heard the gunfire. She hoped Ellie wouldn't see him or give him away.

"He dumped…him…in…in a mine shaft," she rasped around her swollen throat. "He followed Logan and me… yesterday. He knew…we'd…" She should've realized sooner Uncle Hugh had the perfect means to get rid of someone he didn't want found.

Ellie burst into tears. "Papa, no."

Hugh pulled the handkerchief away from his shoulder and irritably looked at the blood. "It should've been a perfect solution." He sneered at Harper. "It was for two years until she came. If someone found him, they'd never know who he was. Accidents happen out here all the time."

Harper risked a glance past Uncle Hugh to Logan. He shook his head in warning and continued across the floor on cat feet.

"He didn't even have a proper burial," Ellie said around her tears.

"He didn't deserve one."

"I'll never forgive you."

"Grow up, girl. I did you a favor. I wasn't going to let some belly-crawling vermin come in here and throw away all I've worked for because you didn't have the good sense to see when you were being used."

Ellie lunged at him and brought the barrel of the gun down on his injured shoulder. It clattered to the floor. Uncle Hugh let out a curse and nearly dropped to his knees. Even with the pain from his shoulder and the knot on his head where Ellie had broken the pitcher, he easily fended her off. He tried to pin her writing figure against him while she scratched and clawed at his face.

Logan's foot crunched on a piece of broken glass. Hugh threw Ellie aside. She fell and slid across the freshly waxed floor. Hugh whirled around as Logan leaped onto the desk and threw himself at the bigger man.

Uncle Hugh was injured, but he was six inches taller and outweighed Logan by at least forty pounds. They fell as one to the floor. Hugh slammed his fist into Logan's face and grabbed the collar of his shirt. He banged Logan's head on the floor. Harper screamed, but no sound came out. Logan kneed Hugh in the kidneys and rolled on top of him. Ellie climbed off the floor and combed her hair out of her tear-soaked face.

"Papa!" she screamed. She grabbed Harper's arm. "We have to get help."

Harper knew there was no time for that, especially with the storm raging outside. She looked around the room for a weapon. Her gaze landed on the fireplace poker. She started around the grappling men to get it. Her foot connected with the gun Ellie had dropped.

Uncle Hugh saw it the same moment and reached for it. Harper tried to kick it out of his reach. His hand closed around the pistol grip.

"Logan," she screamed with barely no sound at all.

A gun blast filled the air. Gunpowder stung her nose. She grabbed the poker and ran back around the desk. Uncle Hugh disengaged himself from Logan and lumbered to his feet. Without looking back, he stumbled from the room.

Harper dropped the poker. Logan lay on the floor. His hands clutched his head just above his ear. She sank to the floor beside him.

"Logan, Logan," she whispered around her aching throat.

He blinked away blood and looked up at her. "Don't let him get away."

She shook her head. "You…" She cast her gaze around the darkened room. "Ellie, light." She motioned desperately with her hands.

Ellie brought a lamp from a corner of the room. Harper could hear Uncle Hugh in his office across the hall. It sounded like he was tearing the room apart, opening drawers and slamming doors.

"What do we do?" Ellie asked.

Harper pulled Logan's hair aside and grimaced at the wound. She didn't see an exit wound. "Stop bleeding. Bring…towels. Boil water."

Ellie set the lamp on the desk. "I have to go for the doctor."

Harper shook her head no. "Stop bleeding." She swallowed hard. "Or he'll die."

Ellie whimpered. She looked down at Logan and squared her shoulders. "Don't you dare die in my house, Logan Kinski. I forbid it."

Logan's lips twitched into a grimace meant as a smile. He opened his eyes. "I'll do my best, Miss Lundy."

Harper burst into tears. "You're alive."

"I'm trying."

The backdoor slammed. Ellie and Harper flinched. "I'll get the towels and some water," Ellie said. She ran from the room.

Harper looked down at Logan. She gently cradled his head in her lap. Blood streamed between her fingers. She knew head wounds could bleed profusely even when there wasn't much damage. The knowledge didn't make her feel better. She wanted to run screaming for the doctor, but she needed to remain calm.

His eyes closed again. His breathing was shallow. "Don't sleep," she whispered. "The doctor."

"Harper?"

"Yes, my love."

He blinked despite the pain. "You called me love."

She flushed. "Did I?"

"You know you did."

"It was…oh, stop talking."

"There's nothing wrong with my voice. I can talk all night."

She narrowed her eyes and scowled.

He laughed, then winced and clutched the side of his head. She laid her hand against his cheek since she couldn't do anything else. He put his hand over hers. "Harper, I love you too."

Her breath caught in her throat. "I thought…you…"

He covered her hand with his. "I love you. I've loved you for almost as long as I've known you."

She shook her head to clear it. "How…"

"Don't talk. Your voice. Just know I love you and I thank God for protecting you tonight."

Harper stared into his eyes. She hoped her eyes said the words her voice couldn't. His gaze moved to her lips. She leaned closer.

Ellie ran into the room with an armload of towels. Harper jerked upright. Ellie handed her a towel, which she promptly put to the side of Logan's head. "The water's on the stove," Ellie said. "I'll get a washbasin."

She set the rest of the towels at Harper's feet and started from the room. The sound of a horse on the shale drive reached their ears. "It's Papa." She ran for the front door.

Harper tried to call after her but couldn't raise her voice above a whisper.

A cold wind blew across the foyer as Ellie threw open the front door. "Papa, don't leave. Come back."

Harper looked helplessly at Logan.

"Go. I'll be all right."

She grimaced at the wound on the side of his head. The towel was already soaked with blood, and the flesh above his eye was beginning to swell.

"Go."

"Don't die. Please."

"I won't. Go to Ellie. She can stay with me while you go for the doctor. Hurry. Don't let Hugh get away."

She lifted his head and put a rolled up towel underneath. She gave him one last look and ran across the room. Ellie stood in the open doorway, looking out into the night. Wind pushed her nightclothes against her narrow frame. Rain and leaves blew in, soaking her and the marble floor. She looked back at Harper and then ran out the front door.

"Papa," she called out.

Harper hurried across the grand foyer as quickly as she dared so she wouldn't slip on the wet floor. A horse whinnied in alarm. A terrible crash sounded on the driveway. Uncle Hugh shouted something Harper couldn't understand.

"Papa!"

Ellie began to scream and didn't stop.

Harper lifted her skirt and ran across the porch and down the marble steps to the drive. Ellie stood helplessly in the driving rain as the horse thrashed a moment before scrambling to its feet. It looked down at Uncle Hugh's prone figure as if waiting for him to get up. Ellie circled the massive horse to reach her father.

Harper's feet slipped and slid on the wet pavement. She grabbed Ellie's shoulders and turned her away from the scene. It was obvious Uncle Hugh was dead. Rain mingled with his blood and flowed like a river toward the gutter.

Chapter Twenty-Nine

Friday morning Harper sat outside on the veranda. She had chosen the spot so she could look out over Willow Wood without anyone from town seeing her through the leaves of the tall trees. She understood now why Uncle Hugh had designed the property the way he had. He wanted to see the world without the world seeing him. Though his property had become an oasis of beauty and serenity, she found it also very sad. Especially now. What good had come from him shutting people out of his life? If he had opened his life and his heart to the people of Willow Wood, and more importantly, to the Creator of it all, maybe the tragedies of the last few days could've been avoided. Maybe he could've known peace and joy instead of suspicion and bitterness.

To repair the damage to Harper's throat, Dr. Dutton had prescribed bed rest, gargling with saltwater, and absolutely no talking. Harper believed the bedrest unnecessary, but nonetheless, she spent all of Thursday alone in her room, thinking and praying and thanking God for sparing her. She hadn't realized how much the experience had traumatized her until she closed her eyes to sleep. Images of Uncle Hugh's face, distorted with rage and murderous intent, filled her mind. Other images flashed in disturbing clarity; the open gash on his head where he'd landed in the rain-soaked drive, his blood washing into the gutter, the majestic horse standing guard over him, Ellie's screams and tear-stained face. Finally, she saw Logan on the floor, his head and face swelling from the bullet lodged under his scalp. In her dreams, Logan's eyes were lifeless until a silent scream jerked her awake.

That night, the rain had ended at nearly the same time Uncle Hugh's life slipped away. Harper had run out the big gate for help and ended up at the door of two neighbors she'd never met. Later, she believed God had directed her to the correct house. The Trego sisters, who owned the leatherworks factory, threw dresses over their nightclothes and hurried over. Belinda, the oldest, roused her own staff and sent them for the doctor, the sheriff, and Mrs. Philips. Another took Uncle Hugh's horse back to the stable.

Felicity, the younger sister, led Harper and Ellie back inside to calm Ellie and to make Logan as comfortable as possible until the doctor arrived. According to Dr. Dutton, the bullet had not penetrated his skull. Besides a mammoth headache and temporarily blurred vision, he would recover.

A few hours later she rode back down the hill with Logan in her carriage while the sheriff took possession of Uncle Hugh's body. Through it all, Felicity Trego stayed with Harper and Ellie while Belinda supervised her staff on the street outside the front gate to forbid entrance of nosy neighbors and peepers.

Harper needed to write a letter to Ma and Pa and tell them what had transpired over the last thirty-six hours. She didn't know where to begin. She still couldn't grasp it herself. It was like a nightmare she half expected to wake up from. She didn't know how she'd find the words to tell them Uncle Hugh had killed Matthew and tried to kill her. Now he was dead himself. There was a lot about that night Ma and Pa would probably never know.

The front door opened slowly. She expected one of the maids, coming to check on her again. It wasn't.

Ellie stepped cautiously onto the porch. She cradled a cup of steaming liquid between her hands. Dark circles smudged her eyes, and her skin was sallow. Harper's sore throat tightened at the sight of her. She'd wanted to talk to Ellie and comfort her since Wednesday night. Now she couldn't think of a word to say. As terrible as the situation had been for her, it was immeasurably awful for Ellie.

"I brought some tea for your throat," Ellie said in a small voice. "Dr. Dutton said you should drink as much as you can." Her hands trembled as she set the fragile cup on the table next to her chair.

Harper's gaze went from her shaking hands to her face that looked ready to crumble. She jumped up and pulled Ellie into an embrace. They cried in each other's arms for several minutes.

"I'm so sorry," Ellie repeated over and over as Harper patted her back.

"Stop apologizing," Harper whispered. After a day and a half, she still couldn't talk at a natural level. The doctor told her not to even try. "I love you. You did nothing wrong."

After a few moments they pulled themselves together. Harper plumped the pillow in the empty chair next to hers and motioned for Ellie to sit.

"How are you?"

Ellie swiped away the last of her tears. "I'm better. I don't know what I'd do without you and Mrs. Philips with me. I want to thank you for everything you and Logan did to get to the truth about Matthew. I'm only sorry we found out…like this."

Her gaze moved toward the driveway where her father's body had lain.

Harper reached out and grasped her hand to make her look away. "I'm sorry for all the pain it caused you."

Ellie's entire body shuddered. She took a steadying breath. "You need to rest your voice. Let me do the talking. I want to tell you what I've been thinking since I found out about…what Papa did."

She closed her eyes as though gathering her strength and her nerve.

"I always wondered what my life would've been like if Mother hadn't died. She had been sick for nearly as long as I remember. She had trouble with her lungs, and she wore out easily. She was very susceptible to illness so Papa fretted over her something awful." She smiled sadly at the memory.

"She couldn't run and play with me, but she taught me how to observe the world around me. She wanted me to find beauty in little things. Drawing and painting became my way to do that.

"Once Mother was gone, Papa tried to take her place. He didn't want me to miss out on anything because I didn't have a mother. He wanted to make me feel like we were a complete family, even though there was a huge piece missing. He gave me whatever I wanted, even when it wasn't good for me. Instead of appreciating his sacrifices, I resented him.

"I've been thinking a lot the last few days about Matthew and why I loved him so completely. After two years of grieving, I had begun to forget. This may sound terrible, but…" She took a deep breath. "Knowing what happened has almost been a relief. I think I already knew he wasn't coming back. I just couldn't face it. I blamed myself. I thought if I had done something differently, or not done something, he wouldn't have left. Now I don't have to worry about him.

"He was a good person, Harper. He had his faults, but he was good to me, and he made me feel like no one else ever did. He was always happy. Carefree. That was the biggest difference between him and Papa. Do you know I never saw Papa laugh? Not once in my whole life. Isn't that the saddest thing? He'd chuckle now and then, but never an out-of-control, belly laugh. I don't think he knew how. He was so…determined. He gave me everything except the knowledge of who he was. Everyone in this state thinks they know Hugh Lundy. But, Harper, I don't. He was so consumed with making money and building his empire, he never learned to enjoy the things his wealth and success afforded him. He never got to know *me*."

She stopped talking and looked out over the treetops. Harper knew she wasn't finished so she waited.

"Matthew was a lot like Mother, I think. He loved life, even though he had nothing. Mother found beauty in everyday things, everyday activities. Just like Matthew. Papa couldn't. It makes me so sad for him. I don't know if he was ever happy. He found pleasure in success and in this house and maybe in people thinking highly of him. But I don't know if he ever experienced true happiness. That's the saddest part of losing him. I wish he could've found joy in life."

Tears filled in her eyes. She pulled a handkerchief from her sleeve and dabbed the corners of her eyes and the end of her nose. Harper thanked God Ellie was working through her thoughts. The more she spoke them out loud, the sooner she would sort through the grief of losing Uncle Hugh. And Matthew.

Finally, she looked back at Harper. "I need to tell you something."

Harper's stomach tightened. Was Ellie about to ask her to leave? She didn't need her anymore. What about Logan? He had said he loved her, but what did that mean? Could they find a way to fit their lives together if Ellie sent her back to Kentucky?

"Matthew and I…we were going to marry. I know that's no excuse. What we did was wrong. But we were in love."

Harper realized what Ellie was telling her. "You don't have to explain anything to me."

"I know, but…I loved Matthew and I loved my baby." Her cheeks colored with shame. "I didn't want to lie to you. I didn't want you to think poorly of me either. I was afraid if you knew, you'd hate me."

"Oh, Ellie," Harper said around her sore throat, "I could never hate you. You're my sister. I wouldn't stop loving one of my sisters because of something they did. What I think doesn't matter anyway. The only opinion that matters is God's."

The tension slid out of Ellie's features. "I loved my baby, but if it had been born, it would've brought so much shame on our family. Isn't that awful? Even now, all I care about is myself and what people think."

She held the handkerchief against her nose for a moment. "It's just that I didn't want to hurt Papa more than I already had. I didn't want to disappoint him further."

She crossed her arms and held them against her breast. "I always imagined my baby was a little girl. It was too early to know for sure, but that's how it felt to me. I had only realized myself a few weeks before I fell down the stairs that I was with child. Then Papa saw me, and he knew."

Harper wondered about her accusation the other night that Uncle Hugh had pushed her. Had she accused him out of loss and grief, or had he truly done it? Harper couldn't ask. Ellie might not know the answer anyway.

Ellie wiped a tear from her cheek. "Anyway, I never saw the baby. After I fell, I started bleeding and couldn't stop. It hurt so bad. I knew what was happening. Papa was the only one with me. I called for Mrs. Philips, but Papa said no. He said there was nothing anyone could do, and there was no point in everyone knowing what I had done. I guess he was right. I had already caused him enough shame. After the baby came, he took her away. He said it was better if I didn't see her. Nothing would change if I did, and she wasn't a real baby anyway."

Her voice broke. "She was a baby, Harper. She was my baby and I loved her. But Papa said if people found out it would ruin my life, and even his. He said people would lose all respect for him if they knew he raised a daughter with no morals. He said it could even hurt the company, and that would hurt the community. I had done enough damage without ruining everything he and Hershel List had built."

Tears spilled down her cheeks. Harper clenched her teeth against a fresh wave of anger toward her uncle. How could he care more about his standing in the community than his daughter's pain? But nothing would be gained by such questions. He was in God's hands now. She opened her arms again, and Ellie moved into them. After the tears had passed, Ellie moved back to her chair.

"Papa never told me what he did with her, but a few days after…well, I saw fresh turned earth in the rose garden. Maybe he loved her a little. Mother loved that garden. It was her favorite spot on the property, especially after she got so she couldn't go out. I like to think that's why Papa put the baby there. So she could be close to Mother. I call her Rebekah. That was Mother's name. And Mother's mother. Now it's my baby's name, too." Another tear slid down her cheek.

"Do you think after you recover and Logan can get around again, we could have a memorial service for the baby? And for Papa?" she added, studying Harper through lowered lashes.

Harper swallowed the lump in her swollen throat. Cold sweat plastered her dress to her back. She hid her shaking hands in the folds of her skirt. She had been praying for God to give her grace toward Uncle Hugh. So far, all she felt was anger. And an irrational fear that assaulted her at the sound of his name. His misguided effort to protect Ellie had made him do what he did. Knowing why, though, didn't help get those hate-filled eyes out of her head.

"I'll do whatever you want, Ellie, but you'll have to give me some time."

"Of course. As long as you need." She took a long breath. "There's another thing I need to ask you."

Harper groaned inwardly. She didn't know how much more she could do.

"After you're stronger, do you plan to go back to Kentucky?"

Harper wasn't sure what to say. Was Ellie gently shoving her out the door? Or was it an invitation to stay?

"I don't know. Uncle Hugh brought me here as your companion. Soon you won't need me."

Ellie grabbed her hands. "I'll always need you, Harper. Maybe not in the same way, but that won't change. When you first came here, you asked me about my dreams. Do you remember that? I told you I dreamed of a sister. Having you here is the first time since Mother died that I felt like part of a family. I lost

Matthew and my baby. And now Papa. I don't know if I can lose you too."

"I can't live here on your kindness. Dixons don't take what they don't earn."

Ellie's jaw dropped. "You don't have to *earn* anything. That's not how families work. You're the one who taught me that."

Tears welled in Harper's eyes. "Oh, Ellie, that's the sweetest thing anyone ever said to me."

"I'm glad. So you'll stay?"

"If you'll have me, I'd like to stay right here."

"Until Logan decides he needs you more than I do." Ellie's eyes took on a mischievous gleam.

Heat filled Harper's cheeks. "What..." She was glad her sore throat gave her an excuse not to answer.

"He loves you, Harper. You must know that. Just like you love him."

"I...um...I don't..."

Ellie squeezed her hand. "When you asked me about my dreams, I asked about yours. You said you wanted to make a difference to someone. To leave a mark. You've done that, Harper. You made a difference in me. You showed me I'm strong. I don't have to hide in my room and worry about what people think of me anymore. You changed Logan too. He was so serious before you came. He only stayed here to take care of me. He thought I didn't know. I know a lot more than people give me credit. He felt obligated to me for some reason. He was like Papa. He didn't know how to laugh or see past the goal he was driving toward. But now he knows love, thanks to you. The two of you can use that love to impact generations to come."

"Oh, Ellie, I don't know. He may not want me in that way."

"Well, then, you better find out. You deserve all your dreams to come true. And I hope they come true right here in Willow Wood."

Chapter Thirty

One of the parlors downstairs had been converted to a recovery room for Logan. Traveling up and down stairs was becoming a strain on Dr. Dutton as her birthing time drew near, and she wanted to visit Logan often over the next few days.

It took Harper an hour after talking to Ellie to work up the nerve to go to the parlor to see him. His words the other night, the look in his eyes when he told her he loved her, had filled her with excitement and dread at the same time. What if he had spoken the words out of fear for her safety? Or delirium? In the light of a new day, with his pain controlled by Dr. Dutton's ministrations, he may have come to his senses, despite Ellie's assurance that he loved Harper.

If he loved her, it didn't mean it was the forever sort of love she dreamed of. For now, Ellie was her main concern. Was Logan willing to delay the fulfillment of his own dreams until Ellie was strong enough for her to leave? No one knew how long that would take. Maybe longer than Logan wanted to wait.

He may not even be thinking of a forever with Harper. She remembered when he told her some men couldn't love a woman who loved him too much. Had he been talking about himself? Was he a man who didn't love enough to marry? Maybe life alone on his farm with fond memories of a Kentucky girl he used to care deeply for was enough for him.

Harper knew two things. Memories of an unrequited love would never be enough for her. And she'd never know what Logan wanted until she asked.

"May I come in?" She knocked and slowly pushed open the parlor door to give him time to cover himself if needed.

She heard movement at the bed. "I wish you would." When she closed the door behind her, Logan finished. "It's better than you hovering in the hallway."

She huffed in mock indignation. "I wasn't hovering. I was—"

"Worrying?" he prodded.

She pursed her lips for effect. "Don't flatter yourself. I was just wondering how long you plan to lie there and take advantage of Mrs. Philips's sympathy. She's in the kitchen now boiling a chicken off the bone. She claims nothing has greater healing power than chicken broth."

"That's what the doc said. She prescribes it for everything from pneumonia to a stubbed toe to dysentery."

Harper pulled a small chair up to the bed.

"How are you?" he asked after she sat down. He looked at the scarf she had wrapped around her neck to cover the angry bruises. She didn't want anyone in the house to see them and get mad at Uncle Hugh all over again. She didn't want to see them herself.

"I'm fine. Well, not fine, but I'm getting better."

He reached out and caught her hand. "Thank God. I've been praying for you. I was so worried."

"About me? After what you've been through you should be thinking about yourself."

"I am thinking about myself." He tightened his grip on her hand. "If something would've happened to you, I don't know what I'd've done. I don't know how…"

His words drifted off. Harper glanced away from the unspoken thoughts in his eyes. "Dr. Dutton said the bullet hit you at just the right angle so it went around your skull and not through it."

"My pappy always said I had a thick head." He chuckled. He winced in pain and lifted his hand to the side of his head.

Harper got up and adjusted the pillows behind him. "You shouldn't move around very much. It can make you sick to your stomach. Dr. Dutton said you lost a lot of blood. She also said you need rest and nourishment. As long as infection doesn't set in, you'll be right as rain in a few days."

"Yeah, well, it's not her head that hurts."

She clicked her tongue in sympathy. "Is it quite terrible? Oh, of course it is." She took the towel that laid across his bandage and went to the dry sink to wet it again.

"Don't bother with that. One of the maids comes in and wets it every few minutes. Just when I drift off to sleep, someone drops a cold rag on my head and wakes me up again."

Harper wrung the water out of the towel and laid it back in place. "Oh, stop being a baby. Do you need more pain medication? You sound cranky. Should I fetch the doctor?"

"Harper." He smiled up at her. "Would you please sit down? You're giving me a headache trying to keep up with you flitting around like a hummingbird. I just want to talk to you."

Panic rose in her stomach. She wasn't ready for this conversation. She couldn't bear to hear those words again.

"Some men can't love a woman who loves them too much."

She did love him. So much she thought she would burst. It could be more than he could handle. She didn't know what she'd do if it was.

She sank into the chair and put her hands over her fluttering stomach.

He didn't look nearly as distressed as she felt. "How's Ellie?"

She exhaled in relief. He hadn't said the words. Not yet.

"Better than I expected. She's struggling with guilt. I don't think she knows how to feel about Uncle Hugh and what he did."

"None of us do. At least we finally know what happened to Matthew. I hate to think he died the way he did, but I'm relieved to have answers. I'll have to write a letter to his sister. They weren't close, but she needs to know."

"I can help you if you want. I've been trying to figure out how much to tell Ma and Pa. I don't want to keep things from them, but I don't want to scare them to death either."

Logan held out his hand toward hers. He couldn't reach her while reclining against the pillows, so she moved closer and took his hand. He pulled her onto the bed beside him. "I'm so thankful you're safe," he murmured into her hair.

"I don't know what would've happened if you hadn't come into the house when you did," she said. "Uncle Hugh—he was out of his head. He was so enraged he may have hurt Ellie, too."

"If she hadn't fired the gun, I wouldn't have known anything was wrong. The first time I heard it, I thought it was the storm. But when I heard the second shot..." His gaze moved to her neck. His jaw clenched. "I'm sorry I didn't get there sooner."

"You were right on time. You saved us both."

"It doesn't seem that way. You could've—"

She squeezed his hand. "But I didn't. God protected us all."

He put her hand to his mouth and kissed her knuckles. "I know you hurt more than you admit. You don't have to be brave. It must've been terrible in that room with him."

Uncle Hugh's twisted angry face flashed through her mind. She shivered. "I'm not brave. I was scared out of my mind. I still am every time I see a shadow out of the corner of my eye."

His gaze softened. "Harper, you're the bravest person I know. You left everyone and everything you love to help someone you'd never met. You fought for Ellie when her friends deserted her. You put yourself in mortal danger to find out what happened to Matthew. You nearly lost your life for her."

Her hand fluttered to her throat. She would do it all over again if she had to. "We don't have to give my parents all the sordid details," she said to lighten the weight of the moment.

"I hope not. I'd hate for them to send one of those brothers here to take you home."

Harper looked down at her hands. "I'd hate it, too."

He tucked a strand of hair behind her ear. "I thought Kentucky would always be home to you."

"I thought so, too. Now I believe Willow Wood is where I belong."

He stroked the side of her face. "You don't know how happy I am to hear that."

She held her breath. "For Ellie?"

"No. Well, for her a little, but more for me. If you went back to Kentucky, I guess I'd have to follow you and talk you into coming back."

"You would do that?"

"Of course. And if I couldn't talk you into it, I'd just have to stay there."

"What about your farm? It's your dream."

"No dream is worth having if you're not a part of it."

"Oh, Logan, I thought you… I thought you loved Ellie."

"I reckon I always have as a sister. But you're the one I love. The woman I've waited for my whole life."

Happiness surged through her. Surely a man wouldn't say that, and then tell her he couldn't love someone who loved him too much.

He combed his hand through her hair. "I already talked to Ellie. She wants us to stay here on the estate after we marry until I build a proper cabin."

"After we marry?"

"If you'll have me, that is."

"Oh, Logan, of course, I will. You're the man I dreamed of my whole life." She sank into his open arms.

The End

Next in the Series:

A Wedding for Felicity:

Willow Wood Series: Book 4

Chapter One

October, 1891

The crash accompanied by cries of pain and surprise, made Felicity Trego jerk away from the mirror where she was finishing her morning toilette. She ran into the hallway, nearly stumbling on the smoothly polished floor. Regaining her balance as she ran toward the sound, her heart thudded in her chest. She dashed to the landing and saw at the bottom of the stairs a heap of gray skirt and faded white petticoats.

"Belinda!" Felicity imagined the worst as she rushed down the stairs as quickly as her trembling legs would allow. Her older sister was always in a hurry. It was a wonder she hadn't fallen down the staircase years ago. At thirty-four, Belinda was as stubborn as the day was long. She never paid heed to how a lady should walk and comport herself. Such matters never gave her a moment's pause.

"Belinda?" Felicity said again when she got no response from the crumpled mass. Dread weighed heavy in her chest. *Oh, Lord, let her be all right*, she prayed. "Sister, can you hear me?"

The gray skirt shifted as Belinda struggled to sit up and her disheveled blond head appeared. One hand went to the side of her head. She groaned, more in impatience than pain. "I must've tangled my feet in this infernal skirt. If I were a man, I could wear trousers and wouldn't have to deal with such indignity."

Relief flooded through Felicity as she knelt beside her sister. If Belinda had the wherewithal to complain yet again about the injustices and confining nature of women's garments compared to the freedom of men's clothing, she would surely survive her injuries.

Running footsteps sounded from the rear of the house. "Oh, dear. Oh, dear. Oh, dear," the housekeeper Johanna Casey cried as she ran into the hallway. She arrived more breathless and red-faced than Belinda.

"Miss Belinda. Whatever happened? Are you all right? Can you move?"

Belinda scooted toward the wall to prop herself up. Felicity put her hand on Belinda's shoulder to keep her from moving further. "Lay back. Don't try to get up. Johanna, we must summon the doctor."

"Oh, dear. Oh, dear. It's that rug on the stairs. It must've come loose again. Miss Belinda, have you gravely injured anything?"

"Stop fussing," Belinda snapped. "I'll be fine as soon as I catch my breath. It's only a bump on my head. And my ankle." She pulled her skirt to her knee to assess her injury. She grimaced at the sight of it. Felicity and the housekeeper gasped aloud. The bruised flesh showed dark through her stocking and was already swelling over the top of her boot.

Not typically a delicate person, Belinda's face turned ashen. She fell back against the wall. "Oh, dear, it does hurt."

The housekeeper wrung her hands. "How awful. I'll get the scissors. We must get rid of that boot before it cuts off your circulation."

"No," Felicity exclaimed. "Yell for Shane to go for the doctor. Tell him to hurry. And then make some ice packs. We can slow down the swelling while we wait."

"Oh, dear," Johanna repeated.

"Go!" Felicity shouted.

Her uncharacteristic bark spurred the older woman to action. Still fretting, she turned about on her squat frame and hurried toward the kitchen from where she had come, calling for her son Shane as she ran.

Belinda groaned again. "Please don't bother the doctor, Felicity. Shane can help me upstairs. The swelling will go down as soon as I prop up my foot."

Felicity was secretly alarmed by Belinda's complexion. Her usually pink cheeks were devoid of color, and dark circles Felicity attributed to the pain had already appeared beneath her eyes. "You can't put any weight on that foot. If you were to go upstairs, it would be with Shane carrying you."

That sparked color in Belinda's cheeks as Felicity knew it would. "No one will carry me anywhere. I'm perfectly capable—"

Felicity cut off the rant before Belinda could get wound up. "Dr. Dutton will be here in a few minutes. You'll go upstairs after she has had a chance to examine you and diagnose the damage."

Belinda scowled, clearly furious with the situation and not a little irritated that Felicity was telling her what to do. No one told Belinda Trego what to do, especially her kid sister.

Felicity bit back a smile. Belinda was eleven years older than her, and had been the one in charge of the household, even before Papa died when Felicity was fourteen.

"Dr. Dutton can't come," Belinda said around a wince of pain. "She just had a baby."

"That was two months ago. She makes house calls in town when she's available, as long as she doesn't have to lift or be on her feet too long."

Belinda snorted. Felicity knew she admired Lisette Pelletier—now Dr. Dutton—the lady doctor who had come to town a year and a half ago and forever changed Willow Wood's views on women in positions of authority. But today, when she was the one in need of a doctor's services, she expressed only annoyance.

Felicity ran into the sitting room and grabbed some cushions off the davenport. She gingerly propped Belinda's foot on two pillows and placed another behind her head.

"I can't believe I did something so stupid," Belinda groused. "I don't have time for this today. I'm expected at the factory in…" She glanced at the watch pinned to her jacket lapel. She gasped. "Ten minutes." She moved to sit up. "I must get moving."

The family's factory Trego Leatherworks had started out as a small leather tooling shop in a shed behind Mama and Papa's house when Belinda was a baby. Now it was a booming plant that took up an entire block and employed thirty percent of Willow Wood's workforce. Since Papa's death, the two sisters had taken over the running of it and it continued to expand.

Felicity put her hand on Belinda's shoulder and pushed her back to the floor. "Just relax. You're not going anywhere. You can get that notion out of your head this instant."

Belinda glared at her again. Felicity enjoyed the momentary rush of power over her strong-willed sister before taking a handkerchief from her sleeve and dabbing perspiration off Belinda's forehead.

"When Shane gets back with the doctor, I'll send him to the factory to tell them you aren't coming today."

Belinda jerked upright. "You'll do no such thing. I'm not laying around this house all day. It's a twisted ankle, for pity's sake."

She reached for her ankle. "My goodness, it is tender. Help me unlash this boot. Don't let them cut it off. I can't bear to waste good shoe leather."

Felicity brushed her hands away. "It's not happening, Sister. We're not taking off that boot and you're not leaving this house. Your ankle could be broken and your boot is acting as a splint."

"This is…"

Felicity glowered, a completely new expression for her. "I don't want to hear another word on the matter. I know you have things to do, but you're not doing them today. As soon as the doctor determines the severity of your injury, I'll go to the factory and take care of whatever matters can't wait until tomorrow."

Belinda gasped. "You? You don't know anything about the factory."

"I guess I'll have to learn."

The sisters glared at each other. Belinda was right. Felicity knew next to nothing about running the plant. She had an office there and showed up nearly every day. She worked mostly with the advertising department where she sometimes contributed input into the sales catalogs mailed around the country. The all-male department patiently listened to her ideas before politely dismissing each one and continuing on with whatever they planned in the first place. Everyone at the plant—and in Willow Wood for that matter—tolerated Felicity, but no one took seriously. She was Belinda's beautiful little sister, and little else.

She didn't have Belinda's grit, that was for sure. After the men in the advertising department explained why her ideas weren't prudent or feasible, as if discussing the matter with a small child, she acquiesced. They were the professionals, after all. All she had were her own experiences as a shopper and ideas about how a product's description in a catalog might appeal to a customer. The rest of the department had combined decades of experience and financial proof the catalogs brought revenue to the company.

Felicity was only in charge of a few small sales accounts that didn't amount to much, which the rest of the staff hoped she wouldn't sabotage. During board meetings, she sat, silent and invisible, in an inferior chair with the rest of the staff. Belinda occupied Papa's former seat at the head of the table while Mr. Hughes, the factory manager, sat at the other end. All decisions were made by Belinda and Mr. Hughes, with little influence from the board members. Felicity left the monthly meetings confused, overwhelmed, and annoyed by her lack of understanding. But she had never done anything about it.

She knew better than anyone that if her name wasn't Trego, she wouldn't be allowed within a country mile of the conference room.

Starting today, that would have to change.

Twenty minutes later, Dr. Dutton arrived in a flurry of green serge skirts. "Shouldn't you be home tending that baby?" Belinda said in greeting.

Felicity scowled at her before turning to the doctor. "How is your little one? I haven't had a chance to love on her yet. At church, she's always surrounded by the older ladies. I can't see a thing beyond a few red curls."

Lisette beamed with maternal pride, even as she crossed the foyer to where Belinda still sat against the wall. "I seldom get a chance to see her myself when we go out. Little Jo is certainly the center of attention. I'm afraid she'll grow up thinking the whole world revolves around her."

Belinda snorted. "Jo? Why did you give her a boy's name?"

The doctor's hands started their examination at the top of Belinda's head and moved down the length of her body. "Her name is Josephine, after Grayson's mother. Josie married Owen when he was on his way down here from Montana to take possession of his ranch."

The housekeeper clasped her hands to her breast. "Theirs was such a romantic story. Willow Wood wasn't much more than a crossroads settlement in those days, but they did a lot for our community. Josie was a right fine lady, and we all miss her to this day."

Lisette smiled appreciatively as she carefully manipulated Belinda's ankle. "Thank you for saying that. I wish I could've met her myself. We'll have to wait till our homecoming in heaven for her to meet me and her little namesake."

She set her medical bag aside and got to her feet. "Good news, Belinda. It appears your injury is confined to your foot and ankle."

"You call that good news."

"Yes, you could've broken your neck. Felicity and I will help you to the davenport in the parlor where I can examine you fully."

It took longer for the two women to practically carry Belinda to the next room and get her settled than for the examination.

"You have a nasty break, Belinda," the doctor announced, "in two places. Possibly three."

Johanna covered her mouth with her hands. Even Belinda paled a few more shades. She quickly recovered. "What does that mean? I won't be able to go to the office for the rest of the week?"

Lisette nearly rolled her eyes. "No, Belinda. Unless you plan to move the factory into this room, you won't see the inside of it for at least two months."

Felicity braced herself, and just in time.

"Two months?" Belinda bellowed. "That's unacceptable. I can't spend two months on this couch like a loaf of bread waiting for my yeast to rise."

Lisette was nonplussed. "I'm afraid your injury has taken the matter out of your hands. You have Mr. Hughes, and Felicity here," she added as almost an afterthought.

"Felicity? Mr. Hughes? Why, I..." Belinda sputtered. She looked apologetically at her sister and took a breath to rein in her frustration. "I'm sure you mean well, Doctor, but this simply won't do. I'll stay home the rest of the week, but then I truly must go back to work. The company depends on me. This town depends on me."

Lisette began putting her instruments into her medical bag. "I certainly can't lash you to this davenport. So I'll wish you the best as a cripple for the rest of your life."

Belinda's face darkened. "A cripple? What's that supposed to mean?"

"It means exactly what you think it means. If you don't give your foot and ankle the proper time to heal, you will do irreparable harm from which they will never recover. You may never walk again. And if you do, it will be with a painful and debilitating limp."

"Oh, Belinda," Felicity said.

Johanna couldn't speak at all.

Reality began to register in Belinda's midnight blue eyes. "Are you... Isn't there anything..."

Felicity had never seen her sister at such a loss.

"It's up to you, Belinda," the doctor repeated. "I realize how difficult this is for you. You surely have no choice. You can lie here and give your body time to heal for a few months, maybe longer. Or you can spend the rest of your life in a wheelchair in unimaginable pain." She glanced around the lavishly appointed room. "You're fortunate. At least you can afford a live-in nurse to tend you around the clock. Most people couldn't. I can help you locate one if you're interested."

She must've known the effect her dismal proclamation would have on Belinda.

"I most certainly am not interested!" Belinda exclaimed.

Her eyes narrowed as she realized the doctor had meant to shock her. Her gaze sought out Felicity. "Sister."

Felicity circled the doctor and sank to her knees beside Belinda. "Everything will be fine, Belinda. There are some matters at the factory you can take care of from right here. We'll set up a desk in this room so you can work while staying off your feet. Is that satisfactory, Dr. Dutton?"

"Of course. In a few days, though. I'll give her pain medication to take the rest of this week. After that, there's no reason she can't see to paperwork or whatever else can be done without moving around. But Belinda, you must not get off this couch. I'll have Shane bring some crutches from my office, but those can only be used to go to the necessary."

Tears of frustration filled Belinda's eyes. Felicity felt like crying herself. For the first time in her life, Belinda needed her. She prayed she was up to the challenge. She learned forward and kissed her cheek. "Please don't worry, love. You'll see. You'll be fine and the factory will be fine."

As she walked Lisette to the door, she silently prayed, *Please, Lord, let Belinda handle her recovery with the same dogged determination she does everything else. And help Mr. Hughes, Johanna, and me survive it."*

Read the rest of

A Wedding for Felicity:

Willow Wood Brides Book 4

by visiting Amazon or your favorite online retailer.
Available in paperback or ebook.

Reader Bonus

If you enjoyed *A Dream for Harper*, or any of the other Willow Wood Brides titles, please take a moment to leave a review on Amazon, Goodreads, your blog, or any other site that allows reader reviews.

Also sign up for my newsletter to stay up to date on new releases, promotions and contests. When you sign up, you'll get a free download of *A Promise for Josie: A Willow Wood Brides Prequel*. See how it all began.

Available to Newsletter Subscribers. The story that started it all.

A Promise for Josie:
A Willow Wood Prequel

After a broken promise and a broken heart, is love worth the risk?

Abandoned at the altar on her wedding day, Josie Segal doubts she'll ever find true love. When a tall stranger on his way south to build his own ranch rides into Josie's life, her dreams of love and adventure are reawakened. Can she move beyond the pain and fear of broken promises to trust Owen Dutton, and her own heart?

Sign up for **my newsletter** and receive a link to download **A Promise for Josie—A Willow Wood Brides Prequel.** Stay up to date on upcoming releases in the exciting Willow Wood Brides series, as well as other books and series in the works. You'll also be among the first to learn of promos, giveaways, and contests.

I love hearing from readers. Email me at **teresa@teresaslack.com** anytime with you about the stories.

About the Author

Teresa Slack loves reading, writing, and falling in love. Creating clean and wholesome western romances where cowboys still sweep independent women off their feet was an easy choice for her.

She writes from her home in the beautiful southern Ohio hills, which she shares with her husband and rescue dog and rescue cat. Any errors and typos she blames on the cat randomly running across her keyboard.